WILDFLOWERS

WILDFLOWERS

BY

Schledia Phillips

THREE KEYS PUBLISHING

UNLOCKING WORLDS, HEARTS, AND MINDS

THREE KEYS PUBLISHING
www.threekeyspublishing.com

Schledia Phillips
www.schledia.wix.com/home
Like her on Facebook at Schledia Benefield Phillips, Author
or follow her on twitter @Schledia
or follow her blog at www.schlediaphillips@blogspot.com

DEDICATION

For all of those who have suffered at the hands of abuse and domestic violence.

Our cries are silent.
Our tears run red.
Listen for the words,
That are not said.

Our wounds run deep.
Our fears well hid.
Look for the signs,
Our veiled grievances bid.

~Schledia Phillips~

ACKNOWLEDGMENTS

First and foremost, I would like to thank God for bringing Three Keys Publishing into my life. TKP has allowed me to bring my story, along with its fictitious characters, to life. A special thanks to my editors, Lynn Thompson and Donna Huber. I would like to thank Angie Bonnett for her creative photography and cover art, and a special thanks to Amy Bonnett for her creative cover design work. Big hugs to the models, Chloe Downs and Dustin Howell. I cannot go without thanking Tonya Harris for agreeing to pre-read Wildflowers and give honest input. Thank you for loving the story, giving me feedback, and all your encouragement. Thanks to my friend and fellow author K. B. Hoyle for all your advice and input. Special thanks to Donna Huber for the back cover review. A special shout out to Julie Watkins for all of your help making police work scenes realistic.

Contents

Chapter 1

The Offer

The door had been left wide open; furious with himself for what he had just done, Aster charged across the room and slammed it shut. The adjoining wall vibrated. His blood raged causing his face to flush crimson. His hands violently shook. The wall's shudder sent a jolt through the small, round table next to the door. The crystal vase that sat upon it and held a bouquet of wildflowers smashed to the floor and shattered.

At the sight of the scattered yellow, white, and blue flowers on the hardwood surface, Aster's thoughts drifted to Susan. He saw her strained smile as she walked through the doorway holding the colorful assortment of flowers. She had placed them there only an hour before. *It's symbolic*, he thought. Susan and his relationship had been knocked to the ground to be smashed and strewn apart, and he had only himself to blame. He wondered how he could have allowed her to walk out after everything she had said to him. Acutely aware of the lust for blood she had left him with, he pinched the bridge of his nose with his trembling hand and inhaled a sharp breath. *Not her,* his mind screamed.

Susan was the person who had saved his life; she led him out of darkness and despair and into a life of hope and love. That darkness was the darkness of a rebellious teenage boy from a broken, abusive home—a home seething with violence, the same violence he now felt coursing through his veins. The savagery she once tamed had been unleashed, and it sought bloodshed.

The kindness of an offer concluded their first encounter. It was the beginning of their senior year in high school, and Susan was new in town. Her family moved into town four weeks into the new school year, so she was unaware of what had taken place the previous year which led to Aster's spending his entire junior year in alternative school, yet she immediately sensed he needed help.

In the beginning she confined her help to tutoring sessions. It was during their shared English/literature class when Ms. Howard grilled Aster in front of his peers about his refusal to read aloud the part she had assigned him in *Othello* that Susan first sensed his need. Something inside her heart asserted he wasn't simply rebelling against Ms. Howard's request. Apparently she was the only one in class capable of seeing through the hard mask of defiance which permeated his countenance. The others ridiculed him by blurting out insults for what they saw as insolence, and Ms. Howard glared at him with contempt. Susan saw past his façade and perceived what she imagined may be his disguise for illiteracy.

Ms. Howard wasn't preparing the students for a performance; they were merely reading the play aloud in class. Aster had trouble reading comic books; he certainly was *not* going to be humiliated in front of his peers by butchering Shakespeare, and there was no way he planned to give in to his teacher's demand. Ms. Howard narrowed her eyes and shot darts of insistence at him. Glaring back with a clenched jaw, Aster tightened his grip on his desk and held his stance. Even if it meant returning to alternative school, he would not be swayed to read aloud.

Susan's dad, a well-to-do doctor, accepted the position as head of the cardiology department at Bayville Hospital in the city of Bayville, Mississippi. Being new, attractive, and wealthy made Susan the target of all the popular guys. Their one problem with her, as Aster had overheard it, was she was *too good,* which for some made her an enormous target. One group of popular guys had their tallies they boasted about to others. Those tallies consisted of the virgins they had conquered. Girls already tainted, whom they were sure to sleep with regardless, weren't worthy to be added to their list of conquests. They only bragged of *fresh meat* as they called it.

It was Susan's second day in class, and her name was called over the intercom system. "Ms. Howard," the brassy female voice called.

Ms. Howard spun to face the intercom. "Yes."

The intercom screeched as she asked, "Do you have Susan Blackman in your class?"

Her eyes quickly scanned the room in search of Susan. "Yes, Ma'am."

"Could you send her to the guidance office,

please?"

"Yes, Ma'am."

Susan stood to gather her books. A slight smile inched across her face in hopes of being changed to an advanced English class. Unaware, she snagged her purse strap on the arm of her desk. As she strode forward, it tugged her shoulder and sent her books tumbling to the floor. Susan blushed when laughter broke out in the room.

"Mr. McGrath, why don't you help carry her books to the office, and then make your way over to Mr. Simmers's office and inform him that you can't seem to participate in class!" Ms. Howard demanded.

Aster glared at Ms. Howard before walking over and snatching Susan's books off the floor with a huff. A shuddery breath escaped Susan's lips as her eyes flickered to his. Her mind whirled as every cell in her body leapt to life, twisting and tingling through her. Susan stepped back an infinitesimal amount, closed her eyes, and whispered something inaudible before reaching for her books.

Her heart pounded and her face flushed as she whispered, "I appreciate it, but I've got it." Her voice was gentle—quite the opposite of Aster's.

Aster knew at that moment there was something about her, something that set her apart from any other girl he'd ever met. Of course, at the time he assumed it was merely the fact she didn't know him that he heard such sweetness in her voice.

Insistent on giving in to this one demand made by Ms. Howard, he refused to hand over her books. "No, I've got it." He gestured for her to exit the room ahead of him with the nod of his head.

Once out of the classroom, she reached out and attempted to take them from him again. Accidentally grazing his hand in the process, the warmth of his hand penetrated her soft skin. Susan's eyes were instantaneously drawn to his. Despite the warmth rushing through her body at his touch, his eyes bore through her with cold indifference.

"Are you trying to get me in trouble?" he complained, pulling the books to his chest.

"No, but I'm not helpless."

Aster gritted his teeth and rolled his eyes. "Of course, you're not."

Hurt reflected through Susan's eyes, yet he refused to allow her feelings to soften the hard shell he had placed around himself; it was strong and secure.

She glanced away from him and whispered, "Just because I'm a girl doesn't mean I need a guy to carry my books."

Despite his hardest efforts, somehow her inability to look him in the eyes broke through his icy exterior. "Look, I don't think you're a pansy girl or anything. I stay in enough trouble as it is. I don't need more. Ms. Howard will be sticking her big, fat nose out that door any minute; I assure you, so do me a favor and pretend I'm being nice to you."

She shook her head and soaked in what he said. She gulped, pushing down the small lump forming in her throat, and asked, "So, is she always that way with everyone, or is it just you she gives a hard time?"

Aster slowed his pace and fell a few steps behind her. He curled his lip and huffed, "Huh, and why would you care if it's just me?"

Spinning around to face him, she arched her neck in order to look him in the eyes. Peering directly into them, she said, "Because I believe in caring about all people, even those who get labeled by teachers as bad seeds."

For a moment he glanced into her deep-brown eyes and caught a glimpse of truth staring back at him. She believed what she said. Susan turned away from him in one quick motion. Aster had never witnessed a shy person stare him down with such boldness. His chest swelled with an odd sense of pride and astonishment all at the same time. Before she had the opportunity to remove her gaze from his, he witnessed true beauty gazing back at him. Although he found her attractive, with her golden hair and chocolate-brown eyes, it wasn't her physical beauty he admired.

Several girls in his senior class were graced with physical beauty, but they were either snobby girls who spent their days admiring themselves in mirrors or flat out mean girls who cared only for themselves. Aster picked up on the fact Susan was different from those girls. Her countenance radiated purity, her smile reflected kindness, and her eyes sparkled with innocence. He was captivated, yet he knew his infatuation would never amount to anything because girls like her weren't interested in guys like him.

Aster opened the door into the spacious office. Susan eyed the secretary as well as several small offices nestled in the back corners of the room. Pointing her in the direction of the guidance counselor's office, he placed her books into her arms, veered to the left, and pushed open the door to the assistant principal's office.

Susan stood speechless and watched him as he entered the office and disappeared behind the door. After the door shut behind him with a light thud, she sighed and strode toward the guidance counselor's office.

Aster sat across from Mr. Simmers. A former college football player for Louisiana State University, he stood a towering six-feet, five inches and weighed at least two-hundred and seventy-five pounds. His stature alone kept most students in line. Aster, however, bowed his chest and gripped the arms of the chair.

"What can I do for you?" Mr. Simmers questioned as he glanced into Aster's sullen eyes.

"Ms. Howard sent me because I refused to read aloud in class."

"Well, McGrath, why did you refuse?"

Aster eyed the closed door. "Because I'm not gonna make a fool of myself. I don't care who she is."

Mr. Simmers's mouth turned down. He grunted and tugged on his jacket. "Do you care to explain to me why you feel you would be making a fool of yourself?"

Aster hung his head and mumbled, "Because I can't read."

"Oh, I see," a disturbed sigh slipped through his lips. "I'm going to send you over to Ms. Glass. Hold on just a minute." He held up his finger to Aster as he picked up the phone and pressed four digits. "Ms. Glass?"

Aster heard Ms. Glass's gruff voice echo through the phone line. After what he had done the previous year, he had spent countless hours in the office with Ms. Glass, so he knew her voice well. Mr. Simmers was on up in age, and it was obvious he was losing his hearing; hence, he maxed out the volume on his phone. Aster could hear word for word what Ms. Glass said.

"Yes, Sir."

"Do you have a minute?"

"Well, Sir, I'm with a student, but I'll be through with her in just a moment. Can I help you with something?"

His deep voice echoed frustration, "Yes, Ma'am, I have a young man in here with me who needs to be placed in some tutoring sessions, and quite frankly, I'm concerned as to why he hasn't already been placed in them."

"Well, who is the student, Sir?"

"Aster McGrath."

"Yes, Sir, I know him. He spent all of last year in alternative school, Sir. Let me get his file. Do you know what subjects he needs tutoring in?"

"He's having difficulty with reading."

"Well, that may explain a lot. I've counseled him a good bit over the last couple of years, but my dealings with him have been concerning his behavior. I never picked up on that issue and no teacher ever reported it, Sir. Does he need counseling in any other area?"

"At this point, I think that's where we need to start. He just told me he can't read."

Ms. Glass glanced at Susan, the student sitting in her office, and said, "Excuse me, dear; I need to help the assistant principal with something real quick. I'll get back with you in just a moment."

"Let me pull his file." She spoke into the phone before setting the receiver on her desk.

Ms. Glass stood and opened the file cabinet labeled *M-S*. Wrestling to remove the folder she sought, she shoved several of them back and yanked out a thick folder. Susan eyed the name typed in bold letters across the label, *McGrath, Aster*. Its thickness heightened her curiosity. Ms. Glass sat down and pulled another folder labeled

After School Tutoring from her desk and flipped through it.

Aster heard the rustling of papers while Mr. Simmers sat in silence. "Sir, the afterschool reading program is currently full. It'll be three months before any of those students graduate out of it," she explained.

Mr. Simmers grunted in frustration. "Can't you squeeze him in?" He picked up a pen and tapped it on his desk in a repeated, steady beat.

"Give me just a minute...no, nuh uh...I'm sorry, Sir, but there's just no way possible," she apologized.

Then Aster heard a familiar, gentle voice. He recognized it from his recent conversation with her.

"Ms. Glass, I'm a straight A student, and I would be more than happy to volunteer my time to tutor anyone who's in need of it. I don't mind, really. I helped to tutor other students back home. I'm more than willing."

Ms. Glass fell silent, and Mr. Simmers's countenance grew wary. "Mr. Simmers, the student I have in my office overheard the gist of our conversation and offered to tutor the young man."

Mr. Simmers cleared his throat. "Yes, Ma'am, I heard."

"Well, Sir, I know it's not standard practice for us to set something like that up, but we really have no availability. What do you think, Sir?"

"Hold on," Mr. Simmers responded. He pulled the phone away from his ear and covered the mouthpiece with his large, rough hand. "Mr. McGrath, our afterschool tutoring class is full, but there is a student who's willing to tutor you. Are you interested?"

Aster hung his head in embarrassment.

Even though he knew who the sweet voice belonged to, he asked, "Who's the student?"

Mr. Simmers withdrew his hand and placed the receiver back to his ear. "Ms. Glass, he wants to know who the student is before he okays it."

"She's our new enrollee Susan Blackman. I have her transcript right here in front of me, and well, quite frankly, Sir, she has the ability as well as the willingness. Her record is remarkable, and she participated in a tutoring program in her former high school. She was a tutor, Sir."

Once again Mr. Simmers pulled the phone away from his ear and covered the receiver with his overly large hand. "Her name is Susan Blackman. She's new to the school, but according to Ms. Glass, her record is impeccable. You won't find a better tutor outside of one of our teachers. Are you interested?"

Aster thought about the kindness she had shown him and the sarcasm he had unleashed upon her. He felt horrible for the way he treated her and wondered if she realized her offer was being extended to him. He knew she watched him enter the assistant principal's office, and Ms. Glass had announced to her she was aiding the assistant principal with an issue. He couldn't help but think she knew he was the one she was offering to help. Aster pictured her beautiful, dark-chocolate eyes and her golden-blonde hair, and before he knew it, he blurted out, "I accept. I'll do it."

Chapter 2

The Library

With each labored breath he took, Aster's chest rose and fell. He stared at the figurative disaster of his life. He lingered over the broken vase and scattered flowers. Kneeling, he picked up the wildflowers strewn across the floor. Just a few hours earlier Susan had walked through the door carrying the bouquet she had picked as a gift for him. They had been handpicked from her field, the field he once referred to as their field.

The hair on the back of his neck stood on ends. Memories he had long suppressed surged to the surface, overrunning his mind. They were memories of the Hell he lived in at home; the constant drunken state of his mother and the absence of his father. He relived the rage he felt at life as a teenager and how he had even taken his frustrations out on the one girl who longed to help him, the girl who sought to save him from himself. During their first misunderstanding, he had lashed out at her with cruel, cutting words. She had held her own and calmed his teeming frustrations that day.

And this is how I repaid her? His blood boiled.

The day after Ms. Howard pushed Aster into meeting Susan by forcing him to carry her books, she required, once again, he read aloud. His instinct kicked in. Lowering his brow, he spit, "I will not."

Insisting he read, Ms. Howard demanded, "You will do your part in this class, or you will flunk this class, Aster."

Aster pressed his lips into a hard line. "No."

Ms. Howard jerked her body around in a swift motion and stomped toward her desk. She yanked a yellow write-up slip from the top drawer, scribbled Aster's name across the top line, and wrote *extreme defiant behavior and insubordination* in bold letters across the paper. Marching back to his desk, she shoved it in his face. "Get out of my class now."

The eyes of his fellow classmates widened as he shoved his desk and ripped the paper from her hand. Aster stormed out of class and slammed the door in order to give Ms. Howard a *real* reason to call him defiant and insubordinate.

Due to the fact Ms. Howard threw him out of the classroom within the first fifteen minutes, he didn't have the opportunity to speak to Susan about their tutoring sessions. He had no idea when they would begin or where they would take place.

He stormed down the hall and punched his locker as he passed it. "Damn it, I needed to talk to Susan before switching classes."

If he planned to graduate, he knew he had to pass that class. As unfortunate as it was, Ms. Howard was his only option for an English teacher. While there were two other twelfth-grade English teachers, one of them taught only advanced English, and the other one split his day between the English department and the history department where he taught the needed credit of government. As a result of scheduling conflicts there, Aster was stuck having to stay with Ms. Howard, and he felt quite certain she held a certain disdain for him that had absolutely nothing to do with his poor reading skills. She seemed to have a high regard for Shane Garrish, the classmate whom Aster had pulverized at the beginning of his junior year which sent him to alternative school for the remainder of the eleventh grade. He had only been allowed to return to Bayville high for his senior year because Shane had dropped the charges against him. It was a deal which mandated Aster spend one year in alternative school. Most of the faculty and town admired Shane for his mercy. Aster could have spent serious time in jail for the condition he left Shane in.

Once, after school, Aster had overheard Ms. Howard making reference to him on her cellphone. He just happened to be strolling past her classroom when he heard her complain, "I can't believe I'm stuck having a murderer's boy in my class. He's already shown his true colors by nearly killing one of the nicest, most respected young men in the school, but they always seem to give me the troubled kids. I can't wait for an opening to come available in Gulfport."

The words *murderer's boy* brought him to a

halt, so he stood outside her door and listened to her spew her contempt of him.

Shane, one of the preppy boys, had the ability to charm anyone and everyone with his smile; even the sternest of teachers were unable to resist adoring him. In Aster's eyes Shane had the ability to smile in your face while stabbing you in the back and make you believe he was somehow trying to protect you. Aster was convinced he was the only sane person in the school not deceived by Shane's apparent charisma. Despite his warnings, his own baby sister had fallen for Shane's allure at one point.

By the time Aster left Mr. Simmers' office, class was almost over, so he headed to his locker to change out his books for the remainder of the day. Aster's mind boiled with anger as he replayed the scene with Ms. Howard over and over again in his mind. Caught up in his repeated instant replay, he didn't realize the curse words spewing under his breath as he slammed his locker door.

Through his peripheral vision, he eyed Susan standing next to him. He jolted. "Damn it, how long have you been standing there?"

"Long enough to hear you're extremely upset with Ms. Howard." She raised her brow, widening her eyes.

"Yeah, the witch won't cut me any slack."

Attempting to change the subject as well as the atmosphere, a bright smile flickered across her face. "So, I didn't have the opportunity to catch up with you before class to find out when and where you want to meet up for tutoring sessions. When the bell rang and I walked out of class, I saw you over here at your locker. I figured

I better catch you now, especially considering I don't see you for the rest of the day. So, what's the plan?"

Her light and airy personality somehow made him forget why he had been angry just seconds before. "Um, there's a small corner out of the way at the public library. We could meet there after school."

"Okay. Where's the library?"

"Oh, that's right, I forgot; you're new here. It's right down the street. It's in walking distance just north of here. Walk out the main entrance to the school and make a right." Aster explained the directions.

"Um, okay." Susan recorded the directions in her mind. Aster looked away, so in order to gain his attention, she gently grazed his arm with her slender hand. "Aster, look, I want you to know these tutoring sessions are between you and me. No one else will know we are meeting together, okay."

Feeling the stabs of all the *goody* girls who wanted to go for rides on his motorcycle up in the country and date him if he took them to Mobile or New Orleans on that date yet were ashamed to be seen walking hand-in-hand with him at school or riding on his motorcycle down Main Street, Aster narrowed his eyes and glared into hers. "So, what am I to you? A charity case? Little Ms. Uptown wants to do a good deed, so you decide to reach out to the bad boy of the school and try to be the saving doctor who fixes him right up keeping him from being the thug who spent almost his entire junior year in alternative school, *but* you're ashamed to let anyone know you're helping him with his school work?" He ripped her up and down with the cruelness of his words.

Susan stepped backward. Her eyes glazed

with a thin layer of tears. Fighting to hold them back, she parted her lips and gasped for air with a gulp. "I...I'm...I'm sorry. I didn't...I didn't even know you spent...Aster, I thought you might be upset if people knew you needed help. I never even considered being ashamed to be seen with you. I didn't mean for you to take it that way. I'm not like that. I'm standing here *at* your locker right now talking to you, aren't I?" Her voice quivered.

Realizing what a jerk he had just been, Aster closed his eyes and shook his head. "I'm sorry, Susan. I've just been having a hard time living down what happened last year. I've been a little pissed at the world, I guess."

"I don't even know what happened last year, nor do I wanna know. I just thought you might be bothered by people knowing I'm helping you with reading. I just wanted you to know I wasn't going to go around blabbing about it is all."

Aster's shoulders slumped. "I get it, and I appreciate it. Honestly, you're right; I don't wanna announce to the entire school that I can't read." He dropped his books to his side. "Look, we better get to class, or we'll be late. I'll meet you outside the library at 3:15, okay?"

"Okay." Susan smiled past the pain his temper and harshness had just inflicted upon her.

As Susan walked to the library after school, a gust of wind whipped past her. She watched as the motorcyclist who caused it drove into the parking lot of the library and screeched to a stop, spraying gravel against the side of the building.

Her eyes fixated on him as he removed his helmet. Aster's dark hair caught her attention. He was tall and well-built with broad shoulders. His chiseled jawline attracted her, but what drew her in were his piercing blue eyes. She paused for a brief moment, closed her eyes, and whispered to herself, "Get a hold of yourself, Susan. Okay, here goes."

Another minute passed before she arrived at the building, and Aster was nowhere in sight. He had not waited outside the building for her as he said he would or as she figured a gentleman would do.

She shrugged off her slight disappointment. "Well, our meetings were supposed to be a secret, I suppose." She glanced around to see if there were any witnesses to her moment of insanity.

Pushing open the heavy glass door, her eyes scanned through the large building overflowing with shelves loaded down with books. Aimless, she strolled through the library in search of the hidden back corner he had mentioned.

"Can I help you find something?" the librarian asked as she stacked books on a cart.

"Yes, Ma'am, I'm looking for an area in the back corner I was told I could study in privately."

"Oh, yes, it's right back that way, dear." She pointed in the correct direction. "But I'm afraid you're a little late. I just saw a young man dash right on back there."

"Oh, okay, thank you. I'll just check it out and see if he's still around." Susan gave her head a nod of thanks before slipping off in the direction the librarian had pointed.

Finding the corner, she slung her backpack off her shoulder and onto the floor and seated herself directly across from Aster. He was kicked back with his feet propped on the table with his hands behind his head while he stared at the ceiling tiles.

The thud of her backpack wrenched him from his daydream. He yanked his legs from the table and sat up straight. Aster smiled. "There you are."

"Here I am. Sorry it took me a minute to get here. You kind of left me in the dust out there."

"Yeah, sorry 'bout that."

"It's perfectly fine." Susan shrugged her shoulders. "It was my idea we keep these sessions secret from everybody else. It wouldn't be much of a secret if they saw us entering the *library* together, now would it?" A slight giggle slipped through Susan's lips.

Susan sat up straight. Her smile faded. "So, I kinda need to know where to start with you. Do you know what grade level you read on?"

Aster fidgeted in his seat, removed his eyes from her sincere gaze, and hung his head. "Ummm...I'm not sure. Never asked. I read Marvel Comic books, but I have a real hard time with them. Mostly I just follow the pictures. It seems to help me understand pretty much what's going on when I can't understand the words."

Inhaling a deep breath, Susan crossed her arms. "Well, I'm not going to pretend this is going to be easy, and I'm not going to pretend to take it easy on you. I've tutored before back in North Alabama, so you just need to know I'm not a push over who doesn't expect you to work hard."

Signaling he got her point, Aster rolled his eyes and changed the subject, "So, is that where you're from, North Alabama?"

"Yep, my dad worked at one of the hospitals in Birmingham. I lived there my entire life."

"Yeah, I heard your dad's a doctor. I guess that means you live on the bay side of town."

"Yeah, it's the only side I know right now outside of the school and now the library, but I haven't even been to the bay yet. So, where do you live?"

"Oh, I live on the east side of town. You don't wanna go into that side of town alone, for sure. Pretty bad crime rate on that side. So, tell me how such an intelligent young girl, like you, got stuck in a class like mine."

Susan sighed. "Well, I guess I got *stuck* because the advanced class was already full...at least that's what Ms. Glass told me." She slightly shrugged her shoulders. "So, tell me how you managed to get to the twelfth grade without reading." She raised her brow.

"Huh," he narrowed his eyes. "You got me there."

Aster's deep voice captivated Susan. She nestled her chin into the palm of her hand and propped her elbow on the table, and without realizing it, she leaned across the small round table. Hanging on his every word, she inched her way closer to him.

"I'm pretty smart in other ways, I guess...So, are we gonna get started?" Aster edged forward. His eyes met hers halfway across the table.

Startled, Susan blushed and jolted back to her side. "Oh, yes, let's get started. I'll be right back." She stood and ambled her way to the librarian.

"Excuse me, where are the elementary level books in this library?"

The librarian pointed and smiled. "In the west side of the library."

"Thank you." Susan smiled back at her. She made her way to the west side and found a book she was familiar with. Making her way back to their table, she whispered, "Okay, here's a book on sixth-grade level. Read as much of it to me as you can, and I'll assess where we should start." She placed it in front of Aster.

Nervous, Aster grabbed the book, opened to the title page and began reading. He stuttered his way through the first couple of pages, often skipping words altogether. Every time he choked on a word, his face hardened with anger, and every time he came to a word he dared not even tackle, he would glance up at Susan. Seeing her eyes wrinkled with concern, he grew frustrated with himself.

Aster took several deep breaths and calmed himself. Susan assumed they were a learned anger management technique.

Close to the end of the second page, Aster slammed the book down. "This is stupid. I can't do it."

"Yes, you can, Aster."

An angry glower contorted his face. He lowered his brow and narrowed his eyes. "And what makes you think you can even help me?" he blurted.

"Because I believe I can."

Her answer was simple, and she didn't find it necessary to expound upon it although she did realize helping him wouldn't be an easy task. Immediately, Susan became aware of the fact he lacked an understanding of phonics. She decided to begin in the beginning. She knew it would be a lengthy process, but she imagined she wouldn't mind it so much. He *was* attractive to look at, and she knew she had heard an inner voice prompting her to help him.

Chapter 3

The Walk

Holding the bouquet of flowers, Aster stood to his feet; he gripped them so tightly the stems crumpled and wilted over his hand. The rage inside him grew, becoming stronger by the second. The memories of Susan's kindness to him back in high school no longer soothed his anger. Grasping for sweet thoughts of her, he scanned his memories for her smile. When they were teenagers, she changed the atmosphere around him with it; it intoxicated him. He squeezed his eyes shut and searched for her voice in his head. The gentleness of it always seemed to quiet the ire in his soul. He longed for it. He needed it to restrain the beast fighting to free itself from within him.

When he could not find her tender words to appease the fury of the fiend clawing its way out, he grew frustrated and began seeing flashes of his mother hammering him in the back with the base of her whiskey bottle. He envisioned the braided metal belt buckle belonging to his father, and he witnessed his mother rear back ready to lash his little sister. He flinched and grabbed his back as he recalled the pain as he shoved Eva out of the way and took her whipping. His remembrance was so vivid he felt the warmth of the blood oozing down his back. He grasped his triceps as he recalled the pain when his mother punished him for dropping a gallon of milk on the kitchen floor; she had snatched his arm, laid her cigarette on the upper portion of it, and slurred how he'd always remember not to drop the milk in the future.

Six full weeks had passed since the beginning of their tutoring sessions. Every day Susan walked to the library after school to meet Aster, and every day Aster rushed past her on his motorcycle. She always found him at the same table in the back corner working with the flash cards she had made him. Aware of his sincerity and commitment to work with diligence, she wondered why no one had ever bothered to offer their assistance before she had. He was never late, and he was never daydreaming when she arrived. They worked together on phonics for at least an hour every afternoon before she would glance at her watch and declare she had to leave.

Aster always crept close to the door and glanced outside to see her climb into a black BMW. From a distance he could see an attractive blonde in the driver's seat. Her mother, he suspected. He wasn't sure why, but he always felt it necessary to wait until they pulled out of the parking lot before he would exit, climb on his bike, and head in the opposite direction. He assumed, despite their new arrival in town (and considering the fact Shane Garrish was from the bay side of town), Susan's parents had probably been forewarned about the local bad boy.

That particular day, leaves crunched behind Susan as she strolled toward the library. She cut her widened eyes from side to side, searching for the culprit in her peripheral vision. Certain someone walked on the sidewalk behind her, her instinct prompted her to turn and see if she was alone. She slowed her strides and inhaled a wary breath. With a slight pivot of her body and a sly tilt of her head, she eyed Aster walking about fifteen paces back. One side of her mouth slanted upward in a half-smile. Stopping, she allowed him the opportunity to catch up. "Where's the bike today?" Her lopsided smile stretched into a grin.

"In need of repair," he uttered. As he approached, he stopped several steps away from her.

"Nothing major I hope." Her forehead wrinkled with concern.

"Nah, nothing major. I just won't have time to fool with it until this weekend. I seem to have a tutor who gives me a lot of homework during the school week," he said, laughing.

It was the first time Susan heard Aster laugh—really laugh. He had chuckled a time or two, but at first he wore a rigid mask of indifference. As time passed between them, his hard exterior changed in her presence. She assumed his increased confidence softened his unbreakable guise. Being able to read helped him in more than one way. Catching herself gazing too intently into his eyes, she pried her eyes from him and started for the library. He fell in step next to her as they made their way down the sidewalk.

"I'm sorry I've been so tough on you." She smiled and gave his arm a shove.

Aster winced in pain, drawing Susan's attention to his arm. He curled his shoulder into his chest and grasped his arm as if her slight prod inflicted serious pain. As he rubbed his arm, he accidentally lifted his sleeve. Susan observed two things for certain: his arm had a serious bruise, and it appeared he had a small, round burn scar at the top of his arm in the triceps area.

Without thinking, she halted, grasped his forearm, and gaped. "Oh my gosh, Aster, what happened?"

"Nothing," he growled, yanking his arm free and tugging on his sleeve to cover the bruise.

Susan raised her brow and blurted, "I'm sorry, Aster. I don't mean to pry, but that is *not* nothing. Did you get in a motorcycle wreck? Is that why your bike is not running?"

"Yeah, that's it...Look, no offense, but I don't wanna talk about it, okay?" he pled.

Susan lifted her hands and backed away. "Okay. I'm sorry. I didn't mean to upset you. It just threw me for a loop is all. That's a really bad bruise. I hope you went to the hospital to make sure nothing was broken or fractured."

Frustrated, he grunted, "I'm okay. Let's just get in the library and get on with our lesson. I have a long walk home."

Susan's eyes widened. "What? You have to walk all the way to the east side of town? Nah uh, no way, my mom will give you a ride."

Exasperated, Aster sucked in a deep breath. "No," he hissed through gritted teeth.

"Aster, I'm not taking *no* for an answer. It'll

be dark by the time you make it home, and you told me yourself the crime rate is high on that side of town. I wouldn't be able to live with myself if something happened all because you had to walk home."

"What do you think I did before you moved into town, Susan? You can't possibly think I had people lining up to give me a ride home, can you?"

"Well, did you stay after school and study before I came into town?"

"No, what does that have to do with anything?"

"Then, I'm sure you just rode the bus home if your motorcycle wasn't running. See..." She pointed to her head. "Not just another pretty face. I've got a brain up there, you know. You can't fool me, Aster."

"I'm not allowed to ride the bus," he bluntly replied.

"Oh...well, I don't care what you did before I moved into town, but I do care about what you do now that I am in town." She stood her ground, folding her arms firmly across her chest.

Aster found himself giving in to the persuasion of her chocolate eyes. "How 'bout we make a deal? I'll let your mom drive me to Broad Street as long as she makes a U turn there. Past Broad Street is when you start getting into the slums. Will you let it go if I do that? I really don't think it's a good idea for a car like your mom's to go past that point."

"Okay, deal." She stuck out her hand for a shake.

They shook on it and walked into the library side-by-side for the first time. The librarian noticed them make their way to the back corner and raised her brow in suspicion.

Everyone in town knew of Aster McGrath and the violence that boiled in his blood. His bloodline was abhorrent; his mother was a drunkard, and his father was a murderer serving a life sentence in the state penitentiary. David McGrath was known for his rage. Aster's mother kept a bruised cheek and a black eye before he was sent away. When his brutality finally led him to beat a man to death outside a local bar over a lost pool game, most folks considered her lucky to be free from his violence; unfortunately, the talk around town was Aster didn't stand a chance. He'd end up like one or both.

Susan inched her chair a little closer to Aster's that day as they sat at the table, and Aster found himself liking the proximity. Several times he found himself drawn to the scent of her hair as he gazed down at her golden locks and admired the profile of her face from that angle. He read through the book she picked out without skipping a word. A sense of pride swelled in his heart over the fact he only stuttered through a handful of them. She had turned out to be an amazing tutor. Aster recognized his regard for her strengthened with each passing day.

When nearly an hour had passed, she checked her watch and whispered, "It's time for us to go."

"All right." He acknowledged the time and closed the book.

"Aster," she breathed as they walked toward the glass door together, "my mom knows I've been helping someone, but she may be a little shocked to find you're a guy. She's protective. Ignore it if she says anything cutting or gives you the evil-eye, okay?"

"I'm used to it, Susan. I'll let it roll off me. Dealing with people who don't like me is one thing I'm good at."

Susan's mother glared through the tinted windows as they approached. Susan opened the front door of the car and stuck her head in. "Mom, can we give Aster a ride to Broad Street?" Her eyes pled with her mother for a *yes.*

Susan's mother, Sharon, tilted her sunglasses, glanced at the attractive young man, and narrowed her eyes. Forcing a smile, she gritted her teeth and answered, "Of course, dear."

Aster climbed in the back seat and shut the door. "Thanks," he uttered.

Eyeing him through the rearview mirror, Sharon asked, "Aster, is it?" Her tone was tense.

"Yes, ma'am," he uttered.

"You'll have to give me directions. I'm sure you realize we're new to town, and I can't recall a Broad Street in any of the areas I've been in."

Aster understood the suggestion in her comment. He knew she had never seen a Broad Street between her home on the bay side of town, the hospital, and the school. The school was situated midway between the upper echelon of Bayville and the slums. Most of those residing in the bay area had heard of Broad Street, a well-known line not to be crossed.

Obscuring the small amount of sunlight left for that time of the evening in late October, dark clouds rolled through the sky. "Take a right out of the parking lot and another right at the end of the road, Ma'am."

As they neared the impecunious portion of

town, Susan witnessed the vast difference in the neighborhoods and homes. She went from seeing lavish homes with impeccable lawns to houses with chipping paint and overgrown yards.

Aster caught Sharon glaring at him through the rear-view mirror several times. Her eyes studied him. Each time, after staring at him, her eyes shifted toward her daughter and watched as she sat still and silent in the passenger seat. Thunder broke through and rumbled, warning of heavy rain. Aster found himself gazing at the floorboard for the majority of the ride. He only looked up to answer a question or give further instructions.

"If you'll get in the left lane, you can make a U turn at the next light. I'll just jump out there and walk the rest of the way." Aster pointed toward the approaching red light. His eyes followed rain drops as they rolled off the polished hood of the car and made their way up the windshield.

"You live close to here?" Sharon's eyes tightened, studying the young man's composure and body language.

"Not too far."

"How far is it?" Susan craned her head to glance at Aster and spoke up for the first time on the trip. Concern over the coming storm filled her voice.

Aster picked up on the fact she seemed to be intimidated by her mother for some reason. "It's just a hop, skip, and a jump thata way." He pointed east.

"I'm sure he'll be fine, dear." Sharon cut her eyes at her daughter.

"I'll be okay. I assure you. It wouldn't be safe for you guys to drive into my neighborhood." He reminded Susan of his concern over their driving him home. "I've walked in the rain plenty of times. It's more dangerous riding my motorcycle in the rain than it is to walk, anyway."

"You drive a motorcycle?" Sharon pried, gathering as much information as she could on the young man her daughter had been spending every afternoon with. Although uncertain, Sharon sensed their time together had not been in a study group, but rather, she seemed to know it was just the two of them—alone.

"Yes, Ma'am. It's broke down right now, but I'll have it running this weekend. It'll only take an hour or so to work out the problem. I just need a few small parts."

Susan pivoted in her seat, facing Aster, and narrowed her eyes in thought. She suspected he had *not* received those bruises from a motorcycle wreck, and now she felt almost certain he confirmed it. She glanced down at his arm for a fleeting moment. She quickly turned back around when he caught her gaze. She noticed the way he tugged on his sleeve to make sure and cover the bruise and scar. She tried to find a picture of his arm in her memory banks. She shifted her gaze and concentrated on what she had seen on their walk to the library that day. The bruise was fresh. She remembered that clearly, but the circular scar was old. It reminded her of one of those after school specials she had seen one time about abuse. The kid in the show had been burnt by a cigarette. She wondered if that was what had been done to him. She even considered he may have done it to himself. She knew a girl back in Birmingham who would cut herself, so she knew it was a possibility.

"So, you do mechanic work?" Sharon questioned.

"I fool around with it a little, mostly on

motorcycles. I built mine from scraps from the junk yard. I've worked on my mom's car. I don't know as much about them, but I'm able to keep it runnin' for her."

"I'm sure she appreciates that. Does your mom work, or is she a stay-at-home mom?" Sharon pried.

"She's disabled, so she's home."

Sharon's voice lowered. "Oh, I'm sorry to hear that."

The car rolled to a stop. Aster opened the door and mumbled, "See ya tomorrow at school, Susan." He shut the door behind him and glanced back to see Susan wave *bye*. As he turned and dashed across the street, the bottom fell out.

Worried, Susan sighed. She stared out the window and watched him jog away from them in the rain.

Chapter 4

The Bay

The crunching and crackling of glass echoed through the room under the weight of Aster's shoes. He paced back and forth, trying to suppress the animalistic rage churning within him. His forehead wrinkled in pain as his memories taunted him. *How could I have done that?* He seethed.

Aster pinched the bridge of his nose and furrowed his brow. The memories were becoming more painful. *She's done so much to help me. How could I do what I just did to her?* He wondered.

It was the day after Susan had insisted he allow her mom to drive him to Broad Street, and it was the end of October which brought with it a change in weather most Mississippians welcomed. Cool morning breezes testified to the arrival of fall, and the crisp, chilly nights brought a sense of tranquility to the coast after the lengthy chaos of summer with its sweltering heat and bustling beaches full of tourists and partying teenagers. As the leaves changed colors and fell, Aster's heart was altered.

Susan ambled down the steps of the school, stopped on the sidewalk, and scanned the surrounding area, searching for Aster. With a huff she started for the library alone. Silence surrounded her. She pondered the previous day and wondered if she had offended him. A light breeze blew, rustling the tree branches and dispersing a shower of leaves. She cut her eyes to the street, hoping to see him race past her on his motorcycle. Disappointment surged toward her heart when no motorcycle passed. As she approached the building, she sought the parking lot for his motorcycle. Again, she found nothing. Considering the previous day, she expected not to see it parked there. What she didn't expect was for him not to be walking next to her. She contemplated it and hoped he had left school early to walk there. With that possibility in mind, she entered the library and made her way to the back. She let out a sigh of relief when she saw him sitting in their usual spot reading. A small smile inched its way across her face.

Susan wiggled her chair in close to assist him as he read. Immediately she sensed the boundary set up between them; he was distant, even more distant than usual. It seemed as if he had dressed himself in a hard shell when he awoke that morning. The personality she had begun to see come out in him had been muted, and his countenance was unsociable. She detected the strong possibility he knew her suspicion of his secret and felt uncomfortable around her now.

A wave of guilt rushed through Aster's mind as he did his best to detach himself. As he rode in the black BMW a day earlier, he immediately picked up on the fact Susan recognized the bruise on the upper part of his arm to be a result of a beating. She had already freaked out on him when she saw it during their walk to the library. He didn't want her probing him with questions, and the only way he knew to ensure she didn't was to turn cold toward her, so he cut his last class to assure she didn't have the opportunity to quiz him on the way to their tutoring session. He considered not showing up at all, but he swiftly shoved that thought from his mind. In order to get a decent-paying job, he needed his diploma.

Aster glanced at Susan's watch. The long hand surpassed her mom's arrival time by fifteen minutes. She continued to flip through the flashcards, oblivious to the time, so he pushed his chair away from the table and grunted, "I guess it's gettin' close to time for me to head on home. Not much daylight left."

Susan's eyes shifted to her watch. "Oh, yeah, we better get going. Sorry, I just lost track of the time. I guess I just didn't feel the pressure to keep an eye on it today," she uttered while grabbing her backpack. Feeling the invisible barrier between them, she dared not glance his way as she packed her things.

Aster couldn't help himself. He nudged a slight crack in the icy shell. "Why not?"

Those two words gave her permission to engage in an actual conversation. She gazed at him for the first time. "My mom flew out this morning with my dad to be at some doctors' convention in Scotland. She doesn't have to be there, but she likes to go visit the places they hold those cardiology meetings. They hold them every year in a different country. She's seen a lot of the world that way."

"You didn't want to go?" He raised his brow.

She stood and began moving toward the door in a fluid saunter. Aster followed. "No, you'll find out I'm not too big on missing school. Haven't missed a day in two years. I did miss a week in my freshman year, but I was in the hospital with pneumonia, so I gave myself a break." She smiled up at him.

"So, did you drive to school?"

"No, I have a license, but my mom said she didn't want me driving while she was gone. I think she was afraid I might drive you home." She snickered.

"Ohhh..." he sighed. "I get it. I don't blame her a bit for not trusting me to be alone in a car with you. Being in a library is at least a public place."

Susan rolled her eyes. "Well, I'm sure she doesn't, but I imagine she was more concerned about her car crossing over Broad Street."

"She pretty strict?"

"In a way." Her voice rose above a whisper as the library door shut behind them. "But it's more of a controlling the direction of my life thing rather than saying I can't have fun or do certain things."

"So, how did it feel for the little rich girl to have to ride the bus to school?" He laughed, making his comment light rather than offensive.

She shrugged her shoulders. "I wouldn't know. My mom arranged for my neighbor to bring me to school."

"So, you have a ride home then, right?"

"Nope, he had things to do, so I told him I had a way home."

Aster came to a standstill. "So, you lied?"

"I did *not!*" Susan's eyes bulged. "I don't lie. I have a way home...my feet. They'll get me there just fine."

The hardness around Aster weakened. "In like an hour. It'll be nearing dark by then. That's not safe, Susan."

"I'm going to the safe side of town, remember?" Her eyes gleamed with jest as she nudged his arm without thinking. Aster cringed. Susan's face fell solemn when she realized what she had done. She wanted to apologize, but she didn't want to draw attention to his injury either. He was finally having a conversation with her for the first time that day. She didn't want him to start rebuilding the barricade she felt he was slowly removing, so she kept her apology to herself. She started walking again and made a left out of the parking lot. Aster followed.

"Are you following me home?" She smiled.

"Nope, just thought I'd go sit by the bay for a while. I've gotta lot on my mind these days, and it helps me to think things through. It's peaceful, you know." He glanced down at her.

"I figured you thought of your motorcycle rides as peaceful," she whispered, gazing into his blue eyes.

"Oh, they are, but in case you forgot, I wrecked my bike." He made another attempt to shift the blame for the bruise on a wreck rather than the reality of what had taken place.

Susan didn't respond to his comment, so the two of them walked side-by-side in silence. Fifty-two minutes had passed when they approached the bay. At that point it became necessary for Aster to shatter the quietness. "Following me to the bay? Or do you live in one of these houses right here on it?"

"Yes and no. No, I live down Driftwood Circle, that way." She pointed in the direction of the road. "It's only a hop, skip, and a jump thata way," she giggled, "and yes, I am following you to the bay. I haven't had a chance to walk along the beach yet. I seem to have a pupil who keeps me busy every day after school." A wide grin spread across her face. "So I thought maybe I'd join you unless you want to be alone, that is."

Aster chuckled at her jest and took a deep breath. He had only followed her to make sure she made it home safe. He had no intentions of actually going to the bay. It was his excuse to follow her, but now he found himself standing in front of her wishing she would go on home yet yearning for her presence. His resolve to shut her out grew weaker by the minute, so he gave in to his longing to be near her and decided a stroll down the beach was just what he desired. "Sure, you can join me," he mumbled.

Making their way closer to Driftwood Circle, they walked down the beach of the bay. The street lights lining the main road flickered on and cast heavy light across the sand, causing the water to glisten. Aster bent over and rolled his jeans up to his knees, slipped his shoes off, looked down at Susan, and asked, "So, you gonna join me or what?"

"Seriously? You're gonna get in that water? It's kinda murky and brown."

"City girl needs a swimming pool?" He teased.

"Ummm...yeah...I do." She laughed. "I have an issue with getting in water creatures live in."

"Roll those pants up right now, or I will." He knit his brow, trying to hold a stern look but couldn't hold back his smile. "You need to loosen up a little and live. I won't let your fancy clothes get wet, I promise."

With a sigh she gave in, slipped off her shoes, and rolled up her pants.

"Okay, follow me." Aster took off sprinting toward the water.

Susan followed. As soon as a small ripple of crisp water splashed over her feet, she froze. "Oh, the water's a little cool."

"Just a little. The shock'll wear off in a minute," he assured her.

Susan didn't budge, so Aster stepped to her side, grabbed her hand, and inched her forward. Starbursts of artificial light shimmered through the water. At ankle deep Susan looked down at her feet and screeched, "Oh, my gosh, there's a kazillion little fish swimming around my feet!"

"Those are minnows. They're attracted to the pink toenail polish. They probably think your toes are food." A playful, half-smile inched its way up one side of Aster's face.

"No way." She giggled. "Okay, that's far enough for me. I'm sure there's bigger fish out there, and I'm not so sure I'm ready to have them thinking my toes are food." She pulled her arm from his and turned back toward the beach.

"That's not what I call loosening up and living." Aster laughed, followed her to the beach, and sat down next to her.

"Well...you may have to learn a little patience with me when it comes to offering my toes as a sacrifice." She chuckled. "So, what do you think it would take to cause me to loosen up and live a little?" She narrowed her eyes and teased.

"A motorcycle ride," he blurted without thinking.

"So, that's the secret to living, huh? You get that motorcycle fixed, and I just may allow you to take me on a ride."

"Really?" He raised an eyebrow. "So you're brave enough to place your life in my hands on a motorcycle but not in murky water, huh?"

"Yep, on one condition."

"Oh, so there are conditions involved?"

Susan joshed right back, "Ummm…if I'm going to put my life in your hands, I have some demands." Her countenance quickly shifted; her smile faded. "Can I ask you something without you getting mad at me or shutting me out?"

Wary, Aster responded, "I suppose."

"Why did you lie to me?" Her eyes pled with gentleness.

Aster inhaled a deep breath. In a slow exhale he released it, along with the remainder of the shell he housed around himself. He wanted to prevent this moment. His eyes shifted away from hers. He glanced out over the water. "It was easier than telling the truth."

"So, what is the truth?"

Aster sat in silence.

"You don't have to tell me if you don't want to, but I would like to think you trust me enough to tell me."

Aster sighed and gave in. "My arm had a couple of run-ins with a broom handle is all."

"Your dad?"

"No, he's in prison. And that bit of information right there is why you probably shouldn't be seen in public with me. I'm branded by this town, you know." He warned her of the label she may get for her help.

"I'm not gonna stop helping you or being your friend. That wouldn't be the right thing to do, so don't try and convince me it is, okay?"

"You're not afraid of the gossip in this town?"

"Nope, people's opinions don't matter. There's only one opinion that matters."

"And whose would that be?"

"God's."

"Oh, you're one of those."

"What does that mean?"

"One of those preppy, goody-two-shoes with a list of dos and don'ts, afraid if she messes up and does the don'ts, she burns for all eternity yet desperately wants to win God's approval by saving the town sinner." His smile withered, and his face turned sour.

"No, I'm not one of those. I'm not trying to save you, Aster. I couldn't if I tried." She raised her brow in a teasing way before dropping them back in sincerity. "I just want to make a difference in your life. You don't have to have the same future as your father, you know." Her eyes flooded with compassion.

Aster gazed into them and found he wanted to believe what she was saying. "I'm a bad seed all around, Susan. It's not just from my dad. My mother's a drunk. That's her disability. She can't hold down a job because she can't stay sober."

"Did she hit you with the broom handle?" Susan's voice quivered.

Aster picked up a hand full of sand and allowed it to slip through his fingers. He watched it build a small pile as it landed. "Yeah, I was three when my dad went to prison. My mom...well...she took to the bottle and resented having to take care of me and my little sister. She usually didn't. We learned to take care of ourselves. We were both put in foster care when I was five because the department of human services found out she had burned me with a cigarette for dropping a gallon of milk and spilling it."

Aster didn't know how or why his story seemed to be rolling off his tongue so easy. He had never shared it with anyone before. Susan sat quiet and listened. "The court forced my mom to sober up or else face jail. I lived on this side of town for a year with a foster family before the court gave me back to my mom. Her sobriety lasted about six months after my return. The case worker stopped by occasionally to check on us, but her visits were always announced, so my mom was sure to be sober and the house was always clean. In the meantime, mom learned how to punish me without leaving marks. Apparently, my dad learned a trick in prison. Soap in a sock doesn't leave marks, but it hurts like hell. It wasn't until I got a little older and the case worker stopped coming by that she stopped caring if she left them."

Susan's eyes welled with tears. "Why do you stay?"

Aster stared at the pile of sand he sifted. "She's my mom. Who would take care of her if I left? My sister ran away three years ago. I'm all she has left." He turned to stare into her eyes for the first time during his story. "See, my family is cursed."

The tears broke past Susan's lids. "No, you are *not* cursed, Aster," she cried. Her compassion and instinct kicked in. Feeling the urge to console him, she threw her arms around him.

Aster gave in to the warmth of her body next to his and allowed himself to feel emotions he had never experienced before. He returned her embrace. Realizing the vulnerability he felt, he squirmed and wrenched himself free of the feelings rushing through him by tugging himself free from her grasp and standing to his feet. "Come on. Let's get you home. I've got a long walk ahead of me.

Chapter 5

The Bike

Aster picked up a shard of glass and squeezed it in his hand. Cutting him, it broke through several layers of skin. He strode across the room to the bookcase and held the glass and the flowers over a small garbage can and dropped them. Blood dripped down the white liner. He lingered there, staring at his own life oozing from his body. He gave in to his nature, the nature he had fought for years to bury. It was the nature passed through his bloodline, his family curse. Nothing good could come from a McGrath; everyone in Bayville knew that, and no matter how hard Aster tried, he was doomed to revert to the sadistic nature passed on to him through his parents.

Aster rubbed his eyes and scanned the bookcase. He caught a fleeting glance of a 5 x 7 frame. His hand was drawn to it. He envisioned Susan strolling across the room and picking it up. He saw her fingertips gently caress the frame. He picked it up and stared at the picture it encased. It was a picture of him on his motorcycle in front of the bay. Susan had taken it the day after he got it running again. As he gazed at the white sand and the blue water in the background, the intense struggle he faced after their first visit to the bay together bombarded his mind. She slowly chiseled her way through the hard exterior of his heart, something no one else had ever been able to do.

Aster had opened up to Susan and allowed her to see a glimpse of his life the day he followed her to the bay, and later that same night his battle began as he lay in bed trying to sleep. It had followed him into the morning along with the sun's light, but it grew in intensity as he pulled out his tools to work on his motorcycle.

Finding out where she lived, Aster walked Susan home the afternoon he spent with her on the beach at the bay. "Thank you for walking me home." She smiled. "You didn't have to, you know, but I'm glad you did." She blushed and looked to the floor of the porch, pulled out her key, and unlocked the door.

"Not a problem," Aster mumbled, turning to walk down the porch steps.

"Aster," she called.

"Yeah?"

"Thank you for sharing those things with me. I know it couldn't have been easy."

Aster sighed.

"I wasn't lying, you know," she uttered, her

eyes capturing his in a gaze.

"About what?"

"You not being cursed. I don't believe it. I don't care who your parents are; when I look at you, I see a good guy." Susan didn't give Aster an opportunity to refute her claim. She opened the door, entered her house, and closed herself in the security of her home just after she whispered, "Goodnight."

Aster watched the door shut. "Goodnight," he mumbled. He stood there for a fleeting moment before shoving his hands in the pockets of his jeans and moseying down the steps. The creak of a door opening caught his attention, and the loud thud of it shutting caused his heart to pound in his chest. He pivoted his body to see if Susan had come back out to say something more, but instead he saw Shane Garrish standing in the doorway of the house right next door to Susan's. He imagined Shane had been Susan's ride to school that day, especially since he was her next-door neighbor. Aster cringed. He found himself more disappointed it wasn't Susan returning to continue their conversation rather than being aggravated over Shane's presence. He yearned to look at her face one more time.

Shane's arms were folded across his chest as if he were warning Aster to stay away. Standing at the edge of his porch, he glared at Aster with malevolence. "Leave, Aster," he growled.

Aster huffed and spit in Shane's direction before flipping him off and meandering his way down the street headed for home.

He took his time walking home that night. Along the way he replayed the moments they had shared that day at the bay. He rewound his thoughts to hearing her giggle over the minnows surrounding her pink toe nail polish. He remembered the softness of her skin as he grabbed her hand and led her a little deeper into the water. He watched her jog back to the beach and plop down in the sand. He pictured her face and the way the soft waves of her golden hair fell across it. He listened to the gentleness in her voice as she asked him why he had lied to her. He witnessed the sadness that had shone in her eyes as he told her his story.

Aster was caught up in an instant replay of the day, which slowed his pace, so it was late that night by the time he made it home. As he approached the shack he referred to as home, the loud banging of slamming doors and the clashing of pots and pans alerted him to his mother's rampage. Passing the steps to the house, he shook his head and headed for his bike. He propped himself against a wooden shelf, folded his arms across his chest, stared at the motorcycle he had built from scraps, and listened for the sound of silence coming from the house. He spent much of the evening in the shed dodging her, which resulted in his not getting to bed until the early morning hour of three a.m., which happened to be the time his mother finally passed out.

When his alarm went off a few hours later, he hit the snooze button. After the fifth time, he recognized what he had been doing and argued with himself over whether or not to get up. *You have school and tutoring today. If you don't go today, you won't be able to see Susan again until Monday.*

Giving in to the constant, annoying beeping, he turned the alarm off and flung his legs off the bed. He sat there for a moment and gained his composure before standing to his feet.

As he walked across the old wooden floorboards, they gave way under his weight and creaked. He locked the bathroom door, turned on the shower, and undressed. Allowing the water time to heat, he stared at the bruise on his arm in the mirror. The bruise was so deep it was still a dark purple. It would take weeks for that one to fade, and he knew it. *Good thing this time of year requires longer sleeves most days,* he reminded himself.

Aster stepped out of the shower and wrapped himself in a towel. Before dressing, he peeked into the living room to make sure his mother still slept. He found her sprawled across the couch lying in the exact spot she had passed out in. She had not budged all night. He dressed himself and grabbed a throw to cover her. With gentle movements, he shifted her body to make her more comfortable, placed a pillow under her head, and threw the blanket over her. He glanced at his watch and knew he had to leave if he were to make it to school.

Just stay home and work on your bike. She said she might get you to take her on a ride when you get it running. Run down to the parts store and find what you need and spend the day working on it, he convinced himself to skip school—not that it had ever been hard to persuade himself to play hooky—but for the first time in his life, he found he looked forward to going to school, and he was certain it wasn't getting an education he was fond of. He ached to be in Susan's presence.

Aster shut the door behind him and took off walking in the direction of the parts store. It happened to be located in the city just to the south of them, so he knew he had a long trek ahead of him. "You know, you are just a rundown piece of junk thrown together from parts found in a junk yard, Aster," he told himself. "You're crazy if you're thinking you have a chance with this girl. She's just a nice girl trying to help you to graduate. She's not interested in more than that. She'd reject you in a heartbeat," he murmured under his breath.

"Wait a minute, mister, *she's* the one who threw her arms around me and hugged me. Why should I just automatically assume she'd reject me?" he argued with himself.

"Then again, her hug was nothing more than a hug of compassion. She's a good Christian girl, and she felt sorry for me because of what I told her about my parents and the bruise and scar she saw." He shook his head in defeat.

Aster made it to the parts store in an hour and a half. He knew exactly what he needed. The plug wires on his Honda 750 had burnt in half, so she wasn't running—at all! All he needed were new plug wires, and he knew exactly how to replace them. He spent the better part of the early morning walking to and from the Honda store in Paradise Shore, the neighboring city located on the Gulf of Mexico. Typically he liked to spend some time in the gulf when he ventured to what he referred to as a *real* beach with crashing waves, but he knew he had no time for that. He had to replace those plugs and get his motorcycle running so he could get up early, take Susan out for a ride, and teach her to loosen up a little.

The walk back home was peaceful. He felt good about the whole idea. He would spend the day fixing the bike and spend the entire next day with a beautiful girl riding on the back of it. It wasn't until he got home and began to work on his Honda that the arguments in his mind started again.

"What are you doing? Man, you're just setting yourself up to get hurt by this girl. Why, oh why, did you let her through? Why did you open up to her and tell her some of the things you've been through? You have no way of knowing if you can trust her to keep your secret or not," he fussed at himself.

He became agitated with himself over the battle brewing between the side of him that liked the way it felt to have her arms around him and the side of him that wanted to harden his heart and keep her out. When it came to girls, his experience showed him they were only interested in what a guy could offer them. It didn't matter if he was nice, opened doors, still believed in picking up the bill, or if he was even a gentleman and gave a simple peck on the lips rather than trying to seduce her at the end of the night. The girls he had been out with wanted a taste of what they referred to as *the wild side* by going on fast rides on his motorcycle. They would even dress in promiscuous clothing and flaunt their bodies, enticing him sexually. They wanted to encounter the elation of having sex with a bad boy, but they were only interested in a one-night or one-date fling because they knew he had no money and no future; therefore, he had nothing more to offer them.

"Susan is not like those girls," he argued with himself as he worked on his bike. "She's kind and generous. She knows I live in the slums, and she doesn't care. She still looks at me the same."

"Of course she does. She's just like them...she asked you to take her on a motorcycle ride, didn't she? She's just looking for you to pull her away from the goody boringness of her life. She wants a taste of the wild side is all."

Aster slung his crescent-wrench against the rundown shack he used as a garage. "Damn it.

Aster! Stop beating yourself up. Go on what you do know. You know how easy it was to tell her things you have *never* shared with anyone else in your life outside of your own sister. You knew she was different the first day you met her. You've been vile and even cruel to her in your choice of words and tone, yet she always responds with kindness. She is not out to hurt you. You can trust her with that part of yourself." He encouraged himself.

Aster defeated himself that day and resolved to show up on her doorsteps the following morning offering to give her a bike ride. His intentions were to allow her to pick the place she wanted to go. He replaced the plug wires and took it out for a test run to Paradise Shore. He found himself pulling up to the beach there. He climbed off his bike and strolled onto the beach. He slipped off his shoes and sat at the edge of the water, allowing the waves to wash his feet while he thought about Susan. He watched the sky turn orange as the sun set over the horizon; it wasn't until the stars began to glimmer that he decided it was time to leave.

When he got back home, he locked his motorcycle up in his make-shift garage and headed in the house. His mother had run out of money, so she was sober, but as Aster had come to learn, a sober drunk is often more difficult to deal with than a plastered one.

He spent the majority of the night arguing with his mother over money and groceries. He had been doing his best to manage the funds they had coming in through his mother's social security disability check. He used it to pay the light bill every month and bought the groceries. For his own spending money, he did odd jobs for some of the wealthier folks in Paradise Shore since they didn't know of his family history or of his personal reputation, so it kept him with a little money to spend on himself.

That night his mother quarreled with him over it. She wanted him to spend his money on her alcohol. She knew it would be at least two more days before she had any money to afford it herself, so she laid into him about how it shouldn't be her responsibility to pay the electric bill from her miniscule income when he was the one using up the hot water. Aster agreed to start putting some of his money toward the bill, but he refused to buy her any alcohol. He put his foot down with her and insisted she would have to use her own money to kill herself with. When she kept nagging him to give her the money, he gave up arguing with her about it, shut himself up in his room, and crawled under the covers thinking of Susan.

Chapter 6

The Ride

Aster affectionately traced his fingertips over the picture of him sitting on his old Honda 750 parked on the beach of the bay. He paused and stared at it before laying it back down on the ledge of the bookcase. As his chest constricted causing his breath to be cut short, he closed his eyes. He drew in a sharp breath to relieve the pain his lungs endured, but the muscles in his chest resisted and tightened all the more, compressing his heart and lungs. He squeezed his eyes in pain. Forcefully, he gasped for air. He clenched the area above his heart with his hand. He knew he wasn't having a heart attack. He had experience with this phenomenon. His body reacted to the stress of the day. Thrust into panic mode, he lost control over his thought processes. Overtaken by the horror of reality and the veracity of the strength rising from the beast within him, his face washed ashen; the monster had been dormant for years, but as each second passed, it clawed its way to the surface.

He stretched his hands on both sides of his head and grasped wads of his hair, gripping them with all his might. He could restrain himself no longer. He had to get out of the room that had become a prison to his memories. He pounded his fist into the picture that caused his present anguish. He knew all too well his torment was a result of his sinful, violent nature rising up against the goodness Susan had brought out in him. The sight of that picture had brought the intensity of the love he felt for her to the surface, leaving his emotions raw. He shook the blood from his hand, charged through the door, and found himself climbing on the one thing he could always count on to bring him peace—his motorcycle.

Aster's fingers wrapped around the clutch as his foot shifted his Honda into fourth gear. The wind rushed past him and blew his dark hair away from his anguished eyes. He discovered while the gusty, fresh air had released his pain and torment, it had not propelled Susan from his mind.

Aster washed up and climbed into bed after spending the day working on his motorcycle with the hope of taking Susan for a ride the following day. Pride over his triumph in the ring with his own thoughts swelled in his heart and raced in his thoughts. He assumed sleep would come with ease since he walked so far to Paradise Shore to the parts store and worked on his bike for a couple of hours. The battle over whether he should pursue a relationship with Susan exhausted him. Finding himself lying in the bed staring at the ceiling, shocked him. He counted the black dots on the tiles, trying to send his mind into oblivion. *...sixty-five, sixty-six, sixty-seven...oh come on!* He struggled with the sand man.

Frustrated, he tossed and turned in a desperate attempt to snooze for at least a few minutes, but it was to no avail. Lying in bed (full of anxiety), Aster awaited the arrival of daybreak. He didn't sleep a wink that night. When the beeping of his alarm blared, he crawled out of bed and stumbled to the bathroom. He stood under the shower head for much longer than usual for him. On a typical day he was in and out in no time, but that day he needed the water to soak in and revive his tired body.

As the warmth of the water saturated his skin, he imagined how he might approach Susan. *I'll just drive over and tell her I came to apologize for unloading my problems on her. Maybe she'll see I got my bike running and ask for that ride. No...I'm just gonna be frank and tell her I like her and ask her if she's ready to loosen up and live a little. Nah, I can't do that. I can't be that forward with her. If she doesn't feel what I feel, it could really mess up our friendship. Damn it, why is she affecting me like this? I've never been this unsure about approaching a girl before. Ok, I'm just gonna drive over and see what happens. I'll just wing it.*

Climbing out of the shower, he wrapped a towel around his drenched body and made his way to his closet. He took his time searching for his nicest shirt only to find it needed ironing.

"Damn it," he grumbled.

Aster tiptoed into his mother's room where she lay sleeping on her bed. It was normal for her to do so on the nights she didn't drink herself to sleep. On heavy drinking nights she passed out wherever she happened to be when she took her last swig. Aster found her in the tub on many occasions and even on the kitchen floor in front of the stove several other times. He always assumed she had decided she was hungry and had gone to cook something to eat only to pass out before having the opportunity to turn the stove on. He was always glad when he found the stove untouched. He often wondered if one day she would turn the stove on before passing out and burn the house down with both of them in it. As long as he stayed sober himself, he hoped he may have enough sense to smell the fire, wake up, and save himself, but he knew all too well that by the time he awoke (if she was indeed in the kitchen trying to cook when she passed out), she'd already be gone when he came to his senses and realized what was taking place. He knew he would do well to get himself to safety, which always left him grateful his sister no longer lived with them. He feared if she were still living at home, he wouldn't be able to save her under such circumstances.

Aster grabbed the iron and the ironing board shoved against his mother's wall. Flinching, he craned his head to peer at his mother when the old, metal ironing board screeched. Folding it closed, he grabbed a hold of it and the iron and crept out of the room. On more than one occasion, his mother had become violent after being awakened by Eva or himself, so he held his breath as he exited her bedroom. Aster plugged the iron into the only outlet in his room and shut his door. He hated ironing, but he cared about what Susan thought of his appearance, so he spent his time making sure to release every wrinkle with the heat of the heavy iron. He glared at the pointed nose of the iron and twisted his body to gaze at the imprint it had made on the back of his upper thigh. That happened on one of the occasions he stepped between his mother and his sister. There had been too many instances to count where he had intervened in order to prevent his sister from being beaten, but that particular evening was the worst of them all.

Aster helped his sister run away that night after she dressed his wound. As usual their mother was drunk. She hollered for Eva to iron her clothes for the following day. Eva, twelve at the time, had been doing her homework. Aster always protected his little sister. He had taken care of her from the time she was barely one and toddling around the house with a saggy diaper. He endured most of the beatings meant for her because he dove in front of her, and that night when he saw his mother's face flush red the way it always did before she unleashed her fury, he threw himself over his little sister just in time. Because he had just taken a shower as it all went down, he wore only underwear, so the tip of the iron seared the hair and skin on the backside of his upper thigh.

Aster remembered all too well the tears flooding his sister's face as she stooped over him and removed the wash cloth filled with ice. He flinched as he recalled the sound of his own scream as Eva rubbed ointment on his burn and wrapped it with gauze.

"I'm so sorry, Aster. It's my fault. I shoulda just done the ironing," she bawled.

"It's not your fault, Eva, but she's gettin' worse. I want you to go pack a bag and go to your friend's house on the bay side. Melody's mom will take you in."

"But what about you?" she cried.

"Don't worry about me. I'll handle it. Mom won't care you're not here. She'll probably be relieved and wish I would leave too. We can see each other at school, okay," he insisted.

"Okay," she whimpered.

After their mother passed out for the night, Aster helped his sister pack her bag. Eva wept as she said her goodbyes and kissed him on the cheek before climbing out the window. "I love you, Aster," she sobbed.

"I love you too. Now get on outta here. I'll see you tomorrow at school."

Aster shook the burning memory from his head and finished ironing his shirt. He slipped on his best jeans and spent plenty of time brushing his teeth and gargling with mouthwash before combing his hair. He opened the top drawer of the clear, plastic, make-shift dresser he had purchased from the isle full of storage units in Wal-Mart and grabbed a cheap bottle of cologne. He doused himself with it before returning it to its spot under his socks.

He left his house at seven-thirty that morning feeling like he was on top of the world. Stopping along the way to fill up with gas, he drove his bike to the bayside of town. When he pulled into Susan's drive, nervousness rushed through his veins. He inhaled a deep breath, ran his fingers through his helmet-hair, and composed himself. Shutting off his bike, he shoved the kickstand in place, jogged up the stairs, and knocked on her door. He knocked several times before he saw her peer through the decorative window of their fancy front door. Seeing disappointment wafting from Susan's countenance as she stared at him through the door, confusion washed through him, and his nervousness resurfaced. His hands shook, so he clasped them together behind his back.

Susan opened the door and folded her arms across her chest with a huff. "You know, I waited for you in the library yesterday, but you never showed up."

"I'm sorry. I figured you'd realize I wasn't coming when you saw I wasn't in English. I had a rough night, so I didn't get much sleep. When I woke up, I was running late, so I decided to stay home and get the motorcycle running so I could take you on that ride," he explained. His eyes searched for forgiveness. "Did you have to walk home by yourself?"

"Yeah, but it was okay. I needed the time to think anyway." She dropped her arms to her side as a sign of absolving him from any guilt. "So, you fixed your bike and want to take me for a ride, huh?" She grinned.

"If you'd like. We can go anywhere you wanna go as long as your parents are okay with it." Aster peered over her shoulder searching for signs of her mother's presence.

"Oh, they're still out of town." She waved him off. "They won't be back until Wednesday evening. They usually call and check in around ten every night to make sure I'm home safe and heading to bed." She shrugged her shoulders.

"So, how long will it take you to get ready?" He raised his brow.

Susan blushed when she realized she stood in front of Aster in her pajamas. "Oh, ummm...come on in and sit in the living room while I get dressed." She held open the door and made room for him to enter. "It'll just take a minute. I'll throw on some old jeans and a t-shirt."

Susan led him to the enormous formal living room adorned with Victorian furniture and elegant pictures. Afraid he may soil the antique, he hesitantly sat on the settee.

"Be right back," she uttered. She darted up the staircase and closed her bedroom door.

Within fifteen minutes she strolled down the stairs sporting jeans, a t-shirt, and a ponytail. *Even dressed down without a stitch of makeup, she's beautiful,* he thought as he gazed at her standing in the foyer, waving for him to come on.

Susan shut and locked the door behind her as they stepped onto the porch.

"Where you headed?" She heard a familiar male voice.

Aster clenched his fists when he heard the voice. Slowly twisting his body, he faced Shane. Susan simply smiled. "Oh, hey, Shane, Aster's gonna take me out on a motorcycle ride. How are you today?" She seemed unaware of Shane's glare at Aster.

"I'm good. Are you sure your parents will be okay with you going off on a motorcycle ride with a practical stranger?" He tried to seem concerned for her wellbeing.

Susan remembered their agreement to keep tutoring private, so she thought her words through before speaking them. "Oh, Aster's no stranger to me. We're friends. My mom has even met him," she assured Shane.

"And she approves of him and where he comes from?" he snapped.

"Shane!" Susan's voice escalated, and her forehead crinkled. "I really don't think this is any of your business."

"She's right; this is none of your business, Shane, so stay out of it," Aster spoke up.

Shane narrowed his eyes and glared at Aster.

Aster pressed his lips in a hard line and threatened, "I'll get into your business if you don't."

Fully aware of what Aster's threat meant, Shane stepped back. His eyes widened and shifted to Susan in fear she understood it as well.

Susan gawked in disbelief. "What's going on between you two? Is there something I should know about?" she pried.

Relieved she was oblivious to their history, Shane folded his arms across his chest and blurted, "No, nothing's going on. Just be careful, Susan. Motorcycles are dangerous." He tried once again to come across as merely being concerned for her safety.

"I will." She waved bye.

Shane stepped back in his house but watched them from the window. Susan, unaware of his eagle-eye, bounced down the front steps. Aster cut his eyes to Shane's house and watched as his hand drew back the curtains. He knew Shane Garrish would be peeking on them. He set his focus on Susan and followed her down the steps.

As they approached Aster's motorcycle, Susan asked, "What was that about?"

Aster glanced toward Shane's house before answering, "I don't like him, and he doesn't like me. That's all." Aster grabbed the extra helmet he had purchased while at the Honda store the previous day and slipped in on her head.

"Do you always carry a passenger helmet?" Susan questioned with a whimsical smile.

A half-smile crossed Aster's face. "No, I picked it up yesterday when I bought the parts to fix my bike."

"Hmmm...Oh, do you have somewhere to stuff this?" she questioned, shoving a small 35mm camera in his face.

"Sure." He lifted his seat exposing a small cubby and took the camera from her. "Planning on taking pictures, huh?"

"Yep." She smiled.

"So, where to?"

"Ride by the bay first. I wanna take a picture of you on your bike in the sand."

Crinkling his forehead, Aster arched an eyebrow. "That's illegal, you know."

"Taking pictures?" Her eyes gleamed and a huge grin spread across her face.

Knowing she knew full well it wasn't taking a picture that was illegal, he shrugged. "Okay, whatever you say."

"Well, you did tell me to loosen up and live a little. Besides, we're not gonna harm anybody by snapping a quick picture before getting on the Interstate."

"The Interstate? Where exactly are you planning on me taking you?" Aster tightened the strap on her helmet, climbed on his 750, turned the key, and cranked it.

"I wanna show you something, but it's at least a four-hour drive, so we've gotta be quick at the bay."

"Ummm...you sure you wanna go off that far?"

Susan climbed on the back of his bike and wrapped her arms around his waist. "Yes, I have something I wanna show you, and it just so happens to be the perfect time of year for it," she hollered in his ear over the roaring of the motor. "I have gas money if you weren't expecting to go so far," she added.

"I'm covered," he assured her, feeling a

slight stab to his ego.

"Okay, then let's go so you can get me back home before my parents call tonight." She laughed.

As Aster took off down the road, he instructed, "Hold tight, and when we go into curves, make sure you lean with my body, okay?"

"Okay."

After turning onto Main Street, he pulled into a parking spot on the bay. Susan climbed off and tugged on her t-shirt. Aster dismounted, retrieved her camera, and smiled. "Take it quick so I don't get arrested," he said, chortling as he threw his leg back over the seat. "They'll use any excuse in this town to pick me up, you know."

"I'll be faster than Speedy Gonzales." She smiled.

He shook his head at her reference, revved the motor, looked all around for any signs of police cars or locals who held a certain disdain for him, and drove into the sand. He slowed to a stop and allowed Susan to snap her picture before heading back to pick her up. "Happy?" His eyes smiled.

She grinned. "Yes, I am." Climbing back on, she secured her arms around his torso.

"So, where to?"

"You'll see when we get there. Just head for Interstate 10 and go east."

Aster looked both ways before entering the street. "Hold on tight," he hollered as the engine roared. He hit Highway 90 and headed for the nearest intersection that led them to the Interstate. The blustering wind surged past them as he laid his bike wide open. He smiled every time Susan laughed as they made their way to Interstate 10. He enjoyed the sensation each time she tightened her grip around his waist, and he found he didn't really care where she led him as long as she was with him.

Chapter 7

The Field

Aster flexed his forearm, pulling his wrist back and opening the engine full throttle. He needed to escape his emotions. It took less than a mile for him to realize the faster the wheels of his motorcycle turned and the harder the wind slammed into his face, the louder his memories screamed in his mind. He needed them to quiet. He was desperate. He cut his eyes to glance at the bay as he passed and cringed at the memories it brought. His deafening thoughts screamed, piercing his mind and distorting his vision. The old-town buildings to his right blurred. He had no idea where he was headed. He just knew he had to get out of town; he had to escape the torment.

After an hour on the Interstate, the pictures in Aster's mind faded, taking his racing memories with them. The peace he often found while on long motorcycle rides draped over him, the reason he loved to set out on Saturday afternoon drives by himself. He had been doing it for as long as he could remember, or at least since he had found and fixed up his first bike.

At the age of twelve, Aster mustered the courage to enter the forbidden, rundown shed behind his house. He rummaged through his dad's old tools and tackle box, searching for a knife and fishing line, when he spotted a tarp in the back of the shed. A shaft of sunlight broke through the dirty window in the back wall and bounced off an exposed piece of rusty metal. It glistened and caught his attention. He climbed over piles of junk to investigate, and that is where he found his dad's old dirt bike. Pulling it out from under the tarp, he grabbed an old cloth and dusted it off the best he could. He pondered how he could get it running and remembered Mr. Hyde, the mechanics teacher at the high school, visiting their school on career day.

Aster rushed inside and found the phonebook. He skimmed through the pages, looking up Mr. Hyde's address. Slamming the phonebook back down, he raced back out and pushed the old bike to the bay side of town. Panting as he approached his home, he knocked on the door.

A stout black man opened the door. "Yes, can I help you?"

"Mr. Hyde, you came to our school a few months back on career day and talked about being a mechanic. I found my dad's old dirt bike and was wonderin' if you could show me how to fix it up?"

Mr. Hyde rubbed his chin in thought. "Yes, I remember that, but I can't seem to place you, young man. What's your name?"

"Aster...Aster McGrath."

Instinctively, Mr. Hyde furrowed his brow. The McGraths' reputation preceded them. "Uh huh...well, why don't you head on out to my workshop right out there." He pointed to a large grey building. "And I'll just inform my wife I'll be out there working."

"Thank you," Aster mumbled as he shoved the bike toward the shop.

Mr. Hyde met Aster by the shop and unlocked the door. That day he instructed Aster in the basics and assisted him in tuning up the old bike. It took them a full day, but it was worth it. Mr. Hyde took Aster under his wings. When the sun began to set, he insisted Aster come back for pointers on engines anytime. Aster spent many afternoons at Mr. Hyde's home learning as much as he could about motorcycles and how their engines worked.

When Aster first began taking his bike out on rides, he found it brought a sense of peace. It became the only way he knew to escape the Hell he lived in; Hell was definitely the best way to describe his home life. Before his sister ran away, he would take her out for rides to a small community north of their hometown. He found a creek tucked away in a wooded area there. It was hidden so well it took him several trips to map out the directions. Sometimes he pitched a tent so they could spend a night away from home. The birds singing and the crickets chirping were therapeutic for them both. They often sat together in silence and listened to the sounds of trickling water. Eva described it as *Mother Nature's music*, and maintained that her melody had a way of bringing tranquility into the direst of chaos.

With a home-life full of pandemonium and utter disorder, serenity was often the only thing to keep Aster sane and calm the rage boiling within his own blood. Time after time, he envisioned having an outburst of wrath and pictured himself standing over the bloodied, beaten body of his mother; it was frequent and frightening. Despite the fact she abused him, she was his mother, and he loved her. He knew he had to resist the impulse to retaliate in such a violent manner. She was sick—terribly sick. What she needed was help, and he knew it, yet he didn't know how he could get her the help she required. He understood there should be consequences which should entail jail time for the things she had done; nevertheless, he always came back to the thought, *she's my mom.*

Before he started doing odd jobs like mowing lawns, weed eating, trimming hedges, replacing brakes and spark plugs, and changing oil for some of the wealthier folks in Paradise Shore, Aster collected aluminum cans and recycled them for spare money. After he got the old dirt bike in good enough running condition to travel out of town on it, he saved money from his recycling adventures to buy an old .22 rifle from an elderly man down the street from him. He set up targets in his backyard and taught himself how to aim and shoot, so when Eva went with him on one of their camping trips, he hunted a rabbit or two and roasted it over a fire for dinner. Eva learned how to make a mean rabbit stew. They feasted on their rabbit meal and talked about their dreams of getting out of the slums of Bayville, Mississippi.

Unlike Aster, Eva had book smarts, so he always encouraged her to study hard so she could get a scholarship and make a better life for herself. He had so much faith in her ability to excel in her education that he took on many of her chores in order to give her ample study time, and thanks to the many visits to Mr. Hyde's for lessons on motors, he had turned out to be a fair mechanic, so he always envisioned himself working in a motorcycle shop fixing their engines. It was the one thing about himself that made him feel proud. When it came to his schooling, he felt completely inadequate.

Aster knew his little sister's chances were better than his, so he worked hard to protect her and those chances. Their mother, Loretta, often called for Eva to do crazy chores while she studied for a test or worked on a project that carried a lot of weight in the grading scale, so Aster jumped in and said he would do it. Often he found himself standing in the middle of one of their rooms with all the clothes on the floor being told to iron them, rehang them, refold them, and put them away, and it wasn't even as if it would need to be done; it was always one of his mother's rages which prompted her to go into a perfectly clean room and destroy it while hollering for Eva to come clean up the mess! Their mother easily convinced Aster she didn't want either of them to better themselves.

On their last camping trip before Aster insisted his sister run away, Eva informed him about her conversation with Melody's mom. "Aster, you remember my friend Melody from school? The one I spend the night with sometimes?"

"Yeah, the girl from the bay side?"

"Yeah, her. You know how you don't like her mom because every time I stay at their house, she combs through my hair lookin' for lice?"

"You shouldn't let people treat you like that, Eva. It really pisses me off she thinks you're dirty or something."

"Well, last weekend when I spent the night with her, her mom came in the room and asked if she could talk to me in private. I thought she was gonna check my head again, but she didn't."

"What did she want?" Aster huffed.

Eva gulped. "I told Melody...how momma beats on you...and how she tries to beat on me, but you get in the way," she said, her voice shaking.

Aster and Eva had a rule not to tell anyone what their mother did to him. They were separated for the year they were both placed in foster care, and Aster didn't want them to be pulled apart again. Eva was only three at the time, so she didn't remember her hand being pried from her brother's and being placed in a car screaming, but Aster remembered the sound of his little sister's screams as they yanked her away from him. After they were returned to their mother's custody and once Eva was old enough to understand, he had made her promise him they would never tell a soul about the things their mother did to him.

The memory of Eva's broken moans and fear-filled eyes were burned in his mind, and it brought more pain than the stinging recall of the cigarette being held against his arm.

Aster groaned.

Eva's chin trembled. "I'm sorry, Aster. I know I promised not to tell. Please don't be mad at me. I didn't know she would tell her momma," she cried.

"She told her mom?" Aster's voice escalated.

Eva's tears turned to sobs. She pulled her knees to her chest and propped her forehead on them. Aster sighed, scooted closer to his sister, wrapped his arm around her, and whispered, "It's okay, Eva. I don't want you to feel like you have to fear me exploding the way you fear momma. I'll deal with it. It'll be okay, I promise."

Eva turned into her brother's chest and hugged him. "I'm so sorry," she whimpered.

Aster knit his brows. "What did Melody's mom want, Eva?" Concern grew in his voice.

Eva pulled herself from Aster's arms. She aimed her eyes at his. "She asked me if what Melody said was true. I told her my mom wasn't the best mom in the world but she never hurt me. I tried to fix it, Aster. I told her you just got a lot of whippings because you've started a lot of fights at school. I didn't know what else to say."

"It's okay. I have been in a lot of fights." Aster shrugged his shoulders. "Did she believe you?"

"Yeah, I think so. She lectured me about how I shouldn't lie to my friends about my mom abusing my brother and trying to abuse me. She told me discipline and abuse was not the same thing. I told her I was sorry. I don't think she really likes you now. She said you sound like a trouble maker and that I'm too sweet to have to live with such a bully."

"A bully, huh?" Aster smirked.

"Yeah, and she also said it sounded like you should be in the juvenile detention center. I think she might report you or something cause she said she wished I could just live with them."

Aster rolled his eyes. "Don't worry. There's nothing she can do. I mean, who's she going to report me to? The school already knows all about the fights I've been in." Aster comforted his sister with a tight squeeze.

That discussion planted the thought into

Aster's mind to send her to Melody's house a few weeks later when his mother went after her with a hot iron. Although he didn't want to be separated from his little sister, he feared one day he may not be there when his mom went after her. Living apart was worth keeping her safe. Besides that, he knew living on the bay side of town would provide his little sister with better opportunities for her future.

Aster assumed mulling over his sister and their secret place of escape would have caused him to take an automatic turn on his bike and head back northwest to revisit the creek. He knew it still existed because he had made a recent trip there for a short visit. He had even pitched a tent and roasted a rabbit for supper. It had been on his mother's birthday, and that day always brought back a struggle with anger and depression, so he naturally searched for a place of peace to calm his state of mind. Instead when he gripped the break on the handlebars, he found himself in Alabama sitting in front of the field Susan had taken him to on their first ride.

The day Aster took off with Susan on his bike, the wind wrapped around him as he followed her directions and headed east on Interstate 10. He stopped at a small gas station in Grand Bay, Alabama, so Susan could use the restroom. A few minutes later, she shoved the heavy glass door open with her hip and came out toting two loaded-down hotdogs and a fountain drink. The wind blew several strands of her hair loose from her ponytail. The flowing tresses wisped across her face. She threw her head back, tossing them out of her eyes, and grinned.

"What is that?" Aster hollered.

"This store has the most amazing hotdogs. We ate here on the move down. You've gotta try one." She shoved his hotdog in front of him.

Aster grabbed it and uttered, "Thanks."

"Come on," she called. She pranced over to a small picnic table situated under a large oak tree.

Allowing himself to get a little closer than normal, Aster sat next to her. Susan took a hefty slurp of the drink and then offered, "Wanna swallow?" She pointed the straw in his direction.

"Ummm...I'll go in and get my own in a minute.

"Oh, come on, now, do you think my germs are *that* bad?" she teased. "I bought a big one just so we could share. I only had so many hands to carry the stuff out, you know. You're gonna hurt my feelings if you treat me like you're afraid I've got some kind of disease."

Aster narrowed his eyes in jest. "How do I know you don't?"

"Uh..." She threw her hand over her heart and sniggered, "Oh...it hurts so bad. I don't know if I'll survive."

Aster snatched the drink from her hand and slurped down a big gulp. "There, happy now?"

She grinned. "Yep."

"It's only ten o'clock. What are we doing eating lunch?"

"Oh, this isn't lunch; it's merely a snack. I'm a growing girl, you know." Susan patted her belly. Aster grabbed the paper the hotdogs were wrapped in and the empty paper cup and chunked them in the garbage can. "Score." Susan jumped and threw her arms up in victory.

Aster cut his eyes toward her and smiled. "You know, I think I'm deciding your shyness in the beginning was all pretend. What happened to that sweet, bashful girl I saw two days ago?"

Susan's bottom lip jutted out in a playful pout. "You no longer think I'm sweet?"

"Oh, you're still sweet, but I think I'm seeing a different side of you."

"Well, mister, let's not forget *you* are the one who insisted I needed to let loose and live a little." She giggled.

"I've created a monster, a beautiful monster, mind you."

Susan blushed. Glancing at the ground, she smiled.

Aster gave his head a nod in the direction of his motorcycle and uttered, "Come on. Let's get back on the road. Apparently we're only about halfway there since we're only two hours into our trip. I'm interested in seeing what it is you have to show me."

They climbed back on the bike and drove back out onto the Interstate heading east. It wasn't long before she instructed him to get in the left lane and merge onto Interstate 65, heading north through Alabama. Aster enjoyed the new scenery. He had never been that far up on his motorcycle. He had been to Mobile plenty of times, but he had never crossed the Dolly Parton Bridge before. He was in awe at the beauty of the state.

They were another hour into their ride when Susan hollered in his ear to take the next exit. He veered off the Interstate and made a left onto a small highway. They drove another fifteen minutes west before she had him slow down while she searched for a marker. When she saw the tattered, red barn on the left, she pointed to the gravel road on the right and instructed him to turn.

Aster feared they may not make it out of the maze she had gotten them into once they turned on the gravel road. They drove another thirty minutes before making a left onto another gravel road and a right onto another one and two more rights before she pointed to a dirt road on the left. When the dirt road ended Aster found himself stopped in front of a large field that had to be at least five-hundred acres. Nestled on the backside of the field sat a nice-sized log cabin. Thousands of wildflowers bloomed across the picturesque field.

Chapter 8

The Wildflowers

The cool November wind cut through Aster's thin clothes as if he stood there in the nude, the only assurance he was still alive and breathing. The stabbing memories drained the life from him. His body ached with each gash, and he sensed all of his vitality seeping from his wounds. Drop by drop, he became numb. At an extremely young age, Aster learned to shut off his emotions as a survival technique. For Aster, numbness was the only way to drown out the physical and emotional pain his mother inflicted upon him for the majority of his life. His mother had always chosen whiskey to mask her pain and suffering, but after being returned to her care at the age of six, Aster found a deadened, emotionless state to work quite well, and as far as he was concerned, he had done a fair job of accomplishing it until Susan showed up.

The violent side of his nature cursed Susan

for removing the binding that revealed his heart. He had suffered countless beatings as he cloaked his soul with an invisible fortress and resolved to let no one pass through. He had kept the core of his being securely hidden from the world until she arrived and began (one layer at a time) unraveling the shroud that protected him. The fiend inside him speared his thoughts and accuscd, *"She's the cause of the rage you now face. I've grown fiercer because she exposed your anguish."*

Careful to stop at the outer edge of the field, Aster walked out into the dying grass. Wildflowers created beautiful blooms in October and November. He gazed at the multiple colors surrounding him and reminded himself Susan had been there earlier and picked that bouquet for him. He wondered which part of the field she had found them in. A sudden and piercing sting shot through his heart causing it to ache and throb. His conversation with Susan earlier that morning surged to the surface, driving him mad. Aster picked a black-eyed Susan; its beauty enraged him all the more. Antagonizing himself, he plucked the petals. He held a golden petal between his fingertips and peered at it. Releasing it, the wind wisped it to a feathery bed on the grass. Picking one petal at a time, Aster allowed each of them to fall to the ground until he was left with a petal-less stem. He stared at the *black eye* of it and reflected on its name. Black-eyed Susan, that was the name he had chosen for her. It had been a long time since he had uttered those words. He found himself whispering, "My black-eyed Susan. Why, Susan? Why?"

When Aster and Susan arrived at the field of

flowers, he went to turn the motorcycle off, but she stopped him. "No, there's a driveway just a little farther up. Pull on up to the house. I need some water and a restroom," she instructed.

Aster shifted his body and craned his head to look at her. "You sure about that? These people have no idea we're coming. They're not gonna see some strange guy driving up on a motorcycle and shoot me on the spot, are they?"

Susan shook her head. "No, silly, this is my parents' vacation home. No one is here but us. I have a key." She pulled the key from the pocket of her blue jeans and dangled it in front of him.

"Okay, if you say so." He shrugged.

Aster turned down the long drive and admired the field of wildflowers as they drove past them. He parked in front of the cabin. Susan climbed off. She removed her helmet, pulled her ponytail holder out, and shook her head. Her golden hair fell in layers past her shoulder blades. Aster crouched over the handlebars of his bike and admired her. When she headed up the steps, he knocked the kickstand in place, removed his helmet, and strode behind her. "Come on in," she suggested when he went to sit on the porch swing.

"I'm all right right here," he assured her.

"Aster, we've been on the road for over four hours, and you didn't go in at the gas station to use the restroom. I'm not gonna make you pee in the woods. That wouldn't be very friendly of me, now would it?" Her look was stern.

He raised his brow and followed her into the cabin at her insistence. "Okay, okay, if you insist. Just thought you might feel uncomfortable in a house out in the middle of nowhere alone with a guy, any guy actually, but particularly a guy who has a really bad reputation. I thought I heard you were a good girl." He chuckled.

"With just about any other guy, I *would* feel uncomfortable, but not with you. I trust you."

"You shouldn't, you know."

Susan narrowed her eyes questioning his comment.

He threw his hands in front of him and quickly retorted, "Not that I'm planning to hurt you or take advantage of you or anything like that. It's just not wise for you to trust people so quickly. You should guard yourself better than that."

"You think me too trustworthy of others?"

"Most definitely. You're all about being kind to everyone and giving them the benefit of the doubt, like you did with me. I've watched you at school and seen the way you treat others. I even overheard you talking to your friend Angie a few weeks back. You were insisting she shouldn't believe what Sean had told her about Leslie. I know Leslie, Susan, and she wouldn't have been so gracious to you had someone tried to spread a rumor about you." Aster paused for a moment. "Why do you trust people so easily? I find trust almost impossible."

"Well, I guess your life has been different from mine, so it's more difficult for you to let your guard down. Me...I believe there's good in everyone, and I try to see that. I think God shows me the good in people," Susan explained.

Aster scoffed, "Your God showed you good in me, huh? I don't believe it."

"He did. I believe He told me to help you that day in class."

Aster rolled his eyes. "Why do you think that?"

"Because I sensed immediately that you weren't just defying Ms. Howard. Oh, I saw clearly that you loathe her." She raised her brow. "But I felt the reason you refused was because you were illiterate. It was just a sense I had. You could say God kinda gave me a nudge in that direction," she explained.

"Is that the word for it? Illiterate?" Aster turned his head in pain.

"Yes, it's the formal word for someone who can't read is all."

"Sounds more like the word for someone stricken with an incurable disease." He stared at the floor.

Susan saw the pain reflected in Aster's eyes and felt enormous guilt for being so insensitive. She hadn't meant to cause him pain. "I'm sorry, Aster. Sometimes I just talk in a formal manner about things. That word does sound horrible, doesn't it?"

Aster didn't respond to her question; instead, he replied, "So, you heard this God of yours tell you to help me when you sensed I was *illiterate*?" He emphasized the word.

"Not really. I didn't hear God tell me anything, not audibly anyway. I simply felt something inside of me prompt me to offer my help, and I just had this overwhelming feeling you were refusing to read because you couldn't."

"Well, tell your God I said thank you."

Susan smiled. "He heard you; now go to the bathroom so I can show you the reason I brought you out here."

"Okay, you don't have to be so pushy." He laughed.

Susan pointed Aster to the restroom. When he came back out, she had poured them both a glass of ice water. She handed him one and said, "Drink up so we can go."

Aster guzzled the cool, refreshing water,

walked to the sink, and cleaned his glass. "We leaving already? I thought this was the place you wanted to show me."

"You didn't have to do that, you know. I would've washed it." Susan eyed him drying his wet hands.

"I'm not helpless. I've pretty much taken care of myself for the majority of my life, Susan. I wash my own dishes and even my own clothes. I iron them too, but I despise doing it. I'm a pretty good cook too." He held his head in pride.

"Hmmm...a woman's dream...a man who cooks, washes dishes and clothes, and even irons," she teased. "We're not leaving, but I didn't bring you out here to see the house. There's something else I want you to see. Come on."

Susan snatched a blanket laid over a rocking chair on the other side of the front door, grabbed his hand, and pulled him behind her and back out onto the porch. She marched down the steps and strolled toward the field of wildflowers. The grass, although dying, stopped about half way up Susan's shins.

Appreciating the view of colorful flowers shooting up all around them, Aster stayed at Susan's side. The field was full of blue, lavender, yellow, and white flowers of different varieties. He had seen most of them growing on the sides of the roads back home, especially the daisies and black-eyed Susans, but there were a couple of varieties he had never seen before.

About center field Susan laid the blanket down and sat Indian style. Signaling for Aster to join her, she patted the spot next to her.

Aster plopped down and gazed around him. "It's real pretty out here. Late October sure does bring some amazing flowers out."

"Sure does. During the entire months of

October and November, this field is covered. They come back in the spring too. This is my special place." Susan smiled. She shared one of her secrets with him since he had shared one of his. "When we go on vacation, I come out here to get away from it all."

"Your mom controlling your life kind of stuff?"

"Pretty much. She's different from me is all. She loves me and wants what's best for me, but her idea of that is different from mine." She shrugged her shoulders. "Sometimes it's a little overbearing. Both of my parents are geniuses, so they have extremely high standards for me in that department. I care about my future and all, but sometimes I just want to be a teenager and *live a little.*" She winked.

"So, is she a pretty strict religious lady?" he wondered.

"Oh, no, my parents don't go to church at all." Susan laughed. "That's one of the things she gets aggravated with me over."

"Whadaya mean? You'd think she'd be glad you have a set of moral values."

"Oh, she likes my morals. It's my belief in a higher power she has issues with. My parents are...uncommonly intellectual and intensely scientific...and they don't think God and science mix. I, on the other hand, can't see separating the two," she explained.

"So, what does your mother want for you that is so overwhelming, besides being a genius?"

"College—which I plan—and marriage into an elite family."

"You don't like the idea of marriage or the elite family?" He removed eye contact and gazed at the blanket.

"Oh, I'm not opposed to marriage. It's my

mother picking out my spouse I have a problem with. She likes to play match maker. She's always pointing out the genetic qualities certain guys carry." Susan used her hands to make quotation marks in the air as she said the word *carry*.

Aster felt himself drawing closer to Susan, not in the physical sense but in his heart. He appreciated her opening up to him just as he had opened up to her. He sat in silence thinking of how he knew her mother would *never* approve of his genetics. After a couple of minutes of silence, he grunted, "I guess life can suck no matter what side of the tracks you're from."

"Huh, yeah, I guess so, but all in all, Aster, I have it pretty good." Susan leaned her head to the side. "You've heard I'm a good girl at school?"

"What?" Aster's eyes shifted in confusion.

"Earlier, you said you'd heard I was a good girl. I'm assuming you heard that at school."

"Oh, yeah." Aster cringed slightly.

"What does that mean exactly, and who has said it?"

"Basically, you're a target for a particular group of guys, and for another group you have a humongous sign posted across your forehead that says *stay away*!" he answered.

Susan nodded. "I get it. I'm used to that sort of thing. It's obvious I don't sleep around, so there are those who are not interested at all and others who see me as a challenge." She shrugged her shoulders. "No need to worry about me though. I like the fact there are those who will stay away, and I'm not dumb to the thoughts of those who have me as a target."

"So, you have morals and brains." Aster laughed.

"Ha, nice way to put it." She giggled.

Aster contemplated the extreme difference

in what was obviously his genetics as compared to Susan's, and he pondered on her belief system and how her mother must hate how she sees good in everyone, and then his thoughts drifted to Shane Garrish and how kind to him she seemed to be. He knew it was her nature to be kind to everyone, but he couldn't help but wonder if she saw good in Shane.

"So, I have a question about what you believe and this God of yours."

Susan sat up straight and said, "Okay, shoot."

"Earlier you said you believe there's good in everyone, and God shows it to you," he started.

"Yes." She widened her eyes and nodded her head.

"Well, what kind of good has your God shown you about Shane Garrish?" He tested.

"None yet," she declared, shrugging her shoulders.

"Hmmm...well, I might be swayed then."

"What do you mean?" she pressed. She narrowed her eyes and searched for truth in his.

"Let's just say if you had told me your God showed you something good in him, I'd tell you your God is crazy."

"And why is that?"

"Because he's not good, and you'd be wise to remember that," was all he said in response.

"Hmmm...I'll keep that in mind. He seems nice enough to me. My mother thinks he has good genes," she teased.

"Your mom is not as intelligent as she thinks then," he huffed.

"So, let me ask you a question."

"What?" he whispered, calming his tone.

"What do you know about your name?"

"Whadaya mean?"

"Do you know where your name came from?"

"My *mom*," he responded in jest. "I don't know other than that. I just always assumed she bought one of those books with a bunch of baby names in it."

Susan smiled. "See, I knew the moment Ms. Howard called your name in class, and I turned to see your blue eyes. You see this flower right here." She leaned over and picked a flower with blue petals and a yellow center that looked similar to a daisy. "This is an aster."

"Huh, really? I had no idea I was named after a flower." His eyes widened.

"Yep, it's always been my favorite of all the flowers out here, and when I heard your name and saw your blue eyes, I immediately thought of my special place and my favorite flower."

Aster couldn't help but smile. "Well, if I'm a flower, then you are too."

"Oh, really." Susan grinned.

"Yep, hang on just a sec." He walked out into the field, picked the prettiest black-eyed Susan he could find, and brought it back to the blanket. "I may not know what all these flowers out here are, but I do know this one." He ran his fingertips over the petals and proclaimed, "See the beautiful golden petals, much like your hair, and see the black eye, which gives it its name, much like your chocolate-colored eyes."

Susan smiled. "I never thought about that before. That's pretty cool; we're both wildflowers." She laughed.

Aster thought about the irony of that and wondered if fate or faith or whatever it's called might be real. He was her Aster, and she was his black-eyed Susan.

Chapter 9

The Gift

Aster's mind played tricks on him. Susan's eye gazed back at him as he stared at the petal-less, dark-brown disk at the end of the stem. At first it was only one of her eyes. Then his view of the picture in his head spread into a panoramic scene, and he saw them both. They were fuzzy in the beginning, but as his thoughts of her eyes intensified, they became clear. Her eyes were bloodshot from her emotional cries as a result of the pain she had just endured, the pain he had caused her. In the next instance he saw a flash of her arm covered in bruises. *How could he do that?* His mind tortured him. Infuriated, he wrapped his hand around the dark-brown disk and crushed it, causing it to crumble to the ground like dust. He couldn't take the pain of being in her field; he had to get out of there. He had to unleash the beast raging within him. He knew he lost the battle with his nature, the nature passed onto him through his father and mother. He needed a target, but the tamed side of him screamed at him to search out an object that would not shed blood.

Aster hopped back on his motorcycle. He forcefully thrust the kickstand and took off like a flash of lightning. A cloud of dust spewed into the sky behind him as his back wheel spun with viciousness and sprayed clumps of the dirt road over the field. Once again, he was unsure where he would end up, but he had to at least try to escape the memories. They provoked him to unbridle the part of him Susan and her God had tamed—until that day.

Earlier that day when Susan showed up with the gift of wildflowers and her confession, she awakened the monster inside him. It had been bound for so long it writhed against the chains. Starved for so many years, the fiend sought blood, the only thing that would satisfy its hunger and thirst. Aster seethed as it churned inside him. The revelation he heard and witnessed that morning had nullified the gift she had given him five and a half years prior. Her gift had been the legacy she used to ensnare the fiend inside him, and now the chains around the monster loosened through her disclosure.

Aster saw a picture of Susan in his mind. He watched as her hand brushed past the side of her face and tucked her golden hair behind her ear. He saw her eyes glisten when the sun's rays danced upon them. Then he observed her countenance fall. Her smile quickly faded as melancholy washed over her features. As the images rushed to the surface of his mind, he raced across the state of Alabama on his motorcycle.

Aster had not seen or talked to Susan since school had let out for their winter break. Early Christmas morning a loud knock echoed through his house. *Who could that be?* He wondered. Jumping from his bed, he picked up the jeans he had worn the night before from the floor and slipped them back on. Barefoot, he tiptoed to make sure his mother still slept. She had been up for most of the night raving about his father and how much she hated him. Aster covered her as she lay on the couch and went to the front door to see who could possibly be at his house on Christmas morning.

He had no peep hole, so he spoke as loud as he could to be heard by the person on the other side and as soft as he could not to awaken his mother. "Who is it?"

"It's me, Aster," the female voice replied.

"Eva!" Aster slung the door open, stepped outside, shut the door behind him, and threw his arms around his little sister. "What are you doing here? It's not safe. Mom was just ranting about how you abandoned her just like Dad did. She went on and on about it last night."

"I brought you a gift."

"What? Why?" he stuttered.

Eva smiled and whispered, "Because it's Christmas, silly...You can come out now."

Susan stepped out from the side of the house. "How do you know about her? And why did you bring her here?" he grumbled.

Susan withdrew. "I'll leave." She turned to head down the road.

"No, wait...stop. I'm sorry. I'm just confused as to how you know my sister. Look, give me a minute to put on a shirt and some shoes, and I'll be right back, okay? It's just not safe for my sister to be here or you for that matter."

Susan stopped, still facing the road, and whispered, "Okay, I'll wait."

Aster slipped the door shut and made his way back to his room, being certain to be as quiet as possible. He donned a shirt and shoes, brushed his teeth and hair, and made his way back outside to join his sister and Susan. Heading back toward the bay side of town, he led them back out on the street. In Susan's hands she held a wrapped gift. Clutching it tight, she pulled it close to her chest. She had not said a word since telling him she would wait. "So, how did you two meet?" he asked once they were a good ways down the road.

Eva glanced up at her brother and began, "Well, I've been seeing you around the bay side an awful lot lately, so I asked around in a discreet manner and found out you had been seen around with the new girl, so I stopped by and had a chat with her last night." Eva laughed. "I wasn't planning on being nice to her either. I went to tell her to keep her paws off my brother, but I like her, so I didn't beat her up."

A smile crossed Susan's face for the first time since they began their trek.

"And what made you two decide to show up on my doorstep this morning—despite the danger?" He raised his brow.

Eva jumped in to respond, "Well, she told me she hadn't seen you in a couple of days, and she didn't have a way to get a hold of ya since school is out for the holidays, and she needed to because she had a Christmas present for ya, so..." His sister shrugged her shoulders. "I decided to walk her here. Besides, I miss you, and it's Christmas...I wanted to see you."

Aster sighed, "I miss you too, but what will the Smiths do if they find out you came to see me? You know you aren't allowed to come to this side of town or to have any contact with me after I beat their nephew to a bloody pulp."

Susan cut her eyes to Aster but said nothing. She wondered who the Smiths were and who their nephew was, and she couldn't help but wonder why Aster had apparently severely beaten someone.

Eva squeezed her eyes shut to stop the flow of tears welling, but she was unsuccessful; they made their way past her lids and ran over her cheeks. "I know. I'm sorry. It's just been so long, and I figured if I was off walking with a girl from the bay side, they wouldn't think I was coming to see you."

Aster hugged his sister. The three of them walked in silence until they passed the road creating the boundary between the bay side and the east side of Bayville. "I'm glad you came to see me, but I still can't believe you brought her past Broad Street. This side of town is dangerous."

"I can handle anything anybody on this side throws my way," Eva huffed, "besides, I wasn't gonna let anything happen to your girlfriend."

"We're just friends," Aster retorted.

From the corner of his eye, he glanced to see Susan's response to his denial and found her clinging to the gift. She let out a soft sigh, but other than that, he was unable to read how what he said had made her feel. Aster knew neither of them had made any profession of liking one another in any way other than that of friendship, but he sensed she was drawn to him as much as he was to her. The way she looked at him and the way she leaned in close to him during their conversations led him to believe she was just as attracted to him, and he was almost positive she was keenly aware of how interested he was in her.

Although ecstatic to see his little sister, he found a part of him desired to be alone with Susan. He fought the urge to reach out and grab her hand. They had only touched one another when reason permitted: his leading her into the water of the bay, her wrapping her arms around his waist as they rode down the Interstate on his motorcycle, and her grabbing his hand to lead him into the field she had taken him to two months prior.

As they neared the bay, Eva turned to Aster and wrapped her arms around him. "Love you, big brother. I better get back home. Wouldn't want to be seen with you. Merry Christmas."

"Merry Christmas," he whispered back and kissed her on the cheek.

"I approve," she whispered in his ear. Aster simply smiled at his sister.

Eva took off, and Aster continued walking toward the bay. Susan passed him up and headed to the pier. She sauntered out to the end and sat on one of the wooden benches.

Aster plopped down next to her. "I'm really sorry I seemed mad you came by the house. I just know how dangerous it is for a girl like you to be walking down the streets on my side of town. It wasn't that I didn't want to see you," he explained.

"Then why haven't I heard from you in a few days?"

"I got a job at a small service center. I've been working. We don't have a phone, so I've had no way to contact you. I'm sorry if you've felt I was ignoring you or intentionally staying away," he apologized.

Susan sighed and let go of her hurt

feelings. "Aster, I know it's probably none of my business, but if your mom was ranting last night about Eva moving out, why hasn't she tried to make her move back? Not that she should move back or anything, but I guess I just don't get it."

"My mom really doesn't want her back. She just wants an excuse to complain."

"Are the Smiths the people Eva lives with?"

"Yeah."

"How do they register her for school each year?"

"They have legal guardianship of her."

Susan squinted. "Why did your mom give them that if she was just going to complain?"

Aster sighed. "She was tricked into signing the papers."

"How in the world did the Smiths trick her into something like that?"

"They didn't. I did. It was the only time I've ever spent any of my money on booze. I promised the Smiths I would get her to sign the papers so everything would be legal. I knew she would never do it willingly, so I gave her some money and told her to buy herself anything she wanted. Naturally she wanted alcohol; on the morning of the court date, I got her good and drunk before driving her down to the courthouse. I didn't even have a driver's license at the time. I convinced her, if she signed the papers in front of the judge, she would be entitled to money, but I warned her not to bring it up to the judge because he wasn't in on that part of it. I told her the Smiths wanted to pay her on the side."

Susan's forehead crinkled. "And she fell for it?"

Aster shrugged. "That kind of thing happens more than you know, Susan. See, there's not good in everyone. Some people are just pure evil."

"What did she do when there wasn't any money?"

Aster inhaled a deep breath. Slowly releasing it, he unlocked another door in his heart and let Susan in. "She waited until I fell asleep that night, tied me to my bedpost, and beat the hell out of me. She broke my leg with my baseball bat. I was laid up in bed for while that time."

Susan gaped, "Oh my gosh, I don't want to hear any more." She shook her head in disbelief at the things Aster had endured to protect his little sister. "I want this to be a happy day. No more bad memories, okay?"

"That's fine by me. I don't like to remember those things anyway."

"Well, I'm sorry I opened up that can of worms...I got you a Christmas present." She smiled. Holding it out for him to take, she sought to change the atmosphere.

Aster assessed from the shape of it that it was a book, so his natural instinct was to imagine she had gotten him a Bible, and despite the kindness and generosity she had shown him, he still wasn't sure if he was interested in knowing anything more about her God. Without thinking twice about his reaction, he blurted, "I get it, today is Christmas, which is a Christian holiday, so you decided to try and convert me by giving me a Bible." He rolled his eyes and pressed his lips into a hard line.

Continuing to hold the gift out to him, Susan sat still. When she spoke, her voice was filled with gentleness, "Aster, I thought you knew me well enough by now to know I'm not the type to shove my beliefs on anyone." She shook the gift. "It's not a Bible. I promise."

Aster's countenance softened. "Then what

is it?"

"You have to open it to find out. I'm not gonna tell you." She smiled, relieving the anxiety that started to grow in Aster's chest.

He stretched his hand forth and took the gift from Susan's hands.

The last time he received a Christmas gift that had been given to him by someone he knew was when he was in foster care. His foster parents, the Sharps, had placed a dozen toys under their tree and labeled them from Santa. He remembered the overflowing joy he felt that Christmas morning when he woke up and tiptoed downstairs to find presents sitting under the majestic Christmas tree decked with golden ornaments. Aster had spent the morning unwrapping them. His foster dad helped him to set up the train set. He laid in the floor for hours watching the caboose rolling down the tracks. Mr. Sharp used his tools to tighten the training wheels on the bicycle they had gotten him before taking him outside and teaching him to ride. It was one of the few happy memories Aster had.

He had been allowed to bring his gifts back home when the system returned him to his mother, but in one of her drunken moments, jealousy consumed her, so she made Aster and Eva watch as she burned the toys they received while in the care of *wealthy folks,* as she called them. They both stood there crying and hugging one another while they watched any hopes of a normal childhood go up in flames. Aster still remembered the stench of melting plastic and rubber like it happened only minutes before. After that the only gifts he ever received were from a program held by the local department store. His mother put their names in every year. She allowed them to keep any clothes and shoes they got, but if they opened up any sort of toy with any value, she sold it for alcohol; albeit, things like that almost never happened. Their presents usually consisted of a Barbie or a baby doll for Eva and toy cars for Aster. When Aster watched his mother trade his first expensive toy for a bottle of scotch, he cried, but when she pried the skateboard from his hands because she had a boyfriend who had a kid and said he'd give her a two bottles of cheap whiskey for it, Aster grew angry for the first time in his life. Once anger unleashed the brute within him, he strived against the urge to fight. He flew off the handle more than once at school and started fights with the boys who picked on him for living in the slums.

Aster reminded himself that violence coursed through his veins, and that was one of the reasons he knew Susan would never be his girlfriend. Despite what she thought of him, she was good, and he was bad. All of the emotions of Christmases past rushed to the surface.

Aster wasn't sure how to handle it; he sat there in silence for a moment. "I...I didn't get you anything. We don't really celebrate Christmas around here, so I didn't think much about it." He refused to take the gift.

"It's okay. I didn't get you something to get something in return. I saw this and thought of you. I think you're ready for it." Her eyes gleamed.

With a little persuasion, he grasped the gift and unraveled the bow tied neatly around it.

Treating the wrapping paper as if it was part of the present, he spent his time pulling the tape loose. He sat staring in pride once he completed his task. In his hands he held a hardbound copy of *The Hobbit* by J.R.R. Tolkien. "You think I'm ready for this? Are you sure?"

An icy breeze blew across the bay. Susan shivered but managed to grin in delight. "Yes, I think you are. You've really been applying yourself, and I know how much you liked *The Lord of the Rings* when we watched it in class, so...I wanted you to have the opportunity to read the book that started it all."

"Thank you." He hugged her without a second thought. Dispelling the frigid cold lingering in the air, the warmth of his body wrapped around her. He wondered if it felt as good to her as it did to him.

"You're welcome, but I do have a secret motive," she informed him.

Releasing her from his grip, he murmured, "Uh oh, what's that?" He grew concerned.

Susan laughed. "I'm going to quiz you on comprehension."

Aster chuckled and glanced at the first gift he had ever received that truly meant something to him.

Chapter 10

The Prayer

Aster continued to drive until he crossed the state line back into Mississippi. He veered off the Interstate in Moss Point and headed south to Pascagoula, making his way to a rundown boxing ring he visited while in the area. He needed to hit something, so he switched lanes and headed to the place he knew he could go. He envisioned his fists punching human flesh. Finding a punching bag to pulverize was his last attempt to conquer his lust for blood and to restrain the curse of his family line. He pulled into Brad's Gym and plowed through the front door. He knew Brad, the owner, so he gave a simple glance in his direction with his blood-red eyes and strode through to a small back room where a worn-out punching bag hung. He did not don gloves; he charged full force into the bag with his bare fists. Attempting to unleash at least a small portion of his fury, he pounded on the bag with repeated, constant thrusts. Frantic, he struggled to relieve some of the bottled up adrenaline bombarding his thoughts and streaming through his blood vessels. His heart beat ferociously, forcing more of the powerful drug released through the adrenal glands to blast through his body. It overloaded his muscles with an onslaught of belligerence. Hostility slammed repetitively into the heavy bag until sweat beads sprouted across his forehead and flowed into his brow.

Aster groaned with each punch. He lost control of the nature he had suppressed in high school. He had handed the reins, which chained his aggressive nature, to Susan five and a half years ago. He had given up the need for vengeance on all who injured him and those he loved, and he trusted in her God to deliver him from himself. He had tried to reject the God she had spoken of, but he found himself desperate to believe. He knew she had never tried to force her beliefs on him. As a matter of fact, she never mentioned God outside of answering a question she had been asked; she lived the faith she held. Aster became convinced she had something he wanted, yet now as his old nature clawed its way back out, bringing with it a murderous spirit that longed to see a heart stop beating and a body drained of its blood, he wondered what good that prayer had done him. *Where are you God? I'm struggling to keep the beast bound, and where are you? Why haven't you protected Susan? She had such faith in you. How could you let her down by endangering her?* Aster's mind wrestled with the God Susan had always loved and served. He desired to gain control over his emotions, but he feared he had lost himself. *Not even God can find me now*, he pondered. *I will be trapped in this darkness and destined to live the rest of my life as a slave to the monster inside of me. Being bound for so long has enraged it and made it stronger than it has ever been. It will not stop until it seeks revenge. I can't control its thirst.* A bead of sweat rolled past his brow and stung his eye. As the salty perspiration hit, his eyes saw a flash of Susan holding a bouquet of wildflowers.

On the eighth of March, Aster stood outside the main entrance of the school waiting for Susan to exit. He finished *The Hobbit* in late February. Susan made out a comprehension quiz to test him and administered it two days prior. She insisted the previous day she would have it ready to go over that afternoon after school. Nervous, he fidgeted, which he found odd.

"Why am I nervous about a fake test? It's not like I'm getting an actual grade or anything," he mumbled under his breath.

Aster realized the answer to his question to be the simple fact he didn't want to let Susan down. He wanted her to feel she had done an amazing job tutoring him. He knew she had. His grades had all improved; it wasn't just his English/literature grade that was affected by their tutoring sessions. He now had a B in math, a B in history, a B in science, and a D in English, although that D was merely one point from a C. Despite the apparent effort and improvement, Ms. Howard never slackened up on Aster; she still made life inside her classroom difficult for him.

Susan stepped out waving a thin stack of papers and grinning. Aster sighed in relief. Her smile signified he hadn't let her down or disappointed her in any way. She raced down the steps to Aster's side. "You did it!" she exclaimed.

Aster jerked his head when he heard Shane Garrish's voice holler, "Have a nice afternoon, Susan. See you this evening."

Susan turned and waved. "See you then."

Aster narrowed his eyes. "Why are you going to be seeing Shane this evening?"

"Oh, my parents have invited his parents over for a barbeque. We've been here since mid-September, and they don't have many friends yet, so they've invited everyone on our street. Putting their feelers out there for new acquaintances, I suppose." Susan shrugged like it was no huge deal.

"Hmmm..."

"You're not jealous, are you?" Her eyes smiled in a teasing way.

Aster huffed. "No."

"Good. There's no reason to be. I haven't forgotten what you said about him."

Susan and Aster walked side-by-side to the library. Her mother flipped out when she heard she had been on a motorcycle and forbad her to ride again. She made Susan a deal: she wouldn't tell her dad about the incident if she promised her that her days of putting herself in dangerous situations were over. Susan tried to refute her mother's claim that she endangered her life by riding on Aster's motorcycle, but in the end she resigned and assured her mother she wouldn't go off like that again, so Aster walked with her to the library every afternoon.

Aster didn't mind not being on his bike for the short distance as long as he walked next to her. As they chatted on their way to the library, he couldn't help but think of Shane being at Susan's house that evening. Shane had a certain charisma that made mothers adore him and desire their daughters to date him. Although that idea attacked his mind, he felt an assurance Susan wasn't the least bit interested in Shane as anything other than a next-door neighbor. Her mother, on the other hand, had plans to set them up. He was quite certain of that. He figured Shane was interested in the set up as well, which was why Aster assumed he had been the snitch who told on her for riding on his motorcycle. He also happened to be one of the seniors in that group of popular guys with tallies on virgins they had conquered, and that irked Aster—seeing he knew ultimately Susan was nothing more than an objective in Shane's mind. He cared nothing about who she was or the standards she held; he longed to add her to his list, and Aster knew it.

"So, I did pretty good, huh?" He quickly changed the subject back to them and expelled his taunting thoughts.

"Sure did. Only missed five of my questions." She beamed.

Aster pushed open the glass door to the library. "Nine weeks exams are next week, so we better buckle down as opposed to celebrating." He frowned. "I really wanna do good on my English exam. Ms. Howard just won't give me a break. Sometimes I think she's disappointed I'm improving."

Susan grabbed his hand, quickly releasing it, and pulled the door back. "Yeah, I've kind of noticed the way she eyes you. She looks like she resents you sometimes. Aster, I know we have exams, and you want to do well on your English one, but...I think maybe you need to loosen up and live a little. I know I'm not supposed to, but would you take me on a ride? My mom is at home getting ready for that barbeque, so she won't find out."

Aster grinned. "Have I created a rebel?"

"I'm not a rebel; I just think we should celebrate is all."

"You sure you wanna risk it?"

"I'm positive." A cheerful smile spread across Susan's face.

Aster held his hand out for Susan's. She glanced in his eyes; her own eyes brightened as she placed her hand in his. He turned and headed back for his bike. He only had his helmet with him, so he slipped it on Susan's head and tightened the neck strap. He cranked his motorcycle and asked, "So, where to?"

"Anywhere, as long as we're back in an hour." Susan wrapped her arms around his waist and laid her head against his back.

Aster drove to the beach in Paradise Shore. It was only a ten-minute drive on his motorcycle, so he knew they'd have a full thirty minutes to enjoy the waves and no one from the bay side of their town would spy on them. He parked in a small parking lot on the beach and pointed to the small waves. "This is one of my favorite places to go. Even though I'm working at the service center, I still do a few odd jobs for some people in this town as well. Both jobs give me the opportunity to visit the beach here every now and then."

"It's great." She jumped from the bike and ran toward the water. "I've never been to the Gulf before. This is awesome."

Aster laughed. "Never been to the Gulf? How? You live on it?"

"Yeah, but I haven't visited any of the towns around us that actually sit right on it. I've only been to our bay. This is so beautiful, don't you think?" Her face gleamed.

Aster gazed at Susan with admiration. "How do you do it?"

"Do what?" She turned and looked in his

eyes.

"How do you always see the good in everything? You always seem so happy. You smile all the time. It's like nature amazes you or something. Don't get me wrong, I appreciate the peacefulness of the water as well as its beauty, but you express such excitement over it."

"I don't know; for one I suppose my excitement right now is because I've never seen waves like this. I guess I look around me at the sky and the clouds and the wildflowers growing in my field and those waves crashing and the amazingness of *how* big the Gulf of Mexico is and the oceans are, and I see God." Susan breathed in the scent of salt water blowing in the breeze. "What do you see when you look at all those things?"

Aster shrugged his shoulders. "I see the beauty of it all. I can't deny that, but I don't know...part of me wants to believe like you do, but I guess I've just seen so much of what you might refer to as Hell in my life, that I question the existence of God. I mean, if He is real, then why has He let me and my sister go through the things we've been through? Isn't He supposed to love everybody? I mean, I love my sister, and that's why I've taken her beatings for her." Aster shook his head. "Why doesn't he stop those kinds of things from happening? Isn't he supposed to be all powerful?"

Susan stood in silence for a moment and thought through her words before she responded, "Aster, what you've done for your sister, that's more or less what Jesus did. He took our beating for us so to speak, but we live in a world where evil exists. He doesn't just wipe it out although I wish He would. I can't answer all of your questions, but I believe God's heart breaks over the things you've suffered. I don't think He wanted any of those things to happen to you or your sister, and don't believe what you hear some people say about how everything happens for a reason, like bad things are somehow ordained by God. That one gets on my nerves. The only reason bad things happen is because of evil. It's never because God does it, but...I do believe God can take bad things and bring good out of them."

"So, what good can you see God bringing out of the bad things I've been through?"

Aster's question was serious rather than sarcasm. Susan immediately picked up on the genuineness of his question. "I'm not really sure at this point, but I do believe He can use it to better your life as well as your sister's. You know, my friends back in Birmingham thought my dad's job change was the worst thing that could've happened in my life, and honestly, I was a little depressed over leaving them, but I trusted that something good could come from it, and I was right." She smiled.

"Really?"

"Of course, if my dad hadn't taken that job and pulled me away from my friends, I wouldn't have met you, Aster." She traced her fingers over the top of his hand.

"That's only good for me." He smiled. "You're the one who's helped me. I've apparently corrupted you to the point that you disobey your mom now." He chuckled.

"You've helped me, Aster. You just don't realize it. You've taught me things I never knew. They just aren't things you learn in school is all; for instance, despite growing up without a father and in such abuse, you still had it in your nature to protect your little sister. You taught me that even those who aren't shown love can still show love."

"Hmmm...never really thought about it that way. So, what does it take to get in good with this God of yours?" Aster pushed the subject a little farther.

Radiance washed over Susan's face. "Faith is all."

"What does that mean exactly?"

Susan scanned the beach front for something she could use to demonstrate faith. She eyed a beach chair a short distance away. "Okay, close your eyes."

"What?" His eyes widened.

"Just close your eyes, Aster."

"Okay," he sighed and squeezed his eyes shut.

"Now take my hand." She held out her hand for his. Aster lifted his hand from his side. Susan grabbed it. "I want you to keep your eyes shut, okay?"

"Whatever you say."

"Now, follow where I lead."

Susan led Aster across the beach to the chair facing the water. She slipped her hand from his and turned his body so the chair sat directly behind him. "Do you trust me?"

"Yeah, I trust you."

"I want you to sit down." She grabbed both of his hands in hers.

"Ummm...I can't catch myself if you're holding my hands."

"Do you trust me not to let you fall or not?"

"Yes, I trust you, Susan."

"Then sit."

Hesitant, Aster bent his knees and edged his way unknowingly toward the chair.

When he was an inch or two away, she released his hands and whispered, "Open your eyes."

Reflexively, Aster placed his hands down to catch himself. He smiled as he felt the wooden chair under him.

"Aster, that's faith. You just trust God to lead you and not to let you fall. You just have to believe in Him and what He did. He's our example, not a set of doctrines handed down by a particular church or denomination."

"So, how is it you met Him?"

"Vacation Bible school." Susan stared over the water and remembered her first encounter. "I read a church sign down the road from our house back in Birmingham advertising a vacation Bible school. I asked to go. My mom didn't really like the idea of my head being filled with that *junk* as she called it, but she was certain I was intelligent enough not to fall for it," she told her story. "I went, and I really felt my heart moved by what they told me about God and how He loved me and how He died for me, so when they gave the altar call, I went down, and I prayed." Susan craned her head to look at Aster. "You know, it wasn't the words I said or anything like that. There's no magic spell. I really believed in my heart God heard me and answered me."

Aster plopped down in the sand next to the chair. "Do you think God can take all of the bad out of me?"

"What bad?"

"Oh, I've got bad in my blood. You can't deny it." Aster hung his head in shame.

"All I know is if you ask Him to and you *believe*, He *will* change your heart, so if you think there is bad in your heart, which I completely disagree with, then that's how you get rid of it," she explained her faith to him.

"So, how do I pray?"

"You just talk to Him just like you are talking to me. God likes honesty. Be honest with Him about how you feel and about your skepticism. He doesn't mind that, you know." She grabbed Aster's hand and began a silent prayer. After a moment she opened her eyes.

Aster gazed into Susan's chocolate-colored eyes and pled, "Will you help me? Will you pray with me?"

Susan caressed the side of Aster's face. "Of course," she whispered.

She led him in a simple prayer before they left to head back to the library. Overtaken with excitement and joy, she threw her arms around him and exclaimed, "This is the best day ever!"

Chapter 11

The Kiss

Aster collapsed into the punching bag and wrapped his arms around it. After an hour of venting his emotions through his fists, his breathing became labored, and his heart beat became erratic. His body earnestly felt the effects of having so many complex emotions churning within him, from love, hate, peace, rage, clarity, confusion, goodwill, envy, to God, to evil, and to Hell. Exhaustion took over his being, and along with the extreme fatigue came a breakdown; he began to cry. His moans were uncontrollable as he held the tattered bag in a tight grip with his arms.

Have I done it? Have I been able to bind the beast again? Or is it already too late? He wondered. *Maybe the monster inside me is just worn out and is only sleeping.*

Sleep, the thought drew him. His body and his mind needed to rest. He needed to feel the peace he felt the day Susan led him in prayer. That prayer, along with Susan, had changed the course of his life, up until that point at least, but now he wasn't sure what he felt for a God who would let them both down the way He had. His thoughts drifted back to the day when he asked Susan why God had not stopped the bad things from happening to him and his sister. Susan's answer had been simple really—bad things happen because of evil. "There's evil in the world," she told Aster that day. Of course, he knew she was right the moment she said it because he knew evil lurked within him, and he knew the beast had already surfaced on more than one occasion.

Aster let go of the bag and crumpled to his knees. He crawled across the floor and leaned against the wall. With his feet flat on the floor and his knees up, he leaned his head back, closed his eyes, and allowed the tears to freely flow from his eyes. He began to see Susan's eyes staring into his, but this time a peaceful memory (a memory so strong he could imagine the softness of her skin and the smell of her hair) invaded his mind. Through his watery eyes, he envisioned her hand grasp his as she bowed her head to silently pray.

Things changed drastically for Aster after Susan led him in that prayer on the beach in Paradise Shore. A calm he had never experienced before in his life trickled through his mind and heart like a peaceful stream. A week later he realized the war raging within him between his cursed family bloodline that sought to be released to seek revenge and bloodshed had surrendered to the side of him that defended the weaker against monsters just like him. There had been an armistice between the two sides. The ceasefire left Aster experiencing an unimaginable peace and an overflowing happiness and joy, and it was those things that led him to believe things could be different for Susan and him. Maybe they had a chance after all. *I'm different now,* he thought.

Despite the stress of nine-weeks exams that week, Aster still found himself feeling happy all day long. He couldn't wait to wake up each morning and get dressed for school. For the most part it was due to the fact he would be seeing Susan, but he also found he enjoyed each day and looked forward to them. He had come to love learning, and even though she never wavered, Aster smiled at Ms. Howard each day as he graced the door of her classroom.

The day of his English exam, she approached his desk and towered over him. "Have you been taking drugs, Mr. McGrath?"

"No, ma'am, I'm just happy is all." He smiled at her.

Ms. Howard took his smile to be cynical. "And what do you have to be happy about, Mr. McGrath?" She glared at him.

"I've changed my ways, and I'm happy about it. I'm real sorry if I was disrespectful to you in the past, Ms. Howard."

"Hmmm," she grunted and picked up the stack of tests and began handing them out.

Aster focused on his test and completed it faster than he had ever completed a test before. Ms. Howard kept an eagle-eye on him that day, searching for any signs of drugs. The way she whiffed as she marched past him made it obvious she sniffed for clues of alcohol as well. Aster simply shook his head each time she passed.

Susan was more than happy over the transformation in Aster; she was exultant! That Friday when the bell rang for them to be released for spring break, Susan's eyes brightened. Aster grabbed her books to carry them when she walked out the front door of the school building. "Oh, no library today. My mom will be here any second. She insisted we didn't need to go study because of spring break and all. I think she's trying to keep us apart as much as possible," she fussed.

"Oh, yeah, sounds about right. Are y'all going out of town for spring break or anything?" Aster secretly cringed at the thought of not seeing her for a week.

Relieving his internal torment, Susan answered, "No, we'll be home the whole week. Dad was already booked with patients." She spotted her mother's car approaching in the distance. "Will I see you in the morning? We can meet at the bay." Her eyes pled.

"Can't. Gotta work, but I'm off Sunday, so I'll see you at church. Where do you go to church, by the way?" He raised his brow in question.

"I walk to the big church a couple of blocks from my house since I have to walk to get there. It's called Bread of Life Church. I like it. Some of the people are a little snobby, but I like the preacher. Service starts at eleven. See you there?" she asked as she grabbed her books and started walking toward the black BMW that pulled in front of them.

"Yeah, I'll be there. Bye." Aster waved.

Sharon, her mother, narrowed her eyes and shot darts at Aster with the full intention of getting a message across; the message was simple—stay away.

That Sunday Aster woke up and showered. After he had gotten off work the previous day, he had driven to the mall and bought him a pair of dress shoes, two pair of nice casual pants (a black pair and a pair of khakis), and two new dress shirts just for going to church with Susan. He ironed the deep packaged wrinkles out of the baby-blue shirt he picked to wear that day and even combed his hair back. He wanted to look his best. Aster showed up ten minutes early to the church Susan had mentioned and met her outside.

Susan couldn't take her eyes off him and finally whispered, "You clean up nicely, Mr. McGrath," as they walked in together and sat in the back pew.

Aster grinned on the outside. On the inside his confidence level rose significantly. Susan's comment strengthened his resolve to act upon his attraction.

Aster was new to religion, so he still felt a little hesitance about being in a church around people; therefore, he desired to be hidden in the back away from judging eyes. Susan agreed to sit in the back with him. She understood his reluctance. The pastor preached a message on baptism and what it symbolized concerning the death of the old man and the birth of the new man. Aster wanted the cursed nature in him to be dead, so when the preacher asked for those seeking to commit their lives to Jesus and desiring to be baptized to come down, Aster jumped up and walked to the front.

Susan gleamed at the sight of him making his way toward the preacher. She remembered the feelings that rushed through her when she made her way down to an altar for the first time, and she was thankful God had allowed her to be a part of making a difference in Aster's spiritual life.

Aster was keenly aware of the whispers as he darted to the front, and so was Susan. "Isn't that the boy who nearly beat that poor boy to death?" They gossiped amongst themselves.

"I think so. Hmmm...he needs to be washed from his sin for sure."

"Probably just seeking to get out of some kind of trouble or something," one snooty lady replied to another.

"Yeah, that's how a low-life is. They get in trouble with the law, and then to make a good impression on the judge, they go running to God and claim to be straightening their life up."

Remembering what Susan mentioned about some of the people being snobby, Aster ignored the comments and spoke to the pastor about praying with Susan and wanting to be baptized. The preacher wrapped his arms around him and welcomed him to the family of God.

Susan knew Aster had admitted to beating someone to a bloody pulp when she showed up at his house with his sister. *That has to be the same person they are speaking of,* she thought to herself. *I wonder if it was really nearly to death as that lady just said?* She contemplated briefly before shoving the thought from her mind. While she wondered, she knew she didn't care. What she saw in Aster was good. He was her wildflower, and she was his, and he had just given his heart and life to God, and to her that meant his past no longer mattered, not that it ever did to her.

Aster wore a huge grin when he approached Susan. "How does it feel?" She grabbed his hand and swung it from side to side.

"Great. So, where to from here?" he asked.

"I wanna go spend the day on the bay,"

Susan responded.

"Then let's go." Still clinging tightly to Susan's hand, Aster walked out the double doors.

They walked a little ways down the street before coming to a crosswalk. Hand in hand they stood patiently waiting for the light to signal they could walk across to the other side in safety. As soon as the light switched, Susan took off running, dragging Aster along behind her. When they reached the other side, she slung her shoes off her feet and left them by the railing. The two of them strolled by the water. It felt natural to Aster for his hand to embrace Susan's as they walked along the bay together.

The warmth of the spring sun shined, and a balmy breeze blew across the water causing the small waves to glisten with starbursts of light dancing upon the bay. Sea gulls and pelicans flew overhead squawking. Aster and Susan found a spot in the sand and sat watching the white birds dive in the water in search of food. Susan leaned back and used her hands to prop herself. She stared into the sky basking in the sun's rays and allowed them to saturate her face.

She broke their silence. "How's it felt?"

Aster knew what her question meant. "Great," he replied.

"Has it helped matters at home?" she gently pried.

"Somewhat. I mean...it's helped me deal with the stress better, I suppose. It hasn't helped my mom. I don't think she's even noticed anything different about me outside of me not smartin' off to her when she's ranting. She may not have even noticed that. Usually I try to bite my tongue to prevent it from being worse anyway, but I eventually just get mad and snap off, which ends up causing me to meet the broom handle."

Aster craned his head to gaze in Susan's eyes. "I've met a cast-iron skillet before too. That one really hurt."

"Have you been praying for her?" Susan wondered.

"Yeah, I have. At first I prayed for God to make her stop drinking and all, but the last couple of days, I just pray for Him to show her she can be happy like I am now." Aster looked out over the water and sighed. "Can I ask you something?"

"Sure, anything."

"Did you used to pray for me?"

"Every day, and I still do, by the way." She nudged him with her shoulder.

"What did you pray, if you don't mind my asking?"

"At first I would just ask God to help me know how to help you with school, and then I began asking Him to help you see Him in me without me having to tell you about Him with words. I think that's the mistake most people make...They pray for God to do things when it is them who should be doing it. God wants people to see our lives and know He exists, not hear our words to know there's a God. I mean, hearing people tell you about someone they believe in doesn't help anyone else to believe, now does it? It's seeing their life and the love they have and the good things they do. That's the way I see it, anyway." She shrugged her shoulders. "I know that's how it worked for me. It wasn't just hearing the message when I went to vacation Bible school; the lady who taught my class helped me to see God in her. She taught us with her words, but there was so much more to it than that. There were two kids in my class that most people would have probably treated bad. It was a brother and sister, and they were obviously being sent there by their parents so they could have a break or something. She didn't treat them any differently than she did the rest of us. I knew both of them from school, and I'd seen teachers make ugly comments to them and treat them like they had some kind of disease, so seeing the way Ms. Ann treated them made an impression on me. She wasn't just saying words. She lived it...So, did my prayer work? Did you see God in me without me having to tell you about Him?"

"Yeah, I think so. I mean...I knew there was something different about you the first day we spoke. When Ms. Howard made me carry your books, you had a kindness in your voice no one else had ever had. At first I thought it was only because you didn't know me and my reputation, but then you would just be nice even when I snapped off at you. It made you even more beautiful to me."

Susan blushed and smiled. Her eyes shifted to the sand beneath her feet. She felt the warmth of the sand rubbing between her toes, so she dug them in a little deeper.

Aster scooted closer to her. His heart beat raced as he reached his hand out and gently grazed the side of her face. Susan's lips trembled slightly. He traced them with his fingertips and leaned in closer. Susan bit her bottom lip and closed her eyes. Aster beheld her beauty and soaked it in like soaking in the rays of the sun. The sunlight glimmered in her golden tresses. Scattering her hair across her face, the wind blew, wafting past them with the smell of spring and saltwater. Aster gathered her hair in his hand and gently slipped it behind her ear. Skimming her jawline, he swept his hand down to her chin and gently lifted her head.

Moving his lips closer to hers, he whispered, "Susan?"

With her eyes still closed, Susan breathed, "Yes?"

Aster's mouth was merely an inch from hers. His breath blew across her face as he softly asked, "Is it okay if I kiss you?"

Susan opened her deep-brown eyes and gazed into Aster's sparkling blue eyes. "Yes."

As Aster brought his lips in and gently touched hers, she closed her eyes again. Lingering, his lips gently grazed hers. He drank in the taste of them before pulling himself away from their first kiss.

Chapter 12

The Threats

Quieting his weeping, Aster gathered himself together, rubbing the heel of his palm over his swollen eyes, and stood. Exhausted, he let out a shuddery breath, sauntered to the restroom, and turned on the rusty faucet. The brownish-red water sputtered when he turned it on, so he stood and watched it spit until the rust cleared the pipes and clean water flowed into the old, white ceramic sink. He gazed at his bloody hands and the opened wound from the vase before shoving them under the crisp water. Aster winced in pain as the water gushed through the laceration in his palm. Splashing his face with the cool stream of water, he washed away the salty sweat and tears on his head, face, and neck. He snatched a towel hanging from a hook on the wall next to him and patted his face dry before staggering back through the main room. He caught a glimpse of Brad seated on a bench with his arms folded across his chest watching a couple of guys in the boxing ring. Aster shifted his gait and made his way toward him.

He reached for Brad's hand and gave it a weak shake, being sure to use his uninjured hand. "Hey, man, you sure you don't wanna take a turn in the ring with this guy. He'll give you a good workout," Brad said, chuckling.

"Nah, I'm exhausted from beating the life out of the old bag. If you'd asked me when I first came in, I'd probably taken you up on the offer," Aster replied.

Brad eyed blood dripping down Aster's fingers. "Dude, you must've really beat the hell out of my bag."

Aster furrowed his brow in confusion. "Sorry?"

"You're still bleeding." He pointed to Aster's right hand.

Turning his palm up, Aster grunted, "Oh, that. Cut myself earlier."

Brad harrumphed. "Come to my office. I've got a First Aid kit. I'll bandage it for you."

Aster followed Brad into his office. The two conversed about boxing while Brad wrapped Aster's hand with gauze.

"Thanks, man," he mumbled before heading back out the front door. Revving up his bike, he climbed back on and headed west on Highway 90, the scenic route back home which took him past the beaches in Biloxi, Gulfport, and Long Beach. At night much of the city sparkled with the colorful lights of casinos. It was exhilarating, but the mesmerizing views were those long strips of highway lined with water and sand glimmering with starbursts of lights created by large street lights and nothing more. The sound of water and waves always brought Aster peace; he found the scenery of the beaches to be a refuge. Despite the peacefulness of the waves and the beauty of the landscape, it was one sided; the view of the north side of the highway was a panorama of devastation. Empty slabs sat where beautiful homes once stood. The sight was sad to anyone who grew up on the beaches of southern Mississippi, so Aster kept his eyes on the backdrop of the seemingly endless Gulf.

Driving back into Bayville, he drove by the bay and turned on the first road past the Bread of Life church. The same building no longer stood there. The building he had been baptized in had been washed away with hurricane Katrina the August after he buried his old man in the water with witnesses looking on. So many things had changed after the storm.

He walked past the door to his office, which still stood open, and eyed the remaining shards of glass scattered across the floor. He ignored it and strode through to the kitchen and flipped the light switch; the light danced across his dark hair, creating a shadow. Metal clattered as he pulled out a pot and filled it with water to boil. He scrambled four eggs while he cooked a pot of grits and slipped bread in the toaster. Pouring himself a glass of juice, he scoffed down a late night meal.

After shoving the dishes he dirtied into his dishwasher, he marched upstairs to his bedroom. He stripped his clothes as soon as he crossed into the master bathroom. He turned on the shower and allowed the heat of the water to get good and piping hot before he climbed in and closed the door. Aster washed his hair and scrubbed his body free from the grim of the day. Trying to douse away everything which happened that day, he leaned into the rushing water and allowed it to rinse his body. He placed his hand against the back wall of the shower and held himself under the steaming hot water. As the water cascaded over his aching body, his mind naturally gravitated to Susan. He saw her head bowed in silent prayer as they sat in the sand on Paradise Shore. He felt the water rushing over his body with tranquility.

Susan's lips were sweet, and their kiss was tender. Her innocence kept Aster from allowing his desire to turn the kiss passionate. He wanted nothing more than to press his lips against hers again, but he refrained himself and simply gazed at her.

Slowly, she opened her eyes and stared into his. "I'm sorry," she whispered.

Aster's eyes widened. "For what?"

Susan removed eye contact and stared at Aster's hand propped in the sand. "For not knowing how to kiss back right." She blushed.

Aster chuckled lightly. "What are you talking about? It was perfect."

Still looking at his hand, she bashfully smiled. "Really? You're just saying that so you don't hurt my feelings."

"Really," he lifted her chin with his free hand. "I wasn't just saying that."

"I've never been kissed before. I'm sure you've kissed lots of girls, haven't you?"

"Does it matter?"

"No, not really. You just did that so well, I figured I don't have the kind of experience you have with that sort of thing is all. I don't want you to feel disappointed, I guess," she nervously stuttered.

"I'm not disappointed in the least." Aster smiled.

"Then why did you stop?" she queried.

"Because...I just think it's wise not to push too much too fast." Aster shifted and propped his free arm on his knee.

"What do you mean? You don't think being friends for six months is long enough or something?"

"No, not that." Aster inhaled a deep breath and thought through his words carefully before explaining, "It's a little different for me than it is for you because you're not the first girl I've kissed, and I wanna be respectful of you and not get caught up in the moment and forget my senses."

"So, you've done more than just kiss other girls, haven't you?" She sat up straight, wrapped her arms around her knees, propped her chin there, and waited for his response.

"Does it matter?" He tried that argument again.

"Yes and no, I mean, technically it shouldn't, but I wanna know." Susan's words ran together in a blur, "It's not that I don't already assume the answer to that question, but if I had an actual answer, my mind wouldn't be left to wonder."

"Yes, I have, but I really don't want to think about that right now."

"How many?" she pried.

"You sure you want to ask these questions?" He tried to change the subject.

"Yes, I am. How many?" she questioned him again.

"A dozen or more. I haven't exactly kept count," he mumbled.

"Were they girlfriends or just friends?"

"Neither, but that was because they wanted it that way. They only wanted to be able to say they went out with the bad boy of the school is all. They weren't interested in being my friend or having a relationship."

"So, they go to our school then?"

"Most of them."

"Hmmmm...am I going to have competition?" She frowned.

"Absolutely not. Number one, they don't want some of their friends to know what they've done...or their boyfriends, but even if they did, they would never stand a chance next to you."

Susan smiled, leaned over, and kissed Aster on the cheek. "Sorry I've been grilling you. I guess I have a little jealous streak I didn't know about."

Aster smiled at the thought of Susan's being jealous over him. He found he liked it. He stood and grabbed her hand. They strolled down the beach for the next several hours talking about trivial things like their favorite foods and television shows before Susan decided she needed to head on home. He walked her to her door and was greeted by her glaring mother. Sharon's eyes bore holes through him.

Susan recognized her mother's evil-eye and recoiled from Aster as if she had no option but to cower down to her mother's obvious disdain. "See you soon," she whispered to Aster. She hung her head and marched straight to her room without saying a word to her mother.

On his way back to the church to retrieve his motorcycle and head home, Aster sensed something behind him. He felt as if he was being watched. He stopped and craned his head to see if he was being followed. When he turned back around, Shane stepped out from behind the local bookstore.

"We need to talk," he huffed.

"I don't have anything to say to you,

Shane." Aster rolled his eyes and heaved a heavy sigh.

Shane stuck his arm out to stop Aster when he tried to pass. Aster cut his eyes to the hand firmly placed on his shoulder.

"I have something to say to you," Shane insisted, keeping his arm steady.

Aster hissed, "Get your hand off me, Shane."

Shane dropped his hand but stepped in front of Aster. "I'm not gonna step out of the way until you hear me out."

"What do you want?" Aster grumbled.

"I want you to stay away from Susan. Her mother wants it too." His eyes pierced through with a threat.

Aster bowed his shoulders. "And why would I stay away from her because of you *or* her mother?" He crossed his arms and held his stance.

"Because you should know how important it is to have a mother who cares about you and wants what's best for you in life...and because you wouldn't want me to tell Susan or her mother that I'm the person you almost killed, now would you?"

Aster glared into Shane's eyes. "Would you like for me to put you back in the hospital?"

"Go ahead. It'll just strengthen my case against you, and Mrs. Blackman's. Hell, Susan may even feel sorry for me and nurse me back to health."

Aster shook his head. "Go ahead, Shane, fantasize. You of all people should know you can't intimidate me. You know what else, I have a feeling you don't plan on saying one damn word because deep down you're afraid I would tell Susan *why* I pulverized you," Aster growled.

"You can't possibly think that Doctor Blackman or Mrs. Sharon would believe the lies and ramblings of a loser from the east side of town who lives in such horrible conditions that his little sister had to run away from the abuse...maybe even the abuse she suffered at his hands...over a nice, clean-cut guy from a family with a reputable name from the bay side, can you?" Shane said, his voice filled with cynicism.

"Susan would never believe you." Aster gritted his teeth.

"Doesn't really matter so much if she does or not. It matters if her parents do or not, and if I'm not mistaken, even the courts have seen me as the good guy who was victimized by the town thug and still asked for them to show him mercy because I felt so sorry for him and what he had to live in." A smug grin spread across Shane's face.

"I'll take my chances," Aster mumbled and shoved his way past the stance Shane still had in front of him.

"If that's the way you want it," Shane hollered as he strutted down the road heading back home.

Aster stormed in his house and slammed the door. "Wherv ya blin," his mother slurred.

"Church and the bay." Aster tricd to remain calm with his mother.

"Ain't no god ou ther. Mi swell give up on tha now." She belched.

"Believe that if you want, Momma."

"Ha ha ha ha ha ha ha ha ha!" she laughed uncontrollably, "Ya can't git rid da evil in ya. Yous bon of it. Is in ya blood," she mocked him. "Jus like tha rot'n fath'r o' yos."

"Stop it, Momma," he begged.

"Ha ha ha ha ha ha ha ha ha, troof hurz, son."

"I said stop it!" he screamed. For the first time since he prayed with Susan, Aster lost control. He grabbed the table lamp off the makeshift end table and slung it across the room into the wall right next to his mother. The lamp shattered. Aster's mother never flinched. She laughed even harder than before.

"I'm outta here," Aster hollered.

He charged out of the house and jumped on his bike. His thoughts went straight to his camp site thirty minutes north. The back tire squealed as he released the brake to take off, but before he could completely let go, a black BMW pulled in his drive and cut him off. The car stopped and Sharon opened the driver's side door and climbed out.

"It's not safe for you to be on this side of town, Mrs. Blackman," Aster warned.

"Yes, I know, which should automatically inform you of the seriousness of what I have to say to you," she began.

"I'm pretty sure I already know," he grumbled.

"Yes, I'm sure you do, but I thought I'd appeal to your *caring* side. Do you mind coming for a ride with me?" She pointed to the passenger side door.

Aster thought about it for a second and shut the motorcycle off. He climbed in the front seat of the BMW and folded his arms across his chest. He was still visibly shaken from the outburst that had left him feeling like a complete and total failure. It was the first real confrontation he had with his mother since praying and giving his life to God, and he failed. He flat out failed. She had prodded him in the spot that caused him to explode.

Sharon cut her eyes at Aster. "Where can we go to talk?"

Aster aimed her in the direction of the northern portion of Paradise Shore. He wasn't about to lead her to his place of peace, but the north side had a sizable park with a well-lit walking track which provided an atmosphere of privacy while remaining public. When they crossed into the city limits, Aster told her to make a right at the first intersection. As the wheels turned, he pointed to the sign that read *Paradise Park.*

Sharon turned into the park entrance, parked the car, shut off the ignition, turned to Aster, and said, "Let's go for a walk, Aster."

"Yes, Ma'am," he uttered just before opening the car door and climbing out into the cool night air.

They walked in silence for at least five minutes before she started in with her polite threat. "Aster, you seem like a nice enough young man, and I've picked up on the fact you are interested in my daughter for more than just a tutor or a mere friend. When Susan didn't return home immediately after church, I drove to her friend Angie's house and inquired about her whereabouts. Angie informed me she saw her cross over to the bay immediately after church with you. I took a little stroll that way to see for myself. I saw you kissing my daughter, so don't try to deny your interest."

Aster coughed. "Yes, Ma'am, I care a lot about her."

"Then if you truly care about her, you will understand why you need to stay away from her. Susan is naive. She is easily swayed by others' philosophies and opinions. She may easily be persuaded to think...believe even...that she has feelings for you as well, but she doesn't know what is best for her. She will receive no assistance from her family to attend college or begin a life if we do not approve of her choices. That being said, I think you would agree you would be ruining my daughter's life if you force her to give up her college education. She'd be stuck having to work and make ends meet just to attend a community college."

Aster silently stared at his feet as they walked. Breaking his silence, he asked. "You would really do that to her?"

"Yes, I would. I cannot foresee investing in a future that would only bring shame upon our family name, and you of all people must understand that. Has your father's imprisonment for murder not shamed your family?" She eyed him.

"You..." Aster stuttered and turned his head.

"Yes, I've heard all about your family. Your mother," she scoffed, "she's not disabled. She's a drunk, and I'll be damned if I allow my daughter to date the son of a drunkard and a murderer. Do you want my daughter to bear that disgrace?"

Aster craned his head, glared into Sharon's eyes, and said nothing.

"Aster, you have nothing to offer my daughter, and I think you are well aware of that fact. I would hate to see my daughter's future ruined because you forced our hand in this matter. She'd only end up hating you for it eventually anyway. Have I made myself clear?"

"Perfectly," Aster responded through a clenched jaw. The threat came across crystal clear.

Chapter 13

The Confession

Once his head was no longer under the weight of the hot water pounding from the shower nozzle, Aster's memory faded along with the muffled sounds of reality. Dense steam filled the room when he opened the glass door of the shower and stepped out. The vapor rolled off Aster's broad shoulders as the heat saturating his body hit the icy-cold air blowing through the vent. He grabbed a towel and wrapped it around his waist, securing it in place. Clearing the haze from the vanity mirror, he swiped his hand across it and created a viewing area just right to stare into his own eyes. He could clearly see his blood no longer boiled; the monster inside had left or hidden itself deep within. He was unsure of which had taken place; he was only certain it was gone at that particular moment. He had always been able to see the beast glare at him through his own eyes. His bout with the devil had finally ended—at least that is what he hoped, yet a part of his mind convinced his heart he would see it surface again. *It's only lying dormant,* he thought.

Chill bumps ran down Aster's arms and across his chest as he ambled toward his bed. The temperature difference from the steamy hot bathroom to the icy bedroom was stark. He shivered slightly at the change in the atmosphere. He sat on the side of the bed and stared out the window for a fleeting moment. His mind was blank for the first time that day. It felt good not having his mind overflowing with racing thoughts, screaming voices, and memories. His brain had finally tired out. Sleep called him. He longed for it. He lay back on the bed and nestled his head into the plush pillow, wrapping his head in comfort.

His body was in dire need of rest in order to recuperate from the exhaustion of warfare, the warfare from within himself. He closed his eyes, but sleep would not come. He tossed and turned in an attempt to induce sleep. He shifted to his side and found himself staring at a framed picture of Susan sitting on his nightstand. He stretched his arm to pick it up and lay back supine. He gazed at the picture of her on his motorcycle in the middle of her wildflower field. He had used her camera that day to take the picture of her. It was their second trip to the colorful field, and it was the day she made a confession that made him realize how right her mother had been.

As soon as Susan's mother dropped Aster off at his house, he charged into the shed, found the bag which held his tent, bungee strapped it to the back of his bike, jumped on, and headed to his camping spot. It had been a while since he had visited the area. Since Susan had entered his life, he found he had not needed that sort of exclusion from the world—until that night. The combination of his run-in with Shane, his incident with his mother, and Mrs. Blackman's threat had overwhelmed him. He needed to think with clarity, and the campsite was one place he could do that.

When he arrived, he found his favorite spot and pitched his tent. Signaling his hunger level, his stomach growled. Aster knew it would be a long night because despite his hunger pangs, he had no appetite, and a hungry, empty belly made for a sleepless night. *I should force myself to eat,* he figured. He pulled his .22 from the bag. He always kept it hidden from his mother in the tent bag. Guns and abusive drunks didn't mix. His only use for it was hunting, so he used it when he went camping. Quietly treading, he hiked through the woods in search of something suitable for dinner. His aim finally landed on two squirrels. He built a fire, pulled out his pocket knife, skinned the critters, and cooked them over the small fire. Despite the knots in his stomach, he force-fed himself, stomped out the fire, and climbed in the tent. A full belly and a warm sleeping bag had him snoozing in no time.

Knock...knock...knock...knock...knock.

Aster rolled over and pulled the sleeping bag over his head. "Who could possibly be knocking?" he mumbled in his sleep.

Knock...knock...knock.

Trying to arouse himself from sleep, Aster squirmed. He stretched his hands, rubbed his eyes, and finally sat up yawning. "That's no knock, that's a woodpecker pecking on a daggum tree," he grumbled. He unzipped the tent and pulled the flap back and poked his head out just enough to see the bird boring a hole in the dead tree to his right. "Must be infested with bugs," he whispered softly. He admired the bird without its knowledge. As it pecked away, it occasionally stopped and looked around. Aster thought the black stripe across its white face made the pileated woodpecker look like it wore a mask. His arm tingled from numbness, so he shifted his weight. The leaves under him crunched causing the bird to stop and search out its surroundings. They eyed one another, and the woodpecker took flight. As it took off to another part of the woods, its black wings spread out wide.

Aster crawled out of the tent and spent the day traipsing through the woods in search of any forms of wildlife. Observing the animals he often came across on his camping excursions was one of the ways he kept his mind free from everyday worries. He trampled through the woods until he realized his stomach had been growling. He made his way back to his tent to retrieve his gun and go in search of dinner. In no time he put a bullet in the head of a rabbit and feasted.

As the sun dropped from sight, Aster sat gazing at the sky and realized he had managed to make it through the day without thinking about Sharon or Shane or their threats, but he also knew he had to think about what they both had said. He had lashed out at his mother for the first time in his life, and he feared what that meant. Sharon was only seeking to protect her daughter from a guy who could potentially end up like either his mother or his father, so he couldn't begrudge her for that. Shane, on the other hand, sought to score, and Aster knew it. Duty demanded he protect her from Shane and his intentions. As soon as Aster came to that conclusion, he knew what he had to do; he had to ignore their threats. He just wasn't sure if he should tell Susan about his encounter with her mother.

Being in the woods helped Aster to think through that much of his problem already, so he decided to spend another night and day there and work through his decision on whether or not he should include Susan in on what was going on. Part of him worried if she thought her mother had come to him in private, she would recoil from him again like she did when he walked her home the previous day. Aster shook his head in an attempt to dispel that notion and crawled back in the tent. He slipped into the sleeping bag and drifted into dream world. Unable to shake the idea from his mind, the thought of Susan withdrawing her affection followed him like a shadow into his dreams.

When he awoke, he brought the plan his mind concocted during sleep along with him. Immediately upon peeling his eyes open, he knew he didn't need to spend the remainder of the day contemplating what to do. He folded up his tent and slipped it back in its carrying case, stuck his .22 in along with it (being sure to flip the safety switch), strapped it to his motorcycle and headed home. Aster drove straight to the old shed and stored his tent and gun before getting back on his bike and driving to the bay side of town.

He headed to Susan's house with boldness, but as he drove down Main Street, he cut his eyes to the bay and saw her walking by herself, kicking at the sand. She folded her arms across her chest. A hard mask covered her face, yet her lips moved as if she argued with herself. Baffled at why she would be at the bay at seven in the morning, Aster pulled in a parallel parking spot and sprinted toward her. When he got a few yards away from her, he hollered, "Look at that black-eyed Susan in the sand!"

Susan's demeanor changed in an instant. Her arms fell to her side, and her face glowed from her smile. "Where were you yesterday?" She sped to his side.

"Went camping. I had to do some thinking," he explained.

Susan's forehead wrinkled. "You...you're starting to scare me a little," she stuttered.

"No need to be scared." Aster grabbed her hand in assurance.

Susan sighed in relief. Looking down at their joined hands, she whispered, "Usually when a guy says he has to think about some things, he's trying to decide if he really likes a girl or not."

Aster furrowed his brow. "Well, we probably should talk about why I went off to think."

"O...kay."

"Don't be nervous," Aster pled.

"Kinda hard not to be. I mean, you kissed me. You stopped kissing me, and when I asked why, you said it was the wise thing to do. I'd never kissed a guy before, so I'm wondering if I wasn't good at it, and the very next thing you do is decide you need to take off because you have some thinking to do."

"It wasn't like that," Aster tried to explain.

"Okay, but you've gotta understand for me...I was left to wonder all day yesterday why you didn't come around. I mean, I kept wondering if I had done something wrong. I didn't know if I had said something wrong, or if you felt some kind of pressure from me because of all of my questions about who you'd been with in the past, or if my acknowledging I felt a little jealous caused you to maybe freak out. I've had a kazillion things running through my mind, Aster," Susan prattled. Her words poured from her as forceful as a gushing waterfall.

"Actually, I kinda liked that you admitted feeling a little jealous, and I didn't feel any kind of pressure from you, and our kiss was amazing. So amazing, in fact, I can't stop thinking about it."

Needing to feel secure in their relationship, Susan threw her arms around Aster's neck and brought her lips to his. Gently caressing his lips with hers, she kissed him repeatedly.

Aster succumbed to the warmth in her lips and allowed the kiss to grow in intensity. He placed his hand in the small of her back and pulled her closer to him. Susan parted her lips slightly and breathed. Without warning, Aster stopped and pulled himself free.

"You've gotta stop doing that to me, Susan."

"I'm sorry. What did I do wrong?"

"Nothing. That's the problem. It was too good." Aster smiled and pulled her back closer to him.

Susan looked at his feet and smiled. "Ummm, you said we should probably talk about why you went camping, so what's up? Why did you need to get away and think?"

Aster inhaled a sharp breath. "Huh, you think you can get away with not getting home until much later today?"

"Yeah, why? She raised her brow in question.

"I'd like to get out of here and go somewhere private to discuss it. I was thinking maybe we could head out to the cabin."

"Okay," she complied.

Aster held Susan's hand tightly as they walked to his motorcycle. He climbed on and took off on the long drive. Neither of them said a word until they stopped at the same gas station and went in to get two loaded-down hotdogs. Aster did his best to keep the conversation away from what he truly wanted to say, so he made small talk by asking her about what she did the day before.

"So, what all did you do yesterday while I was off camping?"

"Nothing really. I spent a lot of time in my room worrying about why you didn't show up at the bay."

"Did you wait there long?"

"A couple of hours." She glanced at her half-eaten hotdog.

"I'm really sorry."

"Oh, it's all right. My room is spotless now. I needed something to do to keep my sanity, so I deep cleaned." She shrugged her shoulders. "It was time for spring cleaning anyways."

"Oh...you spring clean every year?"

"Yeah."

Aster chunked their trash. "You ready?"

"Uh huh," she answered as she swallowed her last bite.

When they pulled up to the cabin, Susan jumped off the bike like a pro. "Oh, yeah, I don't have the key to the cabin on me, so we'll have to just sit amongst our wildflowers."

"That's fine." Aster parked the motorcycle in front of the field of flowers.

"Hey, did I leave my camera in your bike the other day when we went to Paradise Shore?"

"Let me check." Aster lifted the seat and pulled out her small 35 mm camera. "Yep, sure did."

"Shoo, I was worried I had lost it somewhere."

"Sit on the bike and let me take a picture of you." Aster nodded toward the motorcycle.

"Okay." Susan grinned. She climbed on the bike, and Aster snapped his picture. He went to take another, but the button wouldn't budge.

"Hope that one turned out because the film is full," he told her.

"Oh, that's great. That means I can develop them tomorrow. I'll be sure to get doubles for you."

Aster eyed her ancient camera. "So when are you going to go digital along with the rest of the world?"

"When I have no other option." She raised her brow. "I don't really like change."

They walked hand-in-hand into the field and sat amongst their wildflowers. Finally, Susan spoke up, "What is it? What's going on?" she gently pressed him to open up about what he obviously wanted to share in such a secluded place.

Aster had already decided to leave Shane Garrish out of the conversation and focus on her mother's visit. "I had a visitor Sunday afternoon after I got home," he started.

"Yeah," she encouraged him to continue, "Who was it?"

"Your mom." He went silent.

"Hmmm...what did she want, or rather what did she do?"

"She nicely threatened I will be destroying your future if we continue to see one another."

"You told her we were seeing one another?" Her eyes bulged.

"I didn't have to. She went out looking for you Sunday as soon as church let out; she said she saw us kiss."

"Oh, that's embarrassing. Yikes." Susan's face blushed at the thought of her mother watching her receive her first kiss. "How exactly did she nicely *threaten*?"

"She informed me you will basically be cut off if we continue to see one another. She said they won't assist you in any way, shape, or form in attending college if they do not approve of your choices. She nicely pointed out, if I truly care about you, I will not want you having to work just to attend a junior college."

Susan's pink face flushed red. "I'm never going to be out from under her thumb until I can support myself." Susan sat fuming. She looked into Aster's eyes and declared, "I don't care what they do, Aster. I'm not going to allow her to control my life or my happiness anymore."

"I'm sorry. I didn't think you would get this upset by it, Susan. I just thought you should know how desperate your mom is to keep us apart. Apparently, my genetics are not good enough for her." He laughed it off, trying to lighten the situation.

Susan's countenance calmed. "They're good enough for me," she said as she leaned in and softly kissed his lips. Aster wrapped his arms around her and returned her kiss. "Aster," she breathed.

"Hmmm?"

"I have a confession to make."

Aster ran his hands through Susan's hair and mumbled, "What's that?"

Grazing his lips with hers, she whispered, "I'm in love with you."

Chapter 14

The Break Up

Aster ran his hand over the antique frame which held the picture of Susan. In it she sat on his motorcycle in front of the colorful flowers growing in her field, her special place. He flipped the frame over and pushed the clasps that held the velvety black backing in place. He slipped the picture free from its glass prison and slung the frame to the foot of the bed. Caressing the picture he now held in his hand, Aster's eyelids grew heavy. As his head wobbled, he pulled the picture to his chest and mumbled, "I love you too, my black-eyed Susan." As his mind gave way to drowsiness, he drifted off. Finding sleep had always been a struggle for Aster when it came to Susan and the things he had to think about concerning the two of them.

Susan's love for him, her mother's disdain, and Shane's hatred of him wandered into his dreams. He heard Susan whisper *I'm in love with you*, as he drifted into sleep. He had barely passed into the REM stage of sleep when he flinched.

Stunned by Susan's proclamation of love, Aster pulled away from her, stopping their kiss, and for a moment, he simply stared at her without saying a word. Susan's smile faded and a look of horror set in. "I...I shouldn't have..."

Aster knew what she was about to say, and he didn't want her to regret telling him she was in love with him, yet at the same time, he found himself unable to say it back to her. It wasn't that he didn't feel it, but something else happened in him the moment she said those words. The realization of what it meant to love someone kicked him in the chest, knocking the wind from him. To keep her from embarrassment, he impulsively pressed his lips to hers. It was a gentle kiss rather than a passionate one.

Susan seemed appeased with the kiss as a sign of his affection and didn't show any sign of disappointment in the absence of Aster's admittance of loving her in return. Instead she seemed to grasp a hidden meaning in the way his lips softly touched hers and discreetly conceded that, as a result of everything he had been through in his life, he would need more time to be able to vocalize his feelings for her.

As they lay in the grass, Susan nestled herself in Aster's chest. "Aster, have you thought anything about prom? It's only a little over a month away."

"Haven't thought a whole lot about it honestly. I was in alternative school last year, so that kinda put a cramp on me going during my junior year. Would you want to go with me?"

Susan kissed him on the cheek. "Thanks for asking. Yes, I'd love to be your date." Susan lay gleaming for a moment as she daydreamed of her dress. "Aster?"

"Yeah?" He traced his fingertips down her arm.

"Why did you beat that guy up last year?" Susan wrinkled her forehead. "If you don't wanna say, you don't have to," she quickly threw in.

Aster stared into the sky in silence. Sighing, he gave into her request, "Because...he hurt my sister." His answer was short.

"Oh...who is he?" she queried.

Aster inhaled a deep breath and rolled over on his side to face Susan. "I'd rather not talk about all of that if that's okay."

"Okay," she whispered. "I knew you had to have a reason. You just don't have it in you to hurt someone without a cause."

Aster ran his hand through her hair, leaned in, and kissed her forehead. "You think too much of me."

Desperate to change the subject to an area that would prove her point, Susan reminded him, "So, are you looking forward to being baptized Sunday?"

Aster growled, "Yeah, yeah, yeah, point taken." He sat up and propped his arm on his knee. "I'm a little nervous about it actually. They may need to save me until last."

"Why's that? You're not planning on bailing, are you?" Susan responded with goggling eyes.

"Ha, no, but baptism's supposed to wash your sin away, right?"

"In a way." She shrugged. "It's really just symbolic of it though."

"Well, no one will want to get in the water with all the filth of my sin. I'll be the dirtiest one up there." Aster smiled. "All I can say is that better be some pretty powerful water in that tub." He chuckled.

Susan sat up and shoved his shoulder. "Aster, you're so funny."

"Yeah, I turn down offers all the time to be a standup comedian."

Susan rolled her eyes and laughed.

They spent an hour or so lying in the field of flowers before determining they better head back to Mississippi. Aster drove straight to the bay, parked, and let her off where he picked her up. He walked her as far as to her road, kissed her on the cheek, and said, "Better not go any farther. Wouldn't want to cause you any problems. Maybe we should keep things quiet for right now."

Susan tightened her grip on his hand. "Yeah, you're probably right." As she walked away, she smiled and waved. "Bye."

All the way home Aster's mind repeated the words Susan had said to him: *I'm in love with you...I'm in love with you...I'm in love with you.* Her words taunted him and brought everything Sharon said to him to a three-dimensional reality in front of him. He could see the future Sharon spoke of: Susan graduating and embracing him as their caps flew through the night sky was immediately followed by her putting in an application in at the Tiki Torch restaurant, a local seafood place. In the next flash, he saw her sitting in the library at the community college two towns over studying stacks of books, and then he saw her walking down the aisle and placing her hand in his before saying her vows. Aster's imagination jumped ahead and witnessed a notably pregnant Susan carrying an overloaded tray of food to a group of drunken men having a retirement party at the Tiki Torch, and when the baby came, he saw a college withdrawal slip lying on the kitchen table. Aster craned his head, glanced around the room, and recognized his house. Susan now lived in the slums along with him and so did their newborn child, and that was a future he could never allow. Aster knew it would be a natural progression; she loved him, and despite his refusal to tell her, he loved her. The only way Aster knew he could protect her from the future he saw lying ahead of them was to put a stop to the possibility of that future coming to pass, and the only way he knew how to do that was to end their relationship. As much as it stabbed his heart to even imagine being without his black-eyed Susan, he knew he had to save her from the hopeless prospects a life with him would offer.

Aster pulled in his drive and parked his motorcycle. He opened the door, entered his home, and looked around. *She will never have to call a place like this home,* he thought. Aster walked past his mother sitting at the kitchen table. He pulled out a jar of peanut butter and a loaf of bread. As he spread the creamy peanut butter, he uttered, "I'm sorry I broke your lamp, and I'm even sorrier I threw it at the wall next to you."

"What's going on with you, boy?" his mother asked. Her words were clear; she was sober.

"Whatdaya mean?"

"You ain't never apologized to me in your life. Why start now?" She lit a cigarette and coughed.

"I told you; I'm going to church now." He

sat down across from her with a paper towel.

"You ain't told me no such thing, Aster."

"Well, you may not remember, Momma. You weren't exactly in your right mind at the time."

"Huh? Don't remember it. What did I do to make you throw the lamp at me?" Her eyes searched for truth in his.

"You basically told me I had the devil in me, and God couldn't help me."

"Hmmm...well...I guess I deserved that lamp. Probably shoulda hit me with it." She chuckled.

"I'm gettin' baptized Sunday if you'd like to come." Aster scanned his mother's eyes for hope.

"Nah, I'd cause the roof to fall in if I graced the doors," she mumbled.

"Well, at least think about it. I'd like you to be there." Aster took a bite of his sandwich. "Hey, Mom, where did you come up with my name?"

"Why're you askin' a question like that?"

"Just wonderin'."

"Well, if you must know, back when your daddy had some good in 'm, he brought me a bouquet of these blue flowers to the hospital the day you was born. He told me the lady in the flower shop said they were blue asters. I looked down at you in my arms, and you gazed back at me with those big blue eyes, so I named you Aster."

Aster smiled and stood. He pushed the chair back under the table. "Well, I'm off to bed. Goodnight."

"Goodnight, Son."

"Mom?"

"Yes?"

"I love you," he uttered as he shut his bedroom door.

Stunned, Loretta sat at the kitchen table in

silence. She couldn't remember the last time she heard those words pass through his lips, nor could she remember the last time she said them herself.

That night Aster knelt by his bed and asked God to give him the strength to break things off with Susan and to help her deal with the pain. He ended his prayer by asking God to soften his mother's heart and bring her to the church to see him be baptized.

Over the following four days, Aster worked at the service center from dawn 'til dusk. Spring break allowed him to put more hours in at work. He did his best to keep himself busy. During his long, grueling hours at work (which were therapeutic for him), he formulated the best way to handle the break up. He decided he would have to take a walk with her after church and explain to her why it was best if they didn't see each other anymore.

Early that Sunday the morning light shined through his bedroom window and blinded him, causing him to squint. He rolled out of bed and anxiously prepared himself for the day. He was nervous on more than one level. Not only was he taking a step forward in his spiritual life, he was about to break the heart of the girl he loved.

Susan immediately noticed the distance in Aster when he didn't return her hug and could barely look her in the eyes. "Here are your copies of the pictures." She handed him the doubles of the pictures they had taken. "Everything okay?" she asked as they walked through the doors of the church.

"Not really but let's wait until after church to talk about it, okay?" He kept his stance firm.

"Okay," her voice shook slightly.

Aster sat next to Susan, but he set the

envelope of pictures between them, careful to keep a certain distance between them. He never reached out to grab her hand or show any sign of affection.

Susan wondered if it was a part of Aster's plan to keep things quiet between them as he had suggested they should. It was the only way her mind could fathom why he had not been to see her since they went to the field.

The minister of music stepped to the front of the church and signaled for the choir to stand. They sang a few hymns before the pastor stood behind the podium and began, "Today is a special day. We will be baptizing five individuals who have given their lives to the Lord. I'm going to ask them to stand and follow the usher waiting at the back door. He will take you guys to prepare."

Aster shoved the pictures Susan had given him into a small duffle bag toting a towel and a change of clothes and went to meet the man. Concerned over his disposition, Susan watched as he disappeared from sight. The associate pastor stepped to the front and said a few words to the congregation while the pastor entered the baptismal pool.

The back door creaked open and a tall, dark-haired woman entered. Her hair was pulled back and tied in a knot. Her face was hard from years of alcohol abuse, but one could easily tell she had been a beautiful woman in her day. All eyes turned to see her sit on the back pew. Aster had apparently requested to be the last one baptized. When he entered the baptismal, he looked out into the crowd while the preacher spoke about what Aster told him that day. A smile crossed Aster's face when his eyes fell upon his mom. He went under the water thanking God for answering his prayer, but when he came back up, she was gone. She had quietly slipped out without anyone noticing.

Susan approached Aster as soon as the congregation was released. "Was that your mom?"

"Yep," Aster's eyes welled over. "God answered the prayer I prayed last night," he said as he led Susan across the road to the bay, "and that is all because of you really, so thank you for praying for me and talking to me about praying for my mom."

"You're welcome," she said as she sat in the sand and looked out over the water. The warmth of spring and the squawking of seagulls surrounded them. "You seem distant. What's going on?"

Aster sighed. "First, I want you to know I am truly grateful like I said."

"Okay..." Susan's eyes grew in fear of what was coming next.

"I've thought a whole lot more about what your mom said to me, and I do understand where she's coming from. I don't wanna ruin your future, and if your parents control your future, then they have control over our friendship as well."

"What are you saying, Aster?" Susan's heart pounded with anxiety.

"In the past I've always been rebellious to anything and everything someone said or did that made me feel they were trying to control me, but I don't want the same Aster to still be there, and I wanna respect your mother's feelings without letting you go, but I don't know how to make that work, so ultimately it comes down to the fact I can't stand by and watch them take your future away from you all because I want to be with you."

"You're breaking up with me?...I mean, I know we were never officially dating or anything, but…" Susan began to cry.

Susan's tears stabbed at Aster's heart. It was killing him to hurt her, but he knew he had to end it for her sake. "Susan, your mother's right; I have *nothing* to offer you."

"You have you, your heart. That's all I want," her voice broke.

"That's not enough, Susan."

"Aster, please," she begged.

Aster traced his thumb across her cheek bone and wiped away the tears soaking her skin. "This wasn't an easy decision for me. I want you to know that."

Susan's mind raced; she grasped for straws. "But…but…but…what about prom? You said you would take me to prom."

"Get someone else to take you. It would make your mom happy. Don't mess up your future over me, Susan. Just remember you will always be my black-eyed Susan." Aster leaned over and kissed Susan on the forehead, stood, and walked away.

Chapter 15

The Death

Aster's eyes rapidly scanned the back of his lids as they followed the outline of Susan's cheeks and watched as tears rolled over them as she stood in his office. Her heart had been shattered. He tossed and turned in his bed, desperate to arouse himself from the nightmare. His dream world had intermingled with his latest memories; he walked through the holographic images of his recent past as if he were literally there. Abruptly he shot up from under the covers gasping for breath. Clutching his chest, he grasped the photo. As his breathing slowed, he gathered himself together and flung his legs off the bed.

He glanced at the clock on his nightstand and eyed the time, *12:32 a.m.* "A little more than two hours of sleep would be nice," he grumbled. He stepped into his jeans, placed the picture of Susan back into its frame, and set it on his nightstand—being careful to leave it perfectly situated.

Aster slid the drawer of the nightstand open. Angling the lampshade, he shined the light into the darkness of it. Silver glistened. He grasped the silver object, shut the drawer, and turned out the light. He had somewhere he needed to be, and he knew it. He grabbed his jacket off the coat rack in his foyer and slipped it on as he exited his home. He climbed back on his bike and headed to the east side of town where he pulled in the driveway of his old home.

He still owned the rundown house he grew up in. He wasn't sure why he kept it. He opened the door and pulled out the silver flashlight he retrieved from his nightstand and shined the bright light into the blackness. Making his way to his mother's room, he flashed the beam of light on her bed. Aster cringed in pain before shutting the door. He ambled through the house to his old room, opened the door, and sat on the side of his old bed. He thought about the nights he lay there, sleepless, staring at the ceiling tiles. He counted the black dots so many times he still remembered the number.

Walking away from Susan that day at the bay was one of the hardest things Aster had ever done. Telling his sister to run away had been difficult, but he found the sleepless nights after breaking up with Susan to be pure Hell. He constantly questioned himself about whether or not he had done the right thing. Nearly two weeks of unexcused absences to keep from approaching her in English class had passed when he received a knockout punch from Ms. Howard as he ambled through the door.

Ms. Howard lowered her glasses. "It's nice

to see you've decided to join the class, Aster. Do you have your excuse?"

"No excuse. Just didn't feel like coming."

Ms. Howard harrumphed. "Without an excuse, you can't make up the work you missed. That's nine zeros. There's no way you can pass this class now, and without passing English, you don't graduate, Aster." Her face turned down in a frown, but Aster saw a hidden smile lingering beneath her stern mask.

Aster cut his eyes and noticed Susan steadily working on her bell ringer. She didn't even look up at the mention of his not graduating. It stung him worse than a hornet sting. When the bell rang to change classes, Aster stayed behind.

"Ms. Howard, I need to graduate. Would you please allow me to make up the work?"

"I'm sorry Aster. Rules are rules. The handbook clearly states you are only allowed two unexcused absences per semester. You've already missed those. There's nothing I can do for you. You should've thought about it before you just skipped school because you didn't want to come."

"Damn it," he cursed and punched the door on the way out of class.

As soon as Aster stepped into the hall, the pain of Susan's life moving on without him stabbed him in the chest. The knife twisted repeatedly as Shane Garrish, wearing a gloating smile of victory which screamed he had won, approached her standing at her locker. Aster took in a sharp breath, caught Susan's attention, and allowed his devastation to stare at her momentarily before removing eye contact and walking past them.

Susan looked down at the floor and sighed, "I'll see you tonight, Shane."

Aster's ears burned when he heard those

words. If she was trying to make him jealous, she was definitely accomplishing it. He had tried to warn her about Shane. *Does she realize he is dangerous and plan on forcing me back?* He shrugged the thought from his mind and marched out of the school building. He climbed on his motorcycle and spewed gravel as he spun out.

That night Aster found himself going to the local hot spot for all the teenagers. He had to know if Susan meant a date when she said *I'll see you tonight, Shane.* The thought of her going out with Shane Garrish was pure torment. He knew he had told her to find another date for prom, and logically he knew if he ended things with her, then someone else would eventually come along—*eventually* being the key word! What Aster couldn't wrap his mind around was the fact she was choosing Shane Garrish. *Maybe she's just trying to appease her mom at this point,* he thought to himself as he rode his bike down to the square, the place in town where all the teenagers congregated. Then he saw it, and it hurt worse than he could have ever imagined anything else hurting. Walking through the square, hand-in-hand, and heading to the small movie theatre was Shane and Susan.

*Look at that! Huh, they must be a perfect couple in her mother's eyes. Shane...Susan...her mom's name is Sharon. It must be in the genetics. He has the baby face, the blond hair, the uppity look...*Aster's thoughts tormented him.

Aster parked his motorcycle and followed them to the movies. He needed to warn her about Shane. Sure, he had warned her before but not really. He had never revealed to her why Shane was dangerous. He had merely alluded to the fact he was. He eyed them and saw them enter theatre two. Knowing she would eventually have to go to the restroom by the size of the drink Shane bought her, he stood by the restroom door, leaned against the wall, and waited patiently for her arrival. About halfway through the blockbuster movie, Susan sauntered out of the theatre and strolled toward the restroom. She glanced at the floor when she saw Aster standing there.

"Susan, I need to talk to you," he petitioned as she passed.

Susan stopped and stood with her back to him. "What do you want Aster?"

"I want you to be careful, that's all," he stated plainly.

"Really?" She turned around and shot her blood piercing eyes at him. "And see, I would've thought my being careful would be staying away from you!" she blurted.

"It probably is, but you should stay away from Shane too," he warned.

"Hmmm...that's funny because my mom and dad and Shane's parents have all had an interesting discussion about how he hurt your sister and you beat him nearly to death. You said he hurt her. Number one, you didn't tell me it was Shane, and number two, you lied! You made out like you were defending your little sister, but a boy breaking up with a girl and hurting her is *not* the same as him literally hurting her and being deserving of that, Aster. You know, I think I was wrong and you were right about one thing: there is bad in you, Aster McGrath," Susan spit her words forcefully through clenched teeth. Her face flushed red, and her eyes boiled over with angry tears.

Aster had never seen her like that before, and he knew he was to blame. He had shattered her heart, and now she shattered his. He deserved it; he knew it, but that didn't lessen the pain. He hung his head in shame and uttered, "I'm sorry I didn't tell you it was Shane. Just please be careful, Susan," before walking out the front door of the theatre.

Three days later on Monday morning, Aster woke up for work. He slammed his hand on his alarm and sat up. Groggily he threw the covers off, stood to his feet, and went to the closet. As he slipped his shirt over his head, he heard a loud thud. He raced into his mother's room where the noise came from to find his mother lying on the floor beside her bed. "Mom," he cried, but there was no response. He bent over to scoop her into his arms. As he laid her across her bed, he realized her eyes were open and glaring at him strangely. "Momma...Momma," he called as he shook her unresponsive body. He slapped the side of her face in a desperate attempt to arouse her from what he hoped to be a drunken state, but she didn't flinch. Hysterically he placed his ear to her heart to listen for beating, but there was none to be found. Aster grabbed her car keys from her nightstand and shoved them in his pocket. Lifting her dead weight, he raised her lifeless body into his arms and stumbled for the car. Laying the passenger seat back, he placed her in it and sped to Bayville Hospital on the bay side of town.

Carrying her through the emergency room doors, he cried, "Help, she's not breathing, and her heart's not beating."

A male nurse raced to his side while a female nurse retrieved a gurney. Taking her body from Aster, the male nurse placed her on the narrow bed and rushed her to the back. A female doctor came out within thirty minutes and informed Aster they were unable to revive his mother. Aster stood silently for a moment. Finally he uttered, "What am I supposed to do?"

"You'll need to make funeral arrangements, so the funeral home can pick up her body."

"But I don't have that kind of money. I'm in high," he began to cry when he realized he had not only lost his mother but he would not be graduating.

"Where is your father?" the woman asked.

"Prison."

"Oh, what about other relatives?"

"There are none," Aster mumbled. "I have a little sister, but there's no one else."

The female doctor placed her hand on Aster's shoulder trying to console him to the best of her ability. "Do you need to call her?"

"No, this is something I have to tell her in person," Aster sighed. He sucked in a deep breath and pulled himself together. "But I'll have to wait until school lets out." Aster looked the doctor in the eyes. "Thank you for trying to bring my mother back." In a daze he slowly ambled out the door.

When three-thirty rolled around, he found himself banging on the front door of the Smiths' home. Melody's mother answered the door. "You aren't supposed to be here, Aster," she said, her voice sharp and cold.

"Yes, Ma'am, I know. I'm sorry I'm breaking your rules right now, but this is an emergency, and I need to speak to my sister, please," he pled.

Mrs. Smith stood glaring into Aster's eyes and saw the sadness staring back at her. "Come on in," she mumbled. Leading him to the living room, she asked him to wait while she informed her husband and retrieved his sister. All three of them came back into the room. Mr. Smith, unwilling to allow Aster to speak with Eva privately, stood with his arms folded in anger. He didn't trust him as far as he could throw him. His sister's son had been nearly killed by the brute, as he called him.

Despite the fact he did *not* want to tell her the news in front of the Smiths, Aster resigned to their request. He sat on the couch with his hands trembling. He fidgeted around with them trying to gain his composure and speak.

Eva became frustrated, "What is it, Aster? What's so important?"

With tear-filled eyes Aster looked up and whispered, "Momma died this morning."

Eva sat numbly. "Are you okay?"

"Not really. I found her and carried her to the hospital. I don't know what I'm going to do. They said I had to make funeral arrangements, but I don't have that kind of money."

The room grew silent. After several minutes Mr. Smith spoke up, "I have a friend named Philip. He owns a funeral home. He helps people who can't afford funerals. He will do the funeral for a little of nothing."

Aster glanced Mr. Smith's way. "Mr. Smith, I appreciate it, but I seriously have a hundred dollars to my name. I can't afford even the cheapest of funerals."

"I'll take care of it—for Eva. She's like a daughter to us now. I'll pay for it for *her*." His voice was stern yet full of love for Eva.

Broken, Aster sobbed. Eva's deep insecurities, resulting from growing up in a home with a mother void of emotion and love, caused her to fear losing the Smiths' love as well, so she looked to them for approval and rushed to her brother's side. She wrapped her arms around him. "Everything's gonna be better now, Aster. You never have to worry about her anymore," she whispered. "She can't hurt either of us ever again."

On April 13, 2005, Aster walked into the funeral home to say goodbye to his mother for thc last time. With his sister's hand in his, they sauntered into the parlor and gazed at their mom. Much of her youthful beauty had been restored by the makeup artist and hair stylist. She looked peaceful and finally free from the bondage she had lived in during her lifetime. Aster glanced over to see tears streaming down Eva's face.

"You okay?"

"No...I'm a horrible person."

"Why do you say that?"

"Becuz...standing here looking at Momma, I've tried to bring up happy memories of her, but I keep remembering Mom being gone on one of her binges and you having to give me a bath and comb my hair becuz I couldn't. It was a couple years after we came back home from foster care. You were only eight, and you had to search the house for something we could eat. When Momma came home, she started screamin' at you for gettin' into the cabinets. She chased you down, tied you to the kitchcn chair, and then she saw that you used her ponytail holder to fix my hair, so she grabbed the scissors and cut all my hair off. She kept you in that chair for three days, Aster, and she didn't let you eat anything."

"I forgot about that time. I mean, I remember her cuttin' your hair off, but I couldn't remember why. I'm sorry about that, Eva. I'm sorry I caused you to lose all of your pretty long hair." He gazed into his sister's watery eyes and apologized.

"You didn't cause it, Aster; she did." She sobbed. "I hate her, and I don't understand."

"You don't understand what?"

Turning into her brother's chest, she squalled, "Why it hurts to see her there."

Aster wrapped his arms around his sister and quieted her weeping. "Because no matter what she ever did to you or me, she's your mom, Eva. I had a chance to make peace with her; you didn't. You know, she came to see me get baptized."

"Really?"

"Yeah."

"That's good."

"Yeah, it is."

They both said goodbye to their mother, and then Eva said goodbye to Aster. She had decided not to attend the graveside, so alone Aster followed the hearse to the burial plot. His pastor was already there when he arrived.

Approaching Aster, he wrapped his arms around him. "I'm so sorry for your loss, Aster. Will you allow me to read a few scriptures and pray?"

Aster simply nodded in agreement.

After the prayer Aster whispered, "Thank you for being here. Is it okay if I ask to be alone with my mother?"

"Of course, I'll leave you. My wife cooked a few casseroles. Is it okay if she brings them by in an hour or so?"

"Yeah, I'll be home."

Aster stood by himself watching them lower her into the ground. He felt a certain freedom as he watched his abuser being covered with dirt. He had always imagined he would view that day as a day of victory and rejoicing, a day when he could hold his head high and shout out from the rooftops that he would never be beaten again, but he found himself unable to revel in the moment. Despite her abuse, he felt no merriment in the death of his mother. He felt only sadness and loneliness.

Aster left before she was completely covered and drove home. The pastor's wife pulled in behind him.

"I brought you something to eat. I hope you like shepherd's pie and pea salad."

"Thank you. I appreciate it. I'm not really hungry right now, but I'll eat some later this evening." He took the dishes from her hands.

"We'll be praying for you, Aster," she assured him.

"Good. I really need it right now."

Aster headed in the house. He left the front door open, put the food in the refrigerator, and wandered into his bedroom. He plopped down on his bed and curled in a ball and sobbed. He didn't know how much time had passed when he heard the footsteps coming through the front door. He imagined Eva had decided to check on him, so he sat up in his bed and wiped his tears away. When he heard her voice, she was already at his bedroom door.

"Aster," Susan whispered. Aster looked into her chocolate-eyes. "I'm so sorry about your mom." She stood outside his bedroom door. "Can I…"

"Yeah, come on in," his voice shook.

Susan sat on the bed next to him. "How are you doing?" she asked.

"Okay," he mumbled. "How did you find out? It wasn't in the paper or anything."

"Your sister; she came to the house a little bit ago and told me about it. She also told me she never told the Smiths the truth about how Shane hurt her because she was scared they wouldn't believe her over their nephew. You accepted that and were willing to risk the punishment for almost killing him without defending yourself at all. You risked so much to make sure your sister was safe. I should've known you couldn't do such a thing without just cause."

"Did my sister tell you what the truth was?" He searched for truth in Susan's eyes.

"No, I didn't ask. She was getting choked up already. I figured she didn't really wanna talk about it. I don't need to know. I know to be careful, and I know he had to have truly hurt your sister for you to hurt him like that, and that's all I need to know."

"So, you're going to be constantly on guard around him?" he questioned. His eyes pierced through hers. He wanted to know she would be safe.

"Yes, I promise. I'll be extremely cautious," she vowed.

A tear ran down Aster's face. Susan ran her hand over his moist skin and allowed the tear to soak into her thumb. She leaned in and kissed his tear-saturated cheek. As her lips skimmed over his face and found their way to his mouth, she drank in the taste of his sorrow. Her gentle kiss lingered. Aster embraced it and turned his body to face hers. He grazed the side of her face and lightly traced the line of her neck and shoulder with his hand. He gripped her shoulders and pulled her body closer to his. The warmth of her lips breathed up Aster's neck and found their way to his ear where she whispered, "I love you, Aster. I wish I could take away your pain."

Aster began to break; he grasped her tightly in his arms. His weeping turned to sobs.

Susan's longing to comfort him turned into

repeated kisses. "It's okay, Aster." She brushed her lips against his.

His cries quieted as he gave into the passion of the moment. He fervently kissed her. His lips found her jaw line and followed it to her neck. In the rawness of his pain, Aster's longing for more intensified. As his fingertips traced over her blouse, unbuttoning it, Susan's breathing escalated, and her hands trembled.

She pulled herself free from his embrace and placed her trembling hand on the side of his face. She was frightened, but as she looked into his eyes, she saw the aching of his heart and his yearning for her and found herself vulnerable. Aster leaned into her and gently grazed her lips with his. Susan's quivering subsided as they were both overwhelmed by desire and lost themselves in their love for one another.

Chapter 16

The Exit

Sitting on the side of his old bed, Aster laid his head into his hands. The stress of the day resurfaced. Once again flashes of Susan's arm covered in bruises bombarded his mind. He clutched his fingers forming claws with them and ran them down the sides of his face, yet he drew no blood; his fingernails had been bitten down to the quick, a nervous habit he'd developed as a young boy.

He had lived so many years in the torment of never knowing what was going to set his mother off, so he anxiously chewed away on his fingernails as he hid in the closet of his bedroom. Aster glanced toward the closet door and saw a memory play before his eyes of his mother slinging the door open. There he sat bundled in the back corner of the closet biting his nails trying desperately not to look as he tightly squeezed his eyes shut.

Aster's anger seethed as he recalled the intensity of the fear that always formed a tight knot in his stomach. As a little boy his mother's indignant glower always sent a bolt of terror into his belly where it contorted into a tangled mass before rushing through his extremities, so he dared not even look as she lifted his tiny body from the corner by his overalls and dropped him in the middle of the bedroom floor to unleash her fury upon him.

Searching for the love that had saved him from the darkness of his home life, Aster knelt beside his bed and skimmed his hands over the place he had made love to Susan that day after his mother's funeral. The thought of making love to her and feeling the warmth of her body radiating against his soothed his anger. Tears pooled behind his lids as he remembered how it felt to hold her trembling body next to his and watch as her conviction set in causing tears to stream down her troubled face. Her shame and his repentance lingered in his mind. He knew he would never be free of the constant struggle within him. Her love was his torment, and he longed to sever the tie that had bound him for so long.

Susan lay under the covers next to Aster. Feeling multiple scars, she traced her fingertips down his back. Sadness for the things he endured broke to the surface and brought tears to her eyes, and then without warning the realization of what had just taken place gripped her. She gasped.

Lowering his brow, Aster gazed into Susan's

eyes and dried her tears. "Are you okay? I didn't hurt you, did I?"

Susan sat up and pulled the covers around her body. "Huh...I can't believe...we just...how did that happen? Why did I do that?"

Aster sat up and placed his hand on Susan's back. He knew they had both given in to a force more powerful than either of them could fight, and he understood her regret was not a rejection of him. Aster knew she had given in out of compassion for his pain and love for him, yet by doing so, she had broken a vow she made to herself and to God.

Seeking to console her, he took full blame upon himself in hopes to relieve her of any guilt. "I'm so sorry, Susan. I don't know what came over me. I've just felt so...I *never* wanted to take that from you. I know I just caused you to go against your beliefs. Please forgive me," he begged.

Susan's dark eyes gazed into his. Her lip trembled as she spoke, "Aster, there's nothing to forgive you of. You *didn't* cause me to go against my beliefs." She hung her head in shame. "I did that on my own. You didn't take anything from me either, Aster. I gave myself to you willingly. I wasn't thinking straight when I did it because I surely wasn't thinking about the spiritual consequences." She threw her hands in the air and shook her head in frustration and slammed the palm of her hand into her forehead.

Susan's breathing came in short and rapid spurts. Aster nudged closer. He traced his free hand across her cheek and into her hair and pulled her head to his shoulder. "I should've been stronger. I should've stopped it."

Susan clasped her hand around his wrist and pulled his arm away from her. She held her head up and declared, "I'm the one who is supposed to be more spiritual at this point. Not only have I been a Christian longer, Aster, but your mom just died. You had to carry her to the hospital yourself. You were the one who was so vulnerable. I'm the one who caused it to start by kissing you and telling you I love you. On top of that, you've done that before, which makes it more of a temptation. Me..." her voice escalated in hysterics, "I've never been with anyone until now. I should've been able to stop it. When I saw it was going there, I should've stopped and told you it couldn't go any farther. I...I...I've gotta go home. I need to pray; you should too."

Susan went to stand up and realized her clothes were on the floor. "Oh, ummm...close your eyes. I don't want you to see me," she pled.

Aster squeezed his eyes tight to save her from further embarrassment while Susan redressed herself.

Once her clothes were on, she uttered, "You can open them now."

Aster opened his eyes and gazed at her distraught countenance. "Are you gonna be okay?"

"Ummm...yeah...I think. Hey, Aster, can I ask you something?" She bit her bottom lip.

"You can ask me anything, Susan."

"Did you ummm?" her voice broke.

Aster's eyes were full of bewilderment. "Did...I?" he hesitantly asked.

Susan crinkled her brow as if it were disturbing to say, "You know...ummm...see me?"

Aster sighed. He knew it would be devastating for her to think he had. Susan was extremely modest, and he knew it, so he decided one little white lie between the two of them wouldn't hurt anything. "No. I had my eyes closed for most of it."

Susan's chest collapsed as she exhaled all the air she had been holding in her lungs in anticipation of his answer. "Good," she whispered. She leaned over and kissed Aster on the cheek. "I've gotta get home. Will I...see you tomorrow?"

"Tomorrow is..."

"Thursday. Tomorrow is Thursday."

"I'm supposed to meet my sister tomorrow."

"What about Saturday? We could meet at the bay."

"Yeah, I'll be there around nine that morning. I don't have to be to work until noon Saturday."

A bright smile crossed Susan's face. "Okay, see ya then."

As soon as Susan left, Aster collapsed back in the bed. "Oh, God, what have I done? I'm no good for her; that's why I broke things off with her in the first place. How could I do that to her? How could I put my desire before what is best for her?" He beat himself up for succumbing to the moment. "I've got to make things right for her."

Aster spent the rest of the evening working through a plan on how to be accepted by her parents. He stopped by the Service Center and used their computer to look up GED testing and colleges that would accept it. He even looked up army recruitment centers.

At closing time his boss came out of the office. "What are you doing here? Wasn't your mom's funeral today?"

"Yes, Sir, but I needed to use the computer to look up a few things."

"Whatcha lookin' up?"

"I need to get out of this town and get into some kind of school where I can make some real money, so I'm looking up what's out there for me to do," he explained.

"Well, son, what is it you wanna do with your life?"

Aster smiled when he heard Tim call him son. "Marry the most amazing girl in the world, but career wise, I need to be able to support that girl good enough to live on the bay side of town. I'm not going to graduate, so I need to find a school that will accept a GED."

"Oh, I see. Look, you're good at what you do. If you get an education in what you already know how to do, you could seriously end up owning a nicer place than this. I know I don't live in Bayville, but I do have a real nice home here in Paradise Shore," his boss encouraged him.

"Where's the best school?"

"California. Look, let me make a call. I have an old friend from my days back in school who is a mechanics teacher there. I'll see what he can do to get you in."

Aster raised his brow. "Really? You'd do that for me?"

"Are you kidding me? You're the best mechanic I've had working for me in years. I would never hold you back from a real future in the business. I'll be back in a minute," he excused himself, entered his office, and shut the door behind him. Through the large window in his office, Aster could see Tim scrolling through his rolodex in search of a number. He watched him pick up the phone and dial.

Aster continued his searches while his boss tried to contact his friend. Thirty minutes later Tim strolled out of his office sporting a huge grin. "I've got great news for you, Aster."

Aster pried his eyes away from the computer screen to look at his boss. "What's the good news?"

"Nah, good news ain't good enough. This is great news, boy. I just got you into MEDI!"

"MEDI?" Aster knit his brows together in confusion. He knew he wasn't cut out to be a nurse or paramedic or anything of that nature, especially after what he went through with his mom.

"MEDI, Motorcycle Engine Design Institute. They specialize in engine design, but they also have a program for mechanics," Tim explained as he whacked Aster across the back and laughed.

Aster flinched, but he swiftly set aside the bad memories that surfaced due to the way Tim had popped his back. He knew his boss had no way of knowing what he had been through in his life and was merely showing affection. A lot of guys showed affection by knocking each other around and wrestling. "That's great, Tim. So, how long will it take me to get through the course and have a degree?"

"Two years if you work hard and take a full load each semester. And being you won't have your girl there to distract you, you can do it. It's not gonna be easy though."

Aster shoved the computer chair away from the desk. "Thanks, man. I'm sure you had to give your word about me. I won't let you down."

They spent another hour talking about motorcycles and the details Aster needed on how to get to the institute and where he would live and work while going through the program. As he was going to leave the service center, Aster turned and faced Tim. "Tim, I want you to know how much I appreciate you doing this for me. You placed your trust in me when you hired me, and that means a lot to me."

"I've enjoyed your company. I'm just a

lonely old man. My wife and son both died during childbirth. He would've been just a couple of years older than you by now, and honestly, when you came in looking for a job, I thought about him. I guess I've kind of looked at you like a son since that point, and who wouldn't do everything they could to help out their son." He wrapped his arms around Aster and gave him a tight squeeze. "Now get on outta here."

The following Saturday morning Aster woke up excited about the changes he made in his life. He pulled up at the bay at nine a.m. just as he promised Susan he would. He smiled inside when he noticed her feet barely skimming the edge of the water. "Probably afraid of those minnows," he whispered to himself.

A slight smile inched across Susan's face when she saw him approaching, but she couldn't look him in the eyes. Aster knew why. She was still beating herself up for sleeping with him, and he understood why she felt that way. Susan was a good girl, and she held tight to a dream most girls in 2005 didn't cling to, the fantasy of giving herself on her wedding night to the one person she would spend the rest of her life with. To the majority of society, her vision of her life was an unrealistic fairytale—an illusion he had shattered, yet Aster determined within himself to allow her to hold on to at least one aspect of her hope for her life. *She may not be able to take back what happened and wait until she gets married, but she can marry the one person she's been with,* he mused.

Aster grabbed Susan's hand, leaned over, and kissed her forehead. "Good morning."

Susan sighed, "Good morning to you."

Draping his arm over her shoulder and walking toward the pier, he asked, "So, how are you feeling?"

"Honestly?" The edges of her eyes wrinkled.

"Honestly."

"A little depressed. I mean, I can never take back what happened, Aster, and I'm not blaming you, please know that."

Aster stopped and stared into her eyes. "I know you're not, Susan, but I do blame myself. I wanna make it right."

Pulling herself free from him, Susan jogged up the steps of the pier. "It's not something that can be made right, Aster."

Aster caught up to her. "Maybe that was the wrong way of saying it. Could you just stop for a minute and let me talk to you?"

Slowing her pace, she sat on the first bench she came across. Aster sat next to her. Susan sighed. Tears moistened her eyes. "What is it you're trying to say?"

Aster grabbed her hands in his. Looking at them, he mumbled, "I know I can't make it right by taking it back, but I can do right by you, Susan. I *want* to do right by you."

Susan narrowed her eyes. Trying to understand she asked, "What do you mean do right by me?"

"Tim, my boss man, he got me into a college where I can get a degree in motorcycle mechanics. I can open up my own shop one day or even work for one of the big motorcycle companies and make pretty good money. Granted, I'll never be as wealthy as your dad, but I'll be able to give you a good life."

Susan gazed into Aster's eyes. "Are you serious? What about all that stuff you said about not ruining my college education?"

"You can still go to college. Tim got me something similar to a scholarship to MEDI, a college for motorcycle mechanics, but it's in California. If I work hard I can be finished in two years. You can have your first two years of college under your belt by the same time. I'll get out of college, get a good job, and build up a savings over the following two years while you finish up your college. I won't be around here, so your parents won't cut you off. They don't have to know we're together."

"You'd wait four years for me?" Susan cried.

"Yeah, I would. The question is, would you be willing to wait?"

A tear spilled from Susan's eye. "Yes," she nodded her head as the word passed over her lips.

Aster squeezed her hand. "Susan, there's one tiny hiccup to this scenario."

"What's that?" She dried the tear from her face.

"I have to leave tonight. Part of the deal Tim struck for me is I have to work this summer for Carter. He's a teacher at the institute, and he owns his own shop. He'll give me a place to live, food to eat, and pay my tuition as long as I work in his shop. Tim apparently went on and on about how naturally talented I am with bikes."

Susan sniffled. "Huh, tonight? Wow, so fast."

"I know it's soon, but it's our only chance. I have to take the GED test as soon as I get there. I don't see another option. I'm not going to be able to graduate because I missed those two weeks of school."

"Why did you miss those two weeks?"

"I didn't break up with you because I wanted to. I broke up with you because I didn't want to ruin your life. I didn't think I'd have the strength to stay away from you if I saw you right away. Skipping school was the only way I knew to keep from giving in."

"So you're not going to graduate because of me?"

"No, I'm not going to graduate because I didn't think it all the way through before skipping out on classes."

"Do you have an address where I can write you?"

"Yeah." Aster pulled a piece of paper from his pocket with a street address in San Diego, California.

"You'll write as soon as you get set up, right? Set up an email address as soon as you can, okay?" Susan pulled a pen and paper from her purse and scribbled her email address and home address on it and handed it to him.

Taking the slip of paper from her hand, he whispered, "I promise."

"I don't want you driving straight through to California. You have to promise you'll stop and rest each night. I know it'll lengthen the drive, but I won't be able to sleep if I think you're barely holding your eyeballs open and driving a motorcycle across the country," Susan demanded.

It was the first time Aster had heard such sternness in her voice, so he complied. "I'll see Tim in a bit at work, so I'll talk to him about it. He insisted he wanted to give me a little money for the trip. I tried to refuse, but he told me he thought of me as his son, and if his son were still here, he'd do it for him."

"That's really kind of him. What time are you leaving?"

"Five. I'll drive through Louisiana tonight and stay the night in Texas, okay?"

"Okay."

Aster wrapped his arms around Susan for what he knew would be the last time for at least four years. As he held her in his arms, she promised, "I'll wait for you, Aster McGrath."

Chapter 17

The Hospital

Aster knelt at the side of the bed in his old bedroom and wept. As his body and mind drifted into a deep sleep, he dreamt of Susan. The beast was bound once more, which brought peaceful scenes of their times in the wildflower field. *Brrrring brrrring…brrrring…*His cellphone rang. A shaft of light beamed across his face as he awoke and jerked his head. Gaining his bearings, he witnessed the daylight streaming through the window. His face, moist with tears, glistened in the sunlight. He lifted his hands from his old bed, dried his tears, reached to his side, and flipped open his cellphone. Immediately, he looked for the time. *Seven-oh-three*, he wondered how he had slept several hours on his knees.

"Hello," he groggily answered.

The voice on the other end was male and unknown to him, but that was nothing new to him considering the type of work he did. People often called in search of assistance. "Reverend McGrath?" he inquired.

"Yes, this is Reverend McGrath. How may I help you?" He rubbed his swollen eyes.

"This is Detective Marshall with Bayville Police department. I'm hoping you can help identify a woman who was brought to the hospital yesterday around noon. She had been beaten. She's still unconscious and had no identification on her. I found a card in her pocket with your name and church on it. I thought she may be part of your congregation. Can you meet me at the hospital?"

Hot acid gushed through Aster's stomach. He knew exactly who lay in that hospital bed, and he knew he was to blame for her condition. The monster inside him kicked at his gut, begging to be set free, but Aster took a huge gulp and pushed the beast back down. "I'll be there in five minutes. What room?"

"She's on the fifth floor in ICU. I'll meet you in the hall."

"Yes, Sir, I'll see you in a few minutes." Aster immediately dialed another number.

"Hello," the hushed voice answered.

"Tyler, there's been an emergency. I need you to give the message this morning."

"Yeah, sure thing. Is everything okay?"

"No, you may want to be prepared to cover tonight as well."

"All right. Just let me know if there's anything I can do."

"I will." He flipped the phone closed.

Five minutes later, just as he said he would, Aster drove into the hospital parking lot. He parked his Altima and momentarily stared at the towering hospital. The last time he had been to Bayville Hospital was the day he carried his mother's body into the emergency room. His stomach twisted. Naturally he placed his hand over it. Gripping the steering wheel with his other hand, he prayed, "Dear God, please don't let it be as bad as I already know it is. Don't let her die."

Hesitantly Aster stepped out of his white car and shook off his fears before marching through the front doors of the building and making his way to the elevator. Suspiciously he glanced around to see if he recognized anyone.

Bayville had changed since hurricane Katrina. She had wiped out the bayside of town and flooded the lower levels of the hospital. Susan's father had drowned trying to save two of his patients. Aster's sister told him about it when he came back into town in search of her and Susan. He had driven home as soon as they opened the roads for people to return after the storm. Along with everyone else on the bayside of town, Eva and the Smiths lost everything.

The Smiths were wealthy, so as soon as Mr. Smith heard the beast of a storm had reached a monstrous category five and was headed for the Mississippi/Louisiana coast, he loaded them all up and drove to Tennessee. They had just returned to find an empty lot where their home once stood when Aster made it into town. Katrina sucked the bay into her belly and spewed it all out right on top of all the homes on the west side of Bayville. The east side of town was far enough away from the bay to be spared from being washed away from rapid flooding. Most of the damage received on that side of town was due to the strong winds ripping through poorly-built homes. Leaving a heap of rubble, a tornado barreled through the mid-section of town and demolished the library Susan and Aster studied in. Upon sight most of Bayville resembled a war zone.

For the most part Bayville had been rebuilt, but five years later construction sites were still scattered across the town. On top of rebuilding their town, the citizens of Bayville also gained multitudes of newcomers from Louisiana, who migrated a little farther east to reestablish their lives. Immediately after the storm, most of the homes on the east side were still livable, along with Aster's old home. Before leaving to go back to California to finish his schooling, Aster met a family, The Elkinses, from New Orleans. They were in search of a place to live. He offered to allow them to live in his old home until he returned.

The Elkinses signed a two-year lease, so Aster permitted them to live in the rundown shack for two-hundred dollars a month. He figured it wasn't worth more than that, and he knew it would help the family of five to get back on their feet. They ended up staying until Aster moved back to Bayville just six months prior. They had saved their money and built a nice home on the bay side of town. They were now a part of Aster's congregation at Bread of Life Church. Aster found himself to be grateful for being surrounded by strangers now that he was back in town. Talk of his bad blood had been watered down a bit by the departure of many old residents of the bay side.

Aster stepped off the elevator onto the fifth floor and scanned the walls in search of signs pointing to the intensive care unit. He swiftly found the sign, took a deep breath, and headed to the right.

The walls of the hallway started to swell in and out around him causing him to feel dizzy. He glanced around him and envisioned the walls as living tissue. It was then he recognized he was in the throat of the serpent who intended to eat him alive and send him into the pits of his belly to live out his remaining days. Discerning the fact his mind played tricks on him, he stopped and placed his hand against the wall to steady himself.

The acid in his stomach churned, making him feel nauseated. He was losing his composure, and he knew it. He skimmed through his mind in search of techniques he had been trained to teach others in Bible College. He searched the walls for directions to the restroom. It wasn't far off, so he inhaled another deep breath and headed that way. Once he finally made it to the restroom, he stumbled through the door, staggered into the first stall, and retched the remains of his stomach into the toilet. Making his way to the sink, he turned the knob and released a stream of cold water into the sparkling clean basin. He cupped his hands together, gargled, and spit several times. After rinsing out his mouth, he splashed his face several times with the cool, refreshing water. He grabbed a wad of paper towels and dried his face.

He stared into the mirror and chanted, "You can do this, Aster. You can do this. You can face her. You have to. She'll forgive you; she will. It's who she is."

Aster encouraged himself to face what he feared the most—the possibility Susan had been so deeply wounded by him she would be unable to even look at him, much less release him from his sin against her when he begged for her forgiveness. He gained his composure and headed back down the hallway that only a moment ago tried to swallow him alive. In the distance he eyed a man standing tall outside the door to the intensive care unit. As he neared, he noticed the Bayville Police Department logo, three pale-blue, wavy lines stacked one on top of the other with a seagull embroidered above them, worn with pride on his royal-blue polo shirt.

He inhaled a sharp breath before approaching him. "I'm Reverend McGrath." He shook the detective's hand. Guilt washed through him. Instinctively his eyes shifted, unable to be captured in the detective's gaze.

"Thank you for coming, Reverend." His voice resonated with military-like seriousness as he hit the buzzer on the wall by the double doors leading into the intensive care ward.

"Not a problem, Detective."

The door opened, and Detective Marshall led the way into a wide hall. "Reverend, before we go any further, I should warn you; this woman is in pretty bad shape. Whoever did this to her messed her face up pretty bad. The doctor has already stitched the gashes to her face—she was beaten so much her face was busted open. The doctor was certain she hadn't been cut, just beaten. Her face is pretty bruised and swollen though. You may not even be able to recognize her even if she is a member of your congregation, but we'd appreciate any information you could give us on who she is. We're hoping maybe she at least came to you for some sort of guidance."

Aster's stomach lurched. Gulping, he nodded his head acknowledging everything the detective said and braced himself.

Aster followed Detective Marshall through the spacious hall to a circular room. The nurses' station was situated in the center of the room, which allowed them visual contact with all patients encircling them. The rooms were more like glassed-in cubicles surrounding the circumference of the room. All patients could be clearly seen from the nurses' station at all hours. Each room had a glass door to allow some sort of privacy for families. Multiple beeps and bleeps constantly rang in Aster's ears. He wondered how the nurses could stand it. It was already driving him mad, and he had been in the room for less than a minute.

Aster recognized Susan immediately when Detective Marshall led him into the room where she slept.

He gasped and took a step back at the sight of her battered face. Detective Marshall chimed in, "I know it's tough to see, but do you rec—"

"Susan...Her name is Susan Blackman," Aster interjected.

"Are you positive?"

"Yes, Sir."

"Is she a member of your congregation?"

"No, Sir. I went to high school with her. She tutored me."

Detective Marshall eyed Aster's blanched face. "Do you know why she had a card for your church on her?"

"No, she must've picked one up from the church."

"Thanks for coming out here so quickly." He stretched his hand out to shake Aster's.

As Aster's hand met his, he uttered, "Her mother is Sharon Blackman. She lives in Prentiss, Alabama."

Behind the closed door the detective continued to question Aster. Susan's nurse watched the two men converse from the nurses' station. When they exited the room, she approached with Susan's chart.

"Our Jane Doe is Susan Blackman. Reverend McGrath just identified her. I'm on my way out to contact her mother," Detective Marshall uttered.

As the double doors closed behind the detective, Aster turned on his heels and headed back to Susan's room. The nurse entered behind him. "Is your name by any chance Aster McGrath?"

Glancing down at the nurse, he answered, "Yes."

"Well, Reverend, my name is Penny. I'm her nurse. She woke up for a minute about an hour ago and grabbed my hand and mumbled the name *Aster McGrath*. At first I thought maybe she was trying to tell me you were the one who did this to her, but now I see she was asking for her minister. People often realize...well...they, they sometimes ask for their pastor in a time like this..." her voice trailed.

"She asked for me?" A deluge of tears rushed to his eyes.

"Yes, Sir, she keeps drifting in and out of consciousness. Your name is the only thing she has said, outside of asking for daisies. She must love flowers," Penny explained.

"Yes, she does. She loves wildflowers. Is she allowed to have them in her room?"

"Yes, she is. I'm glad you were able to tell the police who she is. She's not any relation to Dr. Blackman who drowned here during Katrina, is she?"

"Yes, he was her father. Do you know where was she found?"

"About a mile from the hospital around noon yesterday is what I was told. My shift started at five this morning. The nurse on shift before me said she had been unconscious since they brought her in."

"How...bad is she?" Aster's throat closed. He choked on his words.

"Pretty bad, Reverend, you may want to...well...you know. The doctor doesn't expect her to make it. His report says he's not sure how she's still hanging on already. There's a lot of internal bleeding they can't get to stop. I'll give you some privacy with her so you can pray." As she went to shut the glass door, she mumbled, "What kind of evil is it that does something like that to someone?"

Aster jerked his head around and stood gaping at the nurse. Her remark stabbed him in the gut. His hands shook as he turned to face the dying woman whom he needed to be praying for him now more than ever. As the glass door shut, silence filled the room. Aster inched his way to Susan's bedside. He stretched his hand and lightly grazed hers.

Three days after receiving the phone call that led him to Susan's side as she lay in ICU, Aster gazed at the white casket covered in a beautiful spray of black-eyed Susans, blue and purple asters, and dozens of daisies. The earth swirled around him. The Bible he held in his hands visibly shook. He feared Sharon recognized his trembling, and he didn't want her to see any weakness in him at that moment. He took three deep breaths and glanced at the little girl with white-blonde hair holding Sharon's hand. A smile played across his lips as he saw Susan staring back at him through the child's chocolaty eyes. In that moment he knew he could do it.

Aster glanced through the crowd standing

in the cemetery and began, "Susan was a rare young woman in this society and world and much too young to be taken from us. She leaves behind her mother, Sharon, a beautiful daughter, and me, the young, reckless boy she saved from a life of hopeless darkness. It is because of her I am the one standing here today as a minister. She is the one who led me to the God I now serve. We see so many Christians in this society running around preaching to people about how they are going to Hell over all the sins they are committing, yet they accomplish very little for God because they are standing in judgment when God Himself is the only one who can do that, but Susan wasn't like that. Her light did not shine through theological words or scriptures being thrown at me or anyone else. She simply was. She showed me a love I had never known, and it wasn't because she preached to me because she never did. Her only mentions of God were when I asked a question and He was honestly a part of her answer." Tears rushed over Aster's eyes and spilled over his lids. He didn't try to hold them back at that point. He simply allowed them to flow.

As he went to continue, his jaw trembled, but he managed to choke out his words in order to honor her and what she had done for him. "I used to see myself as a hopeless cause, a bad seed with no future, and when I would make comments about the evil within me, Susan would always tell me that wasn't true. Her reply was always that she saw the good in me. That's what made her so unusual, I think. Most people want to see the bad in people rather than seeing the good in them. She was a jewel in a dark cavern, shining so brightly because of the love radiating through her heart and life that you could see her from miles away. Her physical beauty paled in comparison to the beauty of her soul. She truly lived what she believed, and she deserved so much more than what the world gave her. Even now as I myself question God about how He could allow such violence to be released on someone who gave only love, I am reminded of the truth in the statement Susan made to me the day she led me to the Lord when I questioned her about how God could allow evil. She looked me in the eyes and said, 'Evil exists, but God can use the bad things that happen to bring about good.'"

Aster read a short scripture, closed his Bible, and prayed. "Thank you, God, for the good You will bring out of this tragedy."

Chapter 18

The Visit

Sharon's countenance was full of grief and pride as she caressed her granddaughter's arm—grief in the loss of her daughter and pride in the child seated next to her. She watched as one-by-one the pallbearers placed their black-eyed Susan boutonnieres on the spray of wildflowers placed atop Susan's pearly-white casket and walked away. They sauntered their way over to Sharon and nodded their heads in acknowledgment of her grief. They obviously knew Sharon well enough to know better than to extend a hug to her.

She had a particular way about her that was devoid of touchy, feely emotion, yet a tear escaped her eye as the last pallbearer knelt before her granddaughter, tousled her white-blonde hair, and whispered, "Your momma will always be with you right in here." He pointed to her tiny heart. The little girl smiled up at the young man, stretched her arms around his neck, and cried,

"Wuv you Doddie."

"I love you too, baby girl." He returned her embrace.

Sharon placed her hand on his shoulder. "Thank you for those words, Dodson. They meant a lot to Mae and *me*."

Dodson craned his head and gazed into Sharon's eyes. "I'm so sorry for your loss, Aunt Sharon."

When he pulled away from her to join the rest of the pallbearers, Mae laid her head against her grandmother's side and cried, "I want my mommy."

"Ssshhhh, it's okay sweetheart; it's okay." Sharon kissed her head and whispered, "Your mommy will visit you in your dreams now." She comforted the child.

"Daddy," she cried.

Sharon cradled her granddaughter in her arms. "Nana's here, sweet pea. Nana's right here."

Aster choked back the tears aching to push their way out. He wanted to throw open the casket, grab Susan in his arms, and beg her to wake up, not just for him but for her little girl. Seeing her tiny heart breaking stabbed him; nevertheless, he held back his tears, and with a long-stem daisy in his hand, he ambled his way over to the dainty image of Susan sitting next to the woman who had given him such grief. As he glanced in Sharon's eyes, he no longer saw hatred glaring back at him; he simply saw a void.

It was obvious to Aster, and anyone else who knew Sharon and the luxuries she was used to before her husband died during hurricane Katrina, life had not dealt well with her since his death, and now she faced the death of her only child. All she had left was her granddaughter, who just happened to be the spitting image of her mother. That knowledge left Aster not only mourning the loss his black-eyed Susan, but an overwhelming sadness for Sharon and her loneliness draped around him like a heavy cloak.

Aster sat next to the blonde-haired beauty of a child and handed her the daisy. "Would you like to walk up there with me and place this flower on your momma's casket?"

The little girl glanced into his eyes, and with a trembling bottom lip, she shook her head *yes*. Aster held his hand out for her to grab. She placed her petite hand in his. He gazed at it for a fleeting moment. Her entire little hand fit within his palm. It amazed him. Holding tightly to his hand, she scooted off the seat and plopped to the ground. As Aster glimpsed upon her resemblance, he remembered the first time he held Susan's hand to lead her into the bay. He smiled a weak smile.

Five days prior to Susan's funeral, Aster sat at his desk preparing his next sermon. His office walls, lined in dark wood paneling, smelled of lemon scented furniture polish. His office sparkled in cleanliness. Not one speck of dust settled on the books covering his bookshelf, but his desk was a different story. It was anything but organized. Strewn about it and opened in varying places were a commentary, a concordance, and three different versions of the Bible.

He flipped through the pages of Matthew Henry's commentary, studying his message. A light knock at the front door drew his attention. He looked up from the book in his hand and glanced around the room. Again a light knock resounded. He placed his notes across the top of the commentary, scooted his chair back, and stood. He wasn't expecting any company that day. Most of his congregation knew it was a day of preparation for him, so they usually called the church secretary if they needed him, and she usually called him rather than showing up at his home.

Unsure of whom it may have been and frightened it might be an emergency, he opened his office door and quickly made his way to the front entrance of his home. He grasped the knob in a firm grip and tugged open the door. His lungs involuntarily wheezed when his eyes fell upon Susan standing with a bouquet of black-eyed Susans, daisies, and asters. The scent of the flowers blended with hers and wafted through the door. Shaken and speechless, Aster stood staring at her for a moment.

Finally, she spoke up, "Hi, Aster." She forced a smile. "May I come in?" The morning light danced across her eyes revealing her nervousness.

Aster caught his breath and uttered, "Ummm...yeah, sure. Come in." He stood to the side and held the door open. She inched her way into his home scanning her surroundings and admired what he had made of his life.

It was the first time Aster had laid eyes on Susan (face to face that is) since the day she told him she would wait for him. When he came back to Bayville after hurricane Katrina looking for Eva and Susan, Susan was nowhere to be found. She had left town for safety purposes and not yet returned. When he moved back into town and took the position of pastor at the Bread of Life Church, he was unaware she had returned to Bayville until he saw her walking the beach by the bay—the place where he first opened his heart to her and allowed her in. From a distance he watched as she held a little girl's hand and led her into the water. She ventured out farther than he had ever been able to convince her to go and that made him smile, yet even his joy was torture. Seeing her from a distance had been so painful he dared not approach her, and now gazing at her beauty close enough to breathe the scent of her hair and feel her skin as she brushed past him (entering his home) and stood before him, the knife of her presence stabbed him repeatedly in the heart.

Aster's heart raced, but he knew he had to control his emotions. With Susan there within his grasp, he had questions he hoped she would finally answer; nevertheless, he knew he needed to distance himself in order to protect his heart from the pain it was likely to endure as a result of her explanations. He decided to keep the visit as formal as possible, so rather than inviting Susan into his living room, he led her to his office where he did all of his studies.

Susan's eyes skimmed over the room and fell upon the small round table by the door. Holding up the vase of wildflowers, she asked, "May I?"

Aster gave his head a slight nod. His countenance was solemn.

"Maybe they will liven up your office a bit." She forced another smile.

"Maybe so," he mumbled. Aster couldn't return her smile. As much as he wanted to be gracious to her considering her kindness to him when he was unlovable to everyone else in town, he simply could not open his heart back up.

"Well, I thought you might like them anyhow. I took my daughter to stay at the cabin with my mom for a week. The field was in full bloom." Susan glanced at the floor and whispered, "I couldn't help but think of you, so I went out early this morning before daylight and picked a bunch." She looked back up at him and shrugged her shoulders. "I stopped at a boutique on my way back into town and bought the vase." Susan glanced back at the bouquet and situated the vase of flowers perfectly on the small, round table.

"So, your mom lives in the cabin now, huh?" Aster made sure the office door stayed open.

"Yes, she couldn't bear to come back here after daddy's death. Katrina ruined so many lives."

"Yes, she did. She caused me a bit of pain myself," Aster sighed.

Susan flinched at his words. Although she was unsure of exactly how it related to her, she was certain it did.

Aster's chest ached. He found making small talk was the best way for him to deal with the pain he was presently suffering. "I was sorry to hear about your father, Susan."

"Yes, it was hard for a while. Daddy made sure we were safe at the cabin while he worked. You know doctors have to work during a storm like that. Things were strained between Momma and me for a while after Daddy's death. It was pretty bad. He was always my buffer with Momma, so for a long time I didn't have any compassion from her on the direction of my life. She was extremely hard-nosed about it."

"Well, it looks like your life turned out fairly well. Maybe your mother did know best."

Susan recoiled slightly. "Maybe so."

Aster pulled out the seat on the opposite side of his desk. "Have a seat."

"Okay," Susan's hands shook as she reached out for the arm of the chair to sit. Her eyes shifted quickly and gazed at the wall behind Aster and the mess across his desk.

"And you have the consolation your father died a hero. I hear he was trying to save two of his patients," he uttered as he sat in his chair across the desk from her. He realized quickly the closer hcr proximity the more his chest constricted, so he put as much distance as possible between them.

"Yes, he did. He had already saved four others. He went back for the remaining two. Despite all of the doctors and nurses hollering it was too late, he wouldn't give up. He went back down to the second floor. When they found his body, they said he had made it all the way back to the elevator carrying one of the ladies. Just a few more yards and he would have made it around the corner to the stairwell," Susan shared the story of her father's heroism with pride. She shifted in her seat. "So, how is Eva? What is she up to nowadays? I haven't seen her in so long. I think the last time was right after prom, but she wouldn't speak to me."

Aster picked up the pen he had been writing with. He rolled it between his fingers, fidgeting with it. "Eva is good. She graduated from Knoxville high school. I'm sure you know the Smiths lost everything in Katrina, so they came back here to gather what they could and moved to Tennessee. She went off to Ole Miss after graduation and met a young guy named Logan who happened to be preppy enough for the Smiths. Despite his extremely yuppie nature, she fell in love with him. He's five years older than her, so he was nearly finished with his degree when they met. She went to college year round and finished last semester. They were married while she was still in college. I performed the ceremony for her wedding. Mr. Smith gave her away. She looked beautiful, and she seems very happy. She's a counselor for troubled teens now, and her husband is a lawyer. They live in Jackson."

"Oh, wow, that's great. I knew they moved to Tennessee, but Shane never kept in contact with them after the storm. I know you're so proud to see how well her life turned out, and look at you, a preacher. No one in this little town would've ever thought it, huh?" Her chin trembled as tears rushed to her eyes.

"Only you would have ever thought it, and I thank you for that. You had faith in me when no one else would." His countenance softened.

Susan wrung her hands together. "You're welcome, I guess. It's good to see you here pastoring the church where you were baptized." She smiled.

"Thanks."

"I hear you're part owner of the service center in Paradise Shore as well."

"Yeah, I got my degree in motorcycle mechanics before I went to Bible College. I paid my way through by working at Carter's shop."

"That's good. I'm happy for you."

"Thank you. I didn't imagine I would find you living here in Bayville when I moved back home six months ago to take the position at the church. I figured your mom had you sent off to an Ivy League college somewhere." He made more small talk.

"Well, life didn't go exactly as any of us had planned, I don't think although it seemed to have gone pretty good for you. Despite the fact I didn't have daddy to buffer Momma's insistence, there were some choices she simply couldn't make me choose, and besides, this is where Shane wanted to raise a family," she began her explanation.

The mention of Shane's name the second time twisted the knife already stabbing Aster in the heart. His ribs ached under the pressure of his pounding heart. "So, a family, huh? And how many children do the two of you have?" He desperately tried to force the aching away.

"I just have the one child, a little girl. Shane tried to talk me into having another baby, but I'm just not ready for another child at this point in my life."

The agony was too much to bear. The idea Susan had shut her heart off to him and married Shane so soon after he left caused him too much anguish. Thoughts of Shane Garrish (the guy she promised him she would be cautious of, the guy he had beaten nearly to death) touching her and making love to her was simply unbearable, so he quickly interjected, "Susan, I don't understand why you're here. What do you want from me?"

Susan looked into Aster's eyes and spoke with boldness, "An answer to the one question that has eaten at me for years..."

Chapter 19

The Letters

Aster's mind whirled with thoughts and memories as he inched his way closer to Susan's casket. Again he glanced at the child holding his hand. Alligator tears streamed down her innocent face. *She shouldn't have to know the pain of losing her mother and definitely not like this,* he thought. Her hand slid out of his palm. She looked back at him, wrapped her hand around his finger, and held tightly to it. As they approached the iridescent chest holding the only woman he had ever loved, he picked her daughter up in his arms and looked into her milk-chocolate eyes. She gazed back into Aster's baby blues, placed her hand upon his cheek, and whispered, "Nana said Mommy intruced you to God an you gonna intruce Mommy to God t'day."

Straightening the bow on her dress, he managed to choke out, "That's what my prayer was about—introducing your momma to God."

"Will God give Mommy her purdy fower?" She stretched the daisy out and stared at it.

A small smile crossed Aster's face. "Yeah, sweetheart, God will make sure she gets your pretty flower. As a matter of fact, I bet your momma has her very own field of wildflowers just like the one at your Nana's house, and I'm almost positive if you sit out in that field when its covered with black-eyed Susans, your momma will be sitting in her field, and it will be like the two of you are there together."

She sniffled. Aster pulled a handkerchief from his pocket and dried the tears from her plump face. He knew he held Susan's heart in his arms; it was the only comfort he had. "Nana said Mommy's gonna visit me in dreams." Her bottom lip jutted out.

"I'm sure she will; I'm sure she will. Okay, you can give her the flower now."

She leaned over and placed her long-stemmed daisy on her mother's casket. Aster kissed her on the cheek and placed her back on the ground. "Go sit with your Nana for a minute, okay?"

"Okay," she whimpered.

Aster removed his boutonniere and set it next to the daisy. Friends and distant relatives loaded back up in their vehicles and drove off. Outside of the funeral home attendants, Sharon, Aster, and Susan's daughter, Mae, were all that remained. Finally Sharon stood, turned to her granddaughter, and instructed, "Wait here, darling." She walked over to Aster, placed her hand on his shoulder, and watched as he pulled a stack of letters from his pocket. Pain shot through her eyes as she stared at the bundle in his hands. "I'll leave you alone with her."

Aster gazed into Sharon's eyes and saw

sorrow staring back at him. "Thank you," he whispered.

As Sharon climbed in her car with her granddaughter, a tear fell upon the top letter in Aster's hands. He stood in silence and stared at the bundle.

Susan glanced across Aster's desk. Her eyes searched for an object to focus on. She didn't want to look him in the eyes, so she stood and paced through his office and wrung her hands. "I told myself I wanted to know, but now that I'm here, I'm not sure if I'll be able to bear the answer."

Aster watched as she scanned her surroundings. Despite her distance his chest constricted.

Susan made her way to the wall of books and traced her fingers over a shelf full of them. "Do you remember all of our afternoons at the library working with flash cards and me teaching you phonics and to read?" An edgy giggle passed through her lips.

"Of course, I do," Aster assured her.

Stopping, she ran her hand down the copy she had given him of *The Hobbit* and declared, "I was so proud of you that day. I always knew you could do it." She pulled the book from its spot on the shelf and opened it to the title page. Written in the top corner, she read her own handwriting,

To Aster from Susan with love. You'll find the book to surpass the movie The Lord of the Rings Merry Christmas.

She skimmed through the remainder of the book quickly before placing it back and making her way farther down the shelf. When she came across the picture of Aster sitting on his motorcycle, parked on the beach at the bay, she picked it up and smiled. "You kept it. I always hoped you would." Susan's fingertips traced the form of Aster's body in the picture she had taken of him during their first motorcycle ride together. "Do you think of me when you look at it?" she wondered, her voice barely audible.

"Yes," was all Aster said in response.

"Hmmmmm...." She sighed. She set the picture down and glanced around the remainder of the office. "You've done well for yourself, Aster, but I have to wonder, how soon after you left did you decide you were called to be a pastor and that I obviously wasn't good enough to be a pastor's wife?"

Pain shot through Aster's chest. Her accusation stabbed straight through his heart. Anger shot like acid up his throat. He gulped, swallowing the fiery breath of the beast within him. "You couldn't be a pastor's wife when I answered God's call; you were already another man's wife, Susan. Finding out about you marrying Shane left me with no one but God. It was during that time when He drew me closer to Him and led me to go to Bible College after finishing at MEDI."

Aster had longed to understand why she had not waited, yet when he moved back into town and found she had moved back herself, he refrained from approaching her and demanding an answer, but now with her allegation severing that which held him back, he unleashed, "You said you would wait for me, but when I came home after Katrina to make sure you were okay, I had to hear from my sister that you married Shane, of all people, Susan. She said you two married on July first, so you waited an awful long time, didn't you?"

"I couldn't wait. You don't understand. It was decided for me," Susan's voice broke.

"Well, I guess I don't understand. We don't live in a day and age of arranged marriages, Susan. You still had to say *I do*. Your mom couldn't force you to marry Shane. I know that's what she wanted, but why did you give in to her insistence?" Silence filled the room for a brief moment. Aster could no longer take it. "So, that's the question that's been eating at you all this time? Wondering why I didn't choose you? I did choose you; you didn't choose *me*."

A gush of tears broke forth from Susan's eyes. "No, that's not my question. I wanna know why," she sobbed.

"Why what?"

"Why you never wrote." Susan's voice was weak. "You said you would write, but you didn't, and I needed you. I used the address you had given me and wrote you, but it was returned. I tried to look you up online, but I couldn't find you. There was no address, no number, nothing. I even had Angie drive me to Paradise Shore looking for Tim's Service Center. I thought maybe he could get in contact with you, but I couldn't find any place called that. I went to the Smiths' house looking for Eva to see if she had heard from you, but they had apparently left to go on vacation the day after school let out. I left a note on the door for her, but I never heard from her. I needed you, but you weren't here. You just abandoned me."

"I never abandoned you, Susan. I emailed you, but they never went through, so I wrote you after I settled in, but every one of my letters were returned as well. I didn't wanna give away that we were together, so I only wrote once a week. I figured you could convince your mom we were merely friends if she found them. I knew daily letters would give away there was more going on between us, but after the third letter was returned, I couldn't take it, so I called from a payphone down the road. I didn't have a phone in Carter's little apartment, and I wasn't going to ask to use his to make a long-distance call. Your mom answered the phone and told me you were dating Shane, but I didn't believe her. I couldn't believe her, so I kept writing, and I kept calling, but she kept answering the phone, and my letters kept being returned. I tried calling Eva too, but she was either off with Melody or her boyfriend. I couldn't just come home. I had a responsibility. I was planning to come home for Labor Day. I was given a week off work. Carter, my boss, knew I was worried about you, so he told me the shop would be closed for a few days anyway, and I could drive home, but then Katrina hit, and when I came home to check on you and Eva, it was too late. You had married Shane. I had already lost you."

Stunned by Aster's proclamation, Susan stood speechless for a moment. "My mother...you wrote...and you called?" she stuttered.

"Yes." Angry, Aster yanked his desk drawer open, pulled out a set of keys, unlocked another drawer in his desk, and pulled out a bundle of letters. A thick rubber band held them together. He walked around his desk and handed them to her. "Here, see for yourself."

Susan removed the rubber band. She flipped through the stack of letters. Each one had *Return to Sender* written across the front of it in bright-red ink. "Huh," she gasped. "I'm sorry, Aster. I didn't know. I should've." She shook her head. "I should've known it was my mother's doing." Susan found the postmarks; they were already in order from the first letter to the last. She lifted the letter post marked April 23 and turned it over, seeing the seal still in place. "At least she didn't read them."

"No, she gave us that much privacy at least," Aster mumbled.

"May I?" Susan asked permission to open the letters.

Aster sighed, "Huh...sure, read them all if you want. It doesn't matter now anyway."

Susan glanced at Aster. A wall of water encased his sapphire-blue eyes. "It matters to me, Aster."

Susan's eyes shifted and fell back upon the letter. For the first time, nearly five and a half years after it was sent, the seal was broken. She pulled the yellowing paper from the envelope, opened it, and read the words to herself:

April 23,

My Black-eyed Susan,

I arrived here in California and settled in a few days ago. I sent a few emails, but for some reason, they didn't go through, so I figured I would write a letter the old-fashion way. Tonight is the prom. I wish I could be there with you. I imagine you will look stunning tonight. You'll have to send me a picture.

Carter is pretty cool. He owns his own shop

and teaches at the school I will be attending. He's thirty-five with a wife and two small children. I can't help but think of the family we will have one day when I see them laughing together. He has a small loft above his garage and that's where I'm staying. I have my own small refrigerator and a microwave. No way to actually cook anything, so I guess I'll be living on frozen dinners, but it's all good. Carter says I can eat all meals with them, but he's going to give me a small paycheck, so I'll probably eat here in the loft a good bit. I don't want to impose on them more than I already am. School starts two weeks after Labor Day. I haven't been to the shop yet to know how that's gonna be, but I'm sure it'll all be good.

I did as you made me promise. I stopped and slept at a motel each night. I'm not going to lie to you though, sometimes it was midnight before I pulled in somewhere, and I was always back up at 6 and back out on the road by 7. It was a really long drive, and I wanted to get settled in here as soon as possible.

I miss you already. I'm not sure if I'm going to be able to survive being away from you long enough for you to get your college education, but I know being so far apart is better because I wouldn't be able to stay away from you if we were close together. We can't take the chance of your parents finding out about us. You may have to outright lie and tell your parents we're just friends if they see any of my letters. I won't write every day. They'd definitely know something is up if I do. I won't mess up your future, Susan. But I think we're going to have to sneak a few visits in somehow. I'll start working on a plan for that right away.

Will write again soon,

Aster

     Susan glanced into Aster's eyes before quickly opening the next letter and reading through it. She skimmed through another letter before she came across the first one Aster had written after making the first phone call.

May 10,

My Black-eyed Susan,

     I've had three of my letters returned to me now. They've all been unopened and marked return to sender, so tonight, I tried to call you. Your mother answered the phone. She told me you had been returning all of my letters and would continue to do so until I stopped writing because you are seriously dating Shane Garrish. I know none of this can be true. I will keep writing every week and keep calling until you happen to get to the mail first or answer the phone and respond to me. I know you wouldn't do this to me.

I miss you so much. I'm gonna talk to Carter about making a trip home to see you for myself if I can't get through to you soon. Being away from you is driving me mad, and not being able to contact you is torture.

I'm not giving up,

Aster

Susan's eyes deluged with watery tears; she gasped. She looked into Aster's eyes; her voice shook as she proclaimed, "I never knew about any of it. I swear to you, Aster, she never told me anything about any of these letters or any of the phone calls. I don't know what happened with the emails. She must've hacked my account or something."

She continued reading through the letters Aster had written her. When she finally came to the last letter, she broke. She sobbed uncontrollably as she read the words his wounded heart had written:

Sept. 12

Susan,

Obviously there is no sense in continuing to refer to you as my black-eyed Susan since you are apparently Shane's wildflower now. I'm not even sure what to say to you at this point. I don't know why I'm even writing; you are obviously just going to scribble return to sender across the top and shove it back in the mail. I can't believe your mother was telling the truth about you and Shane, Especially with your knowing that he hurt my little sister.

I guess I just keep wishing you would have at least written me back and explained your actions to me yourself rather than having your mother answer the phone and in such a coldhearted manner tell me you were with Shane. I thought you cared about me enough to give me that much respect, but I guess I was wrong to think I at least deserved that much.

When I returned to see if you were okay after the hurricane, I had to hear from my sister you were married to Shane. That was a major stab in the gut! But that wasn't the worst of it. She told me about your behavior at the prom. A week after I left, Susan? Really, just a week later and you're publically throwing yourself on Shane, kissing him and laughing in front of the entire school? I drove out to the cabin because I guess I wanted to believe Eva was lying to me, but when I drove up, I saw you through the window. He was kissing you, and I knew. I knew you apparently didn't love me and were unwilling to wait.

Despite all that Susan, there is one thing I do want to thank you for. I want to thank you for introducing me to God and showing me that there truly is good in me. I'm going to finish my schooling here at MEDI, but I plan to attend Bible College when I graduate. I feel God has called me to preach. Maybe that is something good that has come from something bad.

Goodbye

Aster McGrath

Susan folded the letter back and shoved it into the envelope. She glanced one more time at it. "It's not post marked. You didn't send it," her remark was a statement rather than a question.

"No, after writing it, I figured there wasn't any use in sending it. I'm not really sure why I kept it with the others, but I did."

As she handed him the stack of letters, with tears streaming down her face, she insisted, "You need to know about prom. You need to understand why I had to marry him. No matter what you may think of me, Aster, you need to understand I didn't have a choice."

Aster's face hardened. "Please, enlighten me then."

Chapter 20

The Prom

Standing amongst the fallen orange and red oak leaves, the funeral attendants stayed outside of the green canopy covering Susan's open grave. They gave the minister a moment to himself with the person he laid to rest. They both stood shivering in the damp November air. Autumn on the Mississippi coast could be fickle. One day a person may be able to step outside in shorts and a tank top, only to have to pull out a thin winter jacket the following day. The day Susan was buried turned out to be a cold, wet fall day.

Aster waited until Sharon drove away before lifting the casket lid. He broke down and cried over her body for what seemed to the attendants to be much too lengthy for someone who was merely a minister to the deceased. Eventually he lifted her hands and slid the letters under the three wildflowers already placed there. "I'm so sorry I did this to you," he whispered. "I will never be able to forgive myself, Susan. Your mom...she doesn't know, but everyone is soon to find out. They're already investigating all the events of your day that day. They're gonna find out you came by to see me. Your mom will surely hate me then, and I'll never..." Aster's voice broke. After gathering himself together, he continued, "I have to come clean, Susan. I have to tell her the truth. Your mother needs to know what happened. She should know I'm responsible."

Aster dried his tears, shut the lid, signaled to the funeral home attendants he was finished, and walked to his car. He tightly clutched the steering wheel and allowed himself to fall apart while watching them lower her casket into the ground. Through the glass of his windshield, he said goodbye to his black-eyed Susan for the last time. He watched and wailed as the grave diggers came and shoveled the dirt over Susan's casket. As he released all the guilt and shame he bore, he gathered the strength to tell Sharon what he had done, and he knew in his heart once he told her, he had to go straight to the police with the statement he failed to give the detective that day. As Aster collected his thoughts about his confession, he envisioned Susan, her face swollen, bruised, and covered with stitches.

Aster sat behind his desk and stared at Susan. His eyes revealed to her his heart had been shut off. No longer did she hold the key to it. She betrayed him, and now she knew it. For all that time, she assumed he escaped her influence and decided to go on with his life. She often wondered if he found someone else to love soon after making it to California. She knew California was known for its beautiful women and suspected Aster was simply too weak to resist. Maybe he had betrayed her and been unable to face her after that, she often wondered. Her heart's argument with her mind on that subject had always been how strong he had been in abstaining with her, but then her logical side reminded her heart he never confessed loving her and his abstinence was quite possibly more like avoidance; maybe he simply didn't desire her in that way. She would always argue with those thoughts by pointing out they made love once, but her line of reasoning had always been countered with the facts of that day: he never said he loved her, and he was weak and in need of comfort. Maybe that's all that day had been to him, comfort. Her mind claimed anyone else could have satisfied him, and combined with the absence of his letters and emails, she eventually assumed her heart deceived her.

Susan wrung her hands together so tightly her knuckles turned white and her joints ached. Standing back to her feet, she nervously walked to the window and glanced at the fallen leaves covering his lawn. "It's not what you think...not at all," she said, her voice barely above a whisper.

"I think I need to understand then," he spouted, his voice sharp. With harshness he demanded, "Tell me why my sister saw you acting that way with Shane."

Susan inhaled a deep breath. "It all started the night you left. I sat in my room trying to figure out how to go about getting out of going to the prom with Shane. You see, after you broke up with me, him and his family made your sister out to be a little drama queen. You had hurt me, and I was angry with you, so I started going out with Shane. It was the first time in my life I had ever wanted to hurt someone. I wanted you to feel the same pain I felt. It was wrong of me; I know that, but you did tell me to find another date for prom, you know..." Her thoughts trailed off.

"I know what I told you, Susan," Aster responded insensitively.

Susan tried to shake off his callousness. "Anyway...my mother came barging up in my room carrying a gown she had purchased for me that day, a fitted, yellow, sleeveless gown with tiny roses embroidered throughout it. She didn't even allow me to pick out my own prom dress. She insisted it was perfect for me. I knew if I told her I had reconsidered going to the prom with Shane she would freak out and suspect I had gotten back with you. She had already grilled me about your mother's death wanting to know if I had heard from you, so I figured the smart way to play it all out was to go ahead and go to the prom with Shane and pretend I was happy. That was my plan, so it is possible your sister saw me acting like I was happy. I wanted everyone to see that. I needed Shane to believe it so my mother would believe it."

Unsympathetically, Aster interrupted, "Oh, so pretending you were happy meant throwing yourself all over him in front of everyone? You couldn't just go and act like you normally do? You couldn't just smile every once in a while, be kind to him, and dance with him a few times? You had to kiss all over him to convince your parents, who weren't there, by the way, that you and I weren't back together and planning a future?"

Susan flinched. Squeezing her eyes tightly shut, she raised her voice for the first time, "Being normal was my plan, and it was what I did, I thought," her voice lowered to a whisper.

"You thought?" Aster narrowed his eyes.

"Yes. Please allow me to finish," she pled.

"Go on then."

"My mother helped to dress me that day. She even took me to a spa." A small smile crossed her face. "We both had massages, facials, manicures, and even pedicures. She said she wanted us to have mother/daughter time together to serve as a memory. She even brought her camera and had pictures taken by one of the ladies at the Bayville Spa. To spread all of the pictures out in a collage made it look as if I was truly enjoying preparing for that night. It was so difficult having to pretend I was excited about the prom the entire day with my mom. She even brought you up one time. She said, 'So, I haven't heard of that boy Aster being around since his mother died. Have you heard from him?'" Susan did her best to imitate her mother's voice. She turned to face Aster and looked down at the stack of letters he had placed on his desk, and proclaimed, "According to the date you wrote the first one, now I know she knew you *had* tried to contact me through emails, and she knew I truly hadn't heard from you because she made sure of it."

Susan's mind trailed back to the day she prepared for prom. She resumed her story. "Of course, I told her I hadn't heard from you, and I really didn't want to talk about you at all. I even called you a liar. I was unaware you wanted us to play things off as being friends."

Susan couldn't bear to be facing Aster as she recounted the events of that day, so she quickly shifted her body back around and gazed out the window before going on. "You know, prom is supposed to be a magical time in a girl's life. It was my senior year in high school, and I was supposed to be there with you. You were the one who should have pinned on my corsage and escorted me to the dance floor..." Her thoughts trailed again. "But that's not the way things happened, is it?"

Bitterly, Aster interjected, "No, it's obviously *not* how it happened."

"After a day of pretending to be ecstatic about my date with Shane, I learned I had it within me to be a remarkably good liar or actress, whichever you want to call it." She frowned. "When we left the spa, my mother took me to her hairdresser and had Shirley put my hair up in a fancy way. While my hair was being teased and braided and pinned, I had to sit and listen to my mother go on and on about how important it is to look beautiful for an eligible young man who is a potential mate. My mother had apparently already spent countless hours with Shane's mom. She had weaseled her way in and found out the family's history on both sides, and she was convinced they had *great* genetics."

Aster scoffed at those words, "Huh, great genetics. Sounds like your mom had your life planned out for you, so tell me why you went along with it."

Susan ignored his insistence to get straight to the point. She was determined to relive that day and walk him through the entire process. "My mother had me home and dressed by four-thirty. Shane stepped next door to pick me up at four-forty-five. It was like they had plotted it together." A sarcastic giggle slipped through her lips. "My dad kissed me bye on the cheek and told me to have a wonderful night. He told me to be sure to tell him all about it the next day because he was on call at the hospital so he may not be home when I got in, but he insisted he wanted me in by one a.m. 'not a minute later, young lady,' he said to me."

Susan paced the floor again. Reliving that night caused her anxiety level to rise. Her chest constricted, and her breathing became short and rapid. She took several slow breaths. Her hands shook as she grabbed her purse, pulled out a small bottle of water and a bottle of pills. She opened them and swallowed one.

"What was that?" Aster pried.

"Anxiety medicine. It's prescribed. Don't worry. I'm not bringing anything illegal into your home. No matter what you think of me at this point, I hope you know I wouldn't do that. The medicine is needed, trust me," she assured him.

"Trust is not something that can't be asked of me right now," he said, his tone stark and his eyes piercing.

Susan shifted her eyes to his and swiftly removed them. She couldn't bear to see such resentment glaring at her, not from him. "Yes, I know. I also know you want me to get to the point, but I need to explain everything to you in as much detail as possible, so even if you can't trust me, can you at least be patient with me?"

"Sure, I have nothing else to do today. I can be patient." He leaned back in his chair and crossed his arms.

"Thank you." Susan stopped behind the chair she had sat in and placed her hands on the back of it. She gathered herself together before inching her way back to the window. Telling Aster her story was difficult enough; she couldn't bear to look him in the eyes while she did it. "Shane took me out to eat at Lorelli's that night before going to the prom. I started getting nervous, feeling I couldn't go through with it, so I excused myself and went to the restroom. When I returned, our drinks had already been served, and he had already taken the liberty of ordering for me. Apparently my mom had told him my favorite dish. She was really pushing our relationship, and in the end he turned out to be so much like her."

Susan placed her hand upon the window and breathed deeply. "As soon as we got to the convention center, he escorted me to a table, seated me, and said he'd be right back. He came back with two small pieces of cake and two glasses of punch. I tried to insist I wasn't hungry. I mean, we had just left the restaurant, but he insisted we had to have dessert and if we didn't get it right then, there might not be any left by the time I decided I wanted some, so I gave in and ate it. I even smiled while I was doing so. I tried so hard to pretend to be happy. Maybe that's what your sister saw. I was laughing. I don't deny that. I was scared that if Shane told my mother I didn't seem like I wanted to be there with him that she might start keeping a close eye on me and figure it all out. We danced a couple of dances, and then I started feeling sick. I tried to shake it off. I didn't want him to take me home early because I didn't want him to think I was trying to get out of being there with him, but when everything started spinning around, I finally told him I wasn't feeling well. I thought I was going to throw up if the room didn't stop swirling soon. He was a perfect gentleman about it. He said he understood. He walked me back to the table, helped me to sit, knelt in front of me, held my hand, and promised if I didn't start feeling better within thirty minutes, he would take me home. He brought me another glass of punch and insisted it might help."

Tears streamed down Susan's face. Slowly she turned to Aster, hoping to find compassion in his eyes, and whispered, "The next thing I remember is waking up the next morning." She brushed the tears from her face. "But I wasn't in my bed. I was in his, and we were both..." She stared at the floor and choked, "Naked." Her tears forcefully rushed over her cheeks. She sobbed uncontrollably. "I'm sorry. I'm sorry. I'm so sorry, Aster. I don't even know how it happened."

Aster sighed; his countenance softened. He walked around his desk and gently placed his hands on Susan's arms. "Susan, look at me," he insisted.

Shameful, Susan raised her head and lifted her eyes to meet his. "Did he force himself on you?"

Susan removed her eyes from his gaze and cried, "No, apparently, I was more than willing."

Chapter 21

The Storms

Aster watched as a storm brewed in the distance. Dark clouds rolled toward the cemetery. The day had already brought light showers, but now it seemed a downpour was on its way. He cranked his engine and pulled the gearshift into reverse. Backing out of the small road leading to the burial plot, he set his mind on his task.

It was necessary for him to show up at the church with Sharon for the traditional meal served to the grieving family. He was the pastor and the minister officiating Susan's memorial service. He owed her that much and more. After that he would tell Sharon the truth of what transpired that day, and then he would escort her to the police department to give his statement. He wasn't surprised no one had already questioned him further; after all, he was a minister. The police didn't think to ask him about his involvement with her, but he knew it was coming.

Susan had done an excellent acting job in convincing her mother to allow Aster to perform the service. *She must have twisted her mother's arm awfully hard to pull this one off,* he mused.

When he pulled into the parking lot of the church, he parked by the back entrance, the one that opened into the kitchen. He helped the ladies of his congregation with washing the pots and pans they used for cooking before he decided to fix himself a plate. An appetite was something he did not have in the least, but he knew he had to force himself to eat. Sharon saved a place for him next to her and her granddaughter.

Aster didn't quite understand her newfound fondness of him. He chalked it up to something Susan must have said at the hospital when she asked for a few moments alone with her mother. He actually enjoyed the feeling of being accepted by her after so much time passing with hatred seeping through her eyes at him. His stomach contorted into a heap of interwoven knots. He took small bites of his food and followed them with large gulps of iced tea to ensure they went down. They seemed to be getting lodged halfway down his throat. With every bite he took, Aster felt himself choking.

Aster, Sharon, and Mae sat in silence at the table. Aster shoved his fork into a chunk of chicken and stared at it. He cut his eyes to Sharon and watched her piddle with her food and instruct Mae to quite playing with hers. Mae innocently reminded her grandmother she played with her food as well. Sharon sighed and acknowledged what the child said to be truth. As Aster gathered his thoughts on exactly what to say to her, he found himself gazing at Mae and watching her facial expressions. Her gloomy eyes took him back to that day in the field when he broke her mother's heart.

Susan stood in front of Aster's office window with her head hung low. Aster lifted her chin. His touch was gentle. He furrowed his brow in confusion. "No? Are you certain?"

Susan looked into Aster's eyes. "I don't know. I don't remember it. All I had to go on was Shane's explanation of the night. He had been so kind about me not feeling well that it was easy for me to believe him."

"What did he tell you?"

"I need to sit," she insisted.

Aster scooted the chair closer to her. She sat down and placed her face in her hands. "Do you need your water?"

"Yes, please."

Aster picked up her purse and sat it in her lap. She retrieved the bottle of water and took a small sip. "Please, Susan, tell me what he said about that night."

"I will. Just give me a moment. Reliving this is not easy. You have to understand I never meant for you and me to sleep together, but that happened because I love you. I couldn't understand how I ended up with Shane. I freaked out. His parents were out of town that weekend, so when I started yelling at him questioning him as to how I ended up there and what had happened, he didn't even care about how loud I was being. He actually told me I must've just thought he was you because I apparently called him by your name." Susan looked away.

Oddly, somehow it helped Aster to know that.

"He snapped at me a little over that, but then he calmed down and explained to me that after I started getting sick, Josh told him someone had spiked the punch. He told me I probably drank too much of it, and because I had never drunk before, it must've really hit me hard. When we got home, he noticed my dad's car was gone and the lights were out. He figured he didn't want me stumbling in drunk and getting in trouble, so he helped me into his house instead. He decided to wake me up early and help me sneak into my house while my parents were still sleeping."

"Did your parents find out?"

"No, he was right. My mother had not waited up for me. I guess she really trusted Shane. Dad had been called in to do emergency surgery on a man who had a massive heart attack in the middle of the night."

"I calmed down eventually. Aster, he said I was the forward one, which I found hard to believe, but then he explained to me it must have been the alcohol in the punch that caused me to come on to him. He said as I was falling asleep, I called him by your name. He went on and on about how much that hurt him because he thought I had really liked him, and for some reason, I felt bad about that."

Aster sat back on the desk. "So, you felt obligated to marry him because you unknowingly got drunk and had sex with him?" He grasped for an understanding.

"No, not at first, he came over later that day to check on me." The events that transpired over the months following prom consumed Susan's thoughts. As she pondered upon them, she was transported back to the day after prom.

Susan shut her bedroom door, leaned against it,

and stared at her prom dress draped over the footboard of her bed. She jumped when the doorbell rang. She had just made it to the seclusion of her bedroom. All she wanted was to grieve over what she had done. She just spent the better part of the day pretending to be happy about the previous evening and listening to her father regale his story of saving Lester Dennis's life in the operating room. Her mother pressed her for details of the evening with Shane. She wanted to know how many times they danced and if he kissed her goodnight or not. Susan glanced at her dad and hung her head before answering, "Yes, Mom, he did."

"So, is he a good kisser?" Sharon laughed.

"Mother!" she yelped. She stared wide-eyed at her dad searching for a rescue.

"Oh, come on. Don't look at your father that way. It's not like we don't know young lovers kiss."

"It's not like that, Momma. It was prom. It's not like I would've kissed him otherwise."

"Oh, be real, Susan. It's not like I don't already know you've been kissed before." Her mother eyed her.

Susan gulped, "Okay, I'm outta here. I'll be in my room until supper." She darted upstairs.

She had only been in her room for a few moments when the doorbell rang. "Susan, Shane is here to see you," Sharon hollered.

Shane stood next to Sharon at the bottom of the staircase waiting patiently for Susan to come rushing down. Reluctantly Susan headed downstairs to see what Shane wanted, secretly hoping and praying her mother wasn't downstairs grilling him about the events of the night.

As soon as she made it to the bottom step, he leaned over and kissed her on the cheek. "Hey, how are you today?" He smiled.

Susan forced an infinitesimal smile. "I'm good. How are you?"

"Perfect. Can we go sit on the porch and visit?"

Susan looked to her mother for approval. Sharon glanced at what she not only presumed but hoped to be two young lovers seeking alone time and insisted, "You two go on. I've got plenty to keep me busy in the office. I'm planning the next medical conference trip for your dad. We'll be gone for four days this time, and these things have to be planned well in advance if we are to get the best rooms. It takes time for me to do a layout of all the sightseeing I will be doing." She waved the two on and made her way to her husband's office.

Shane grabbed Susan's hand and led her to the swing on the front porch. "I'm real sorry about last night. I hope you realize that. If I would've thought you didn't really want to, I wouldn't have gone through with it. I swear, Susan." He worked to persuade her of his integrity.

"The fact you knew I had been given alcohol without my knowledge didn't make you more cautious?" Hurt reflected through Susan's eyes.

Holding tightly to her hand, Shane admitted, "It did, but when I got you in the house, you started kissing me pretty intensely. I'm sorry. I guess I just gave in. I should've been stronger than that. I promise, Susan, if you won't hold it against me, I won't lay another hand on you."

Susan glanced into Shane's eyes searching for truth. His persuasiveness convinced her of his sincerity; it was just a mistake both of them had made. "Okay, let's just wipe the slate clean between the both of us, but I don't wanna pretend to my parents like we are involved or anything. I think it's best we just remain friends. Is that okay with you?"

"Oh...Yeah, that's fine, I suppose. I just really like you, and I'd like for you to give me a chance, but I understand maybe you need some time," he assured her.

"Another thing, you haven't told anyone, have you?"

"Of course not, I wouldn't do that to you, Susan. I know you're a good girl. Everyone will still believe you're a virgin. Scouts honor." He held his hand in the traditional signal of a boy scout.

Susan gulped. She knew she couldn't make that claim before prom, but she refrained from admitting otherwise. The dread of having to confess to Aster what she had done bombarded her mind. *He won't care for me anymore when he finds out I betrayed him,* she worried.

Graduation night brought with it a severe thunderstorm and torrential rains. The weather confined the graduating class of 2005 to the gymnasium of Bayville High. A series of storms unleashed themselves upon Susan that day. That morning she woke up sick with signs of a stomach virus. She graduated Salutatorian, so she couldn't be late for rehearsal. She pressed through the sickness and made her way to the high school gym.

"Are you all right, dear?" her mother asked as she dropped her off.

"I think I have a virus or something, but I can't miss. They won't allow us to walk if we miss. I'll just have to deal with it, Mom." Susan climbed out of the car and entered the building.

Angie, one of her friends from the youth group at Bread of Life Church, approached her as she walked through the double doors. "Are you okay? You look like death warmed over."

Susan glared at her. "Gee, thanks. Nice to know I look horrible, but I suppose it's fitting; I feel horrible too. I'm sick is all," Susan assured her friend.

Angie's eyes bulged. "You sure you're not pregnant?"

Susan gawked, "No! Why would you even think such a thing?"

"Well, rumor is your name was added to someone's tally," she whispered.

"What? Who said that?" Susan's face washed ghostly white.

"Well, it's really more or less what some suspect. I overheard the talk amongst the guys the Monday after prom. They were all in the gym. I had left my duffle bag, so I had to sneak in to get it. They didn't see me or anything," she swore, "I promise, but when I heard all the guys pressing Shane for details of the night wanting to know if he scored, I stuck around to hear. He told 'em he didn't kiss and tell. Several of the guys started hollering saying, 'Yeah man, you did, didn't ya. You banged the most frigid girl in the school, you smooth talker.' Shane was real quick to give a rebuttal saying he didn't say that."

Susan grabbed her stomach. "I'm gonna be sick." She ran into the restroom, slung the stall door open, and vomited.

Angie rushed in right behind her. "You okay?" She grabbed a wad of paper towels and wet them. "Here, clean your face."

Susan wiped her face off, pushed herself up from the floor, nervously paced to the sink, and turned on the faucet. She rinsed her mouth and spit back out at least four times.

"Angie, why didn't you already tell me this?" Angie was the closest female friend Susan had, which is why she was shocked she hadn't already forewarned her of what some were saying.

"I'm sorry, Suze, I guess I should have, but honestly, I just shrugged it off until I saw you looking so sick. I didn't think it was possible." Angie's face fell. "It's not really possible, is it?" She cringed.

Susan glared in the mirror above the sink. She took a deep breath, and announced, "No," but as she did so, she lumbered through the restroom looking under the doors to see if they were alone. As soon as she saw the coast was clear, she grabbed Angie's arm. Before broaching the topic, she asked, "Can I trust you?"

"Of course, you can," Angie confirmed.

"Shane said that Josh told him that the punch had been spiked at prom. I drank at least two glasses that I remember, and it must've been too much for me, but I don't remember anything after that. I only remember waking up next to him. We did, but I don't remember it. I swear."

"Is it possible you just passed out?"

"No, he said we did. I haven't told anyone though. Did you drive here today?"

"Yeah, why?" Angie raised her brow.

"Will you help me? After practice will you take me to the drug store in Paradise Shore, so I can get a test?"

"Yeah, sure thing." Angie shook her head.

"Please don't tell anyone, Ang."

"I won't. You have my word."

As soon as graduation rehearsal ended, Susan called her mother with the cell phone her dad had given her as a graduation gift. "Mom, Angie has to run some errands and asked if I could go with her." The lies began. "I'll get her to bring me home, okay?"

"Sure thing, sweetheart, don't be out too long though. We've got a graduation dinner to make," Sharon insisted. "I'll have your dress ready and waiting on you."

"Okay, thanks, Mom."

The girls drove through the rain to the Save Rex in Paradise Shore. They bundled up in the restroom searching for the answer to Susan's question.

"Angie, I don't know what I'm gonna do. It's been over a month, and I haven't heard from Aster."

"What does Aster have to do with this?" Angie cocked an eyebrow.

"We...we kind of slept together before he moved off," Susan admitted.

Standing akimbo, Angie stared at her friend with incredulity. "Please tell me you're joking."

Susan's head fell in shame. "I'm not joking around. I love him. Neither of us meant for it to happen. I went to see him after his mother's funeral. It just happened."

Angie looked askance at Susan. "That's worse than your getting drunk and sleeping with Shane. So, who's the father?"

"I don't know, Ang. It was just a little over a week before prom. I don't know what to do."

Angie crossed her arms firmly across her chest. "Aster McGrath is bad news, Susan. I can't believe you ever trusted him. He probably intended to get lost in California. As far as I'm concerned, you'll probably never hear from him again."

"But he promised we would stay in contact while he went to school out there and that we would marry after I finish college."

"And you believed him?" Angie pursed her lips.

"Don't look at me that way, Angie. I don't know what to do."

"This is what you're gonna to do, Suze. You're gonna forget Aster; he's obviously already forgotten you, and you're gonna tell Shane that he's gonna be a daddy."

"I don't know."

"What's not to know? You're in a serious predicament. Shane's family has money. Aster's gone forever, and you need someone to be there for you. Tell Shane."

Susan gazed at her friend in acquiescence before heading back to Bayville to prepare for their high school graduation.

Susan was quiet most of the night, which seemed normal to her parents. She was a quiet girl. Heavy rain pelted the metal roof of the gym as they gathered together to begin the ceremony.

Susan approached Shane as they lined up in the back. "Shane, will you be sure and find me after we throw our caps. I need to talk to you about something," she whispered.

Shane's countenance brightened. "Sure thing, anything for you, Susan. Missed me huh?"

Susan frowned. "Just meet me, please."

"All right, all right." He waved his hands with a gesture of peace.

Knots formed in Susan's already aching belly as Shane approached her while all the other students embraced their parents and siblings. "So, what's up?" he inquired. "Can we be quick about this? My parents are waiting, and I imagine yours are looking for you as well."

"Follow me," Susan demanded as she led him to the girls' locker room and opened the door.

"So, you really did miss me," he gloated as

she grabbed his hand and led him into the pitch-black room.

"Please be serious for a minute. I need to tell you something, Shane," her voice shook.

"What? What's so secretive?" He laughed.

"I...I'm pregnant."

Chapter 22

The Choice

Aster found himself being pulled from his trance-like state by the sound of Sharon's voice calling him. "Aster...Aster...Have you heard anything I've said?" she complained.

Shaking off the memory that captured him, he shuddered. "I'm sorry, Sharon. I just slipped away for a minute there. You were saying?"

Sharon huffed, "A minute my butt. I've been talking to you for ten solid minutes before I realized you weren't nodding or responding. I was saying Susan's friend Angie approached me as we were getting here. She was asking about the investigation into her death and how it was going and all. I told her I planned to go visit the Lieutenant after the day was finished to see where everything is at. She offered to babysit for me. I'm going straight to the police department from her house. I wanted to see if you wanted to ride with me."

"Oh, yes, of course." He nodded his head.

Things fell into place. Aster knew he had been faced with a choice, and in a matter of minutes, on their way to the police department, he was choosing to tell Sharon everything that transpired that day. Aster cleared the table while Sharon took Mae to the restroom to wash her hands and face. He followed her to the parking lot and watched the way she smiled down at her granddaughter. Opening the passenger door, he climbed into her car. Sharon buckled Mae into her booster seat and headed to Angie's house.

Along the way they turned down Aster's road to get to Seacliff Drive where Angie lived. As they passed his home, he cursorily glanced at the office window Susan had been staring through just a few days prior. She had stood there and recapitulated the events that had taken place in her life since his departure. His mind was swiftly taken back to the bay. He saw Susan's hair glisten in the sunlight. He felt the warmth of her lips as his fingers gently grazed them.

Susan stood and marched back to the window in Aster's office. "So, you see, Aster. I didn't just marry Shane out of obligation because I had slept with him. I was pregnant. There were only a few choices I had. I nearly made the wrong one."

Aster plopped into his seat and rubbed his forehead. He hadn't abandoned Susan during that time, but he felt the effects as if he had. "Susan, I'm so sorry I wasn't there for you."

Susan craned her head to face him. "Aster, there's no need for you to apologize. You would've been there for me had you known, and I know that now. Thank you for showing me the letters.

It's not your fault, you know. My mother shares the blame, along with Shane. They both got what they wanted out of it all."

"How did Shane respond when you told him?"

Susan shrugged her shoulder. "The typical way…he told me he had enough money saved up for his senior trip to be able to pay for the trip and an abortion."

Aster scoffed, "You didn't even consider that, did you?"

Susan hung her head in shame. "No, not at first." Tears welled up in her already blood-shot eyes. "I told him there was no way I could. He left the next day for his senior trip, and against Angie's advice, I spent the entire week trying to find you, but I couldn't. I was so frightened. I was almost afraid to find you. I wasn't sure how you would react. I figured you would be angry at me for betraying you, but I hoped you would consider the circumstances in which it all took place and forgive me."

"I wouldn't have blamed you, Susan. I know Shane very well. He probably spiked the punch himself. If your mother hadn't intervened, I would've married you, you know," Aster insisted. "I wouldn't have cared that the child was Shane's. She is Shane's, isn't she?"

"I never told Shane about what happened between you and me, so there was never a blood test to be positive, but she was born February 8. She would've been due January 18, had she been yours. Trust me; I calculated the days a thousand times in my mind. My due date of February 1 was based on an ultrasound. I've always been horrible at keeping track of my cycle, so they couldn't give me one based on that. They ended up having to induce me because I carried her over by a week. I know you would've been there for me, but my mom did intervene, and I was left with only three choices: One, I could have an abortion like Shane suggested and live the rest of my life pretending it never happened; two, I could tell my parents, forget college, and live in the shame of having a child out of wed-lock for the rest of my life...or three; I could marry Shane if he would agree to it, so when Shane returned from his senior trip, I went to see him..." Susan's mind was whisked away back in time to the day Shane returned home from his senior trip in Cancun.

Susan stood patiently at Shane's door waiting for him to answer the doorbell. The summer heat had already invaded the South, and sweat beads formed across her forehead. As he opened the door, she swiped the back of her hand across them, drying them up. Standing before her, his face revealed a hint of reluctance. "Hey, Susan, come on in," he offered.

"That's okay. I'd rather talk somewhere in private." She looked over his shoulder eyeing his mom in the background. "It's probably better that we do."

"Hi, Susan." Shane's mother waved.

"Hi, Mrs. Garrish." She waved in return.

"Okay, we can sit on the porch." Shane stepped out and nonchalantly shut the door behind him. He loped over, kicked back in the rocking chair, and pointed to the one next to him. "Sit." He gestured. Susan sat down. "So, you reconsidered my offer? I figured you might, so I set the money back."

Looking at the painted wood planks of the porch, she whispered, "Yes, I'll do it. I'll have an abortion."

A malicious smirk crept across Shane's face, but Susan didn't see it.

"I know that was a real hard choice for you to make, but I promise it's for the best. This way you won't mess up your future, and neither will I. I'll go with you. I'll stay with you the whole time."

Susan glanced into Shane's eyes. "Really?"

"Really," he said, his tone sincere.

"Thank you," she cried as she threw her arms around his shoulders and hugged him.

Shane returned her embrace, marking his success in swaying her to end her pregnancy. "I'll even make the appointment for you so you won't have to, okay?" he whispered in her ear as he ran his hand through her golden hair. "There is one thing I would like out of it."

"What's that?" She pulled away from his embrace, leery of what he wanted in return.

"I want you to consider dating me again. I'm just asking you to consider it is all. I care about you, Susan. I'll be good to you, I promise."

Susan nodded her head and whispered, "Okay, I can do that."

Within three days Susan found herself sitting in a crowded clinic in Paradise Shore with Shane at her side. The colorless room was icy cold; she sat hunched over wringing her hands while Shane gently stroked her back. Susan quickly noticed most of the young girls in the waiting room sat alone. After what seemed to be hours, the door to the back opened. A tall, slender woman dressed in green scrubs stepped out. Susan jerked her head around to see who had stepped through the door. As she did so, the room started to spin, and she became confused. Muffled sounds passed through the woman's lips. Susan, unable to distinguish what she said, knit her brow in confusion. Again the woman opened her mouth. It seemed to be moving in slow motion to Susan. She stared intently at the woman's lips trying to discern what she said.

Finally Shane placed his hand on Susan's cheek and pulled her face toward his. "Susan, she's calling for you to go back," he claimed. "Didn't you hear?"

"Wh..y? she stuttered.

"You're just confused from the medicine you had to take earlier. It's time. Come on." He stood, grabbed her hand, and led her to the nurse. "I'll be right here waiting for you," he assured her with a kiss on the cheek.

The nurse grasped Susan's hand and led her to the back. As she did, Susan turned to scrutinize Shane's demeanor. He seemed genuinely concerned for her wellbeing, so she submitted to the directions the nurse gave her and sluggishly followed her to the back.

The nurse led her to a small, white room where she instructed her to undress and drape herself with a cotton gown. "Your boyfriend seems real nice," the nurse stated.

"Yeah, seems to be," Susan slurred.

"You're lucky, you know. So many girls show up without the support of a boyfriend."

"Yeah, I suppose I am."

Susan took the gown from the nurse, stumbled to the bed, and anchored herself. As she unbuttoned her blouse, Aster's voice screamed at her. "No, Susan, don't do it! You have to stop what's about to happen. God can take even this bad thing in your life and use it for good!"

Susan's eyes frantically scanned the room

searching for Aster. "Aster?" she called, but she heard no response. She felt as if the walls were closing in around her. She trembled and cried, "I have to go. I can't..." She grabbed her purse and darted out the door.

Running through the hall, she heard the nurse demand, "Where are you going?" She stumbled as she shoved open the door into the lobby.

Shane jumped to his feet. "What's wrong?"

"I can't...I can't do it, Shane. I just can't," she cried.

Shane embraced her and whispered, "It's okay. We'll figure something out. Come on. Let's get outta here."

Susan gazed at him and shook her head *okay*. Shane kept his arm tightly around her waist as he escorted her to his car. By that point Susan barely stood on her own two feet. He drove to a fast-food restaurant, went through the drive-thru, and bought Susan a hamburger, fries, and a Coke before driving to the beach to allow the medication time to wear off. Susan's head wobbled back and forth. Shane parked the car and handed her the drink. She took a few sips of it and set it back down.

Shane shifted his body to face her. "You'll be okay in a little while, Susan. We'll stay here until the medicine wears off. Your parents think we're off at the beach in Gulfport anyway."

"Thank you for not pushing me to go through with it, Shane. I don't know what came over me. All of a sudden I just realized I couldn't do it. I'm sorry if you feel this is going to mess up your life," she apologized.

"Don't worry about that, Susan, but I was just thinkin'; since you couldn't go through with it, maybe we could make this right by getting married," he offered.

Susan's eyes watered. Her heart wanted nothing more than to marry Aster, the guy she loved, but it was already June, and she hadn't heard a word from him. She had tried to find him online to no avail; consequently, she was left with only two choices at that point. She could either live her life in what she considered to be a shameful state, or she could marry Shane. Susan didn't feel there was much of a choice for her. Her conscience told her she had to do the right thing, and her morality told her it was better to marry and maintain some of her integrity, so she gazed at Shane and mumbled, "Okay."

Shane furrowed his brow in astonishment. "Really? You'll marry me?"

Susan gulped, "Yes, I will. It's the right thing to do, but I don't know how I'm going to tell my parents."

"We'll push for a quick wedding. Nothing fancy, just a small church wedding. How about July first?" He threw a date out. "We can make out to everyone that we've been seeing each other since prom. I mean, we did go out before prom too. Our parents will buy it."

"Okay. I don't want anything big and the sooner the better, so when and how are we going to tell our parents?" she pressed.

"Today, we'll tell them today. I'll insist you want to maintain your purity, so it's better if we marry quickly. Our dads will understand. It's our moms I'm worried about. Your mom is probably gonna want a big to-do."

"I'll handle that. She knows me. She knows I'm bashful and don't really get into all the fancy parties."

Shane leaned over and kissed Susan. They spent another four hours on the beach. Susan slept in his arms on the beach towel. He had shoved it in his car in order to make it seem they were truly going to the beach that day. Once the medication wore off, he drove her home and prepared to make the announcement to her mother and father.

A chair screeched across the floor and loud footsteps paced through the room. Susan paused in the midst of her story and watched Aster from where she stood. Eventually he stopped and focused on her standing by the window examining his every move.

Maintaining eye contact, she continued, "Telling my parents that day was difficult. We decided not to tell them I was pregnant until a few weeks after the wedding. Shane made me feel he truly cared about my honor. He didn't want my parents or anyone else for that matter to think bad of me. At least that's the way I saw it..." Her thoughts trailed. "We were married on the first of July just as Eva told you. It was the only choice I felt I had in the end, Aster."

"My father made sure Shane and I both went with my mother to the cabin when the storm came through. Shane's parents refused to leave; his dad was pretty stubborn about it all. He claimed he had survived plenty of other storms in his life. Daddy knew though. He sensed it was a bad one." Her voice softened when she mentioned her father. "Shane's parents both died in the storm. We stayed in Alabama with my mother until the insurances came through and Shane rebuilt his parents' home for us." A slight smile crossed her face as she revealed, "I gave birth to a little girl at a hospital in Alabama. My daddy never had the chance to meet his granddaughter. I had gotten pretty good at lying to my mom, so she was under the impression I gave birth a little early. When she found out they were inducing me, I lied and told her Shane and I had slept together around graduation." Susan scoffed, "She wasn't even mad at me for losing my virginity before marriage or lying to her about wanting to get married quickly because of it. She just snickered and said she expected as much."

Susan clasped her hands together and continued her story, "Shane did his best to move us back here as quickly as possible. It was a year and two months after Katrina before the house was livable."

Aster ambled across the room toward Susan. He came within inches of her before he spoke. Gazing into her eyes, he reminded her, "Earlier when you mentioned what happened between you and me...you said you love me, not loved but love—present tense."

Susan turned away from him. "Yes, I know what I said."

"You shouldn't love me, Susan. You're a married woman. You need to forget the past and move on."

"I can't forget the past, and I'm trying to move on. I came here to see you and to see if...if there was still a chance...if maybe you still had feelings for me," she whispered.

"Susan, what are you saying?" He narrowed his eyes. "How I may or may not feel about you really doesn't matter anymore, so why do you want to know?" Concern grew in his voice.

"Because, Aster. I left him. I left Shane. That's why I took my little girl to my mother's place. I couldn't take it anymore. I couldn't deal with living a lie not a minute longer. I'm filing for a divorce. I want us to be together, like we were supposed to be."

Aster sighed, "Oh my...*Susan,* you want me to walk away from my faith? The faith you led me to? The fellowship I'm ordained through won't allow me to marry anyone who's been divorced."

"I just want you to love me," she cried.

"I can't believe this. I can't believe that this is why you're here. I figured you were looking for some form of closure, but honestly, Susan, you can't be serious."

"I am serious. I've been forced to live a lie. I don't love him. I never did. I know I made the choice, but it was the wrong choice, Aster. I just want my life back.

Aster hung his head. A part of him wanted to grab her in his arms, kiss her, and tell her everything would be okay, but he couldn't. "Go home," he whispered. As much as it panged him to say, he instructed her, "Go home to your husband and try to work things out. Seek some counseling if you need to, but honor your vow."

Tears spilled from Susan's swollen, red eyes. Her vivid recollections of the past as she shared her story with Aster, revealed her brokenness. His response wasn't what she desired. Her heart longed to have his arms wrapped around her and his lips caressing hers the way they did when he made love to her, but instead, he told her to go home to the man she loathed to look upon. Wounded, she grabbed her purse and started for the door.

As she rounded the corner at a swift pace, her sleeve caught on a hook and ripped, exposing the upper portion of her arm. Aster's eyes fell upon the bruises left on the woman he still loved, the woman he had unknowingly just sent back to an abusive man.

Chapter 23

The Awakening

Sharon pulled in front of Angie's house and stopped the car. She left it running. Aster watched the raindrops fall on the windshield as she opened her umbrella and unbuckled her granddaughter. Warmth rushed through his heart as Mae waved goodbye to him and smiled. "Bye bye. Nana, can I see Daddy?"

"Not right now, sweetheart." Sharon's sullen countenance turned to chagrin at the thought of Shane Garrish.

Aster waved bye to Mae. He turned the knob on the heater down slightly and sat waiting for Sharon to return. He thought about the first time he rode in a car with Sharon and how it rained that evening as well. It was the day she made her disdain of him apparent through her cutting words and piercing glares through the rearview mirror. The same glower contorted her face when she marched into the hospital room, but now sadness and compassion replaced anger and hatred.

While he waited for Sharon to return, he searched his memories again—this time finding himself standing in his office fuming after Susan ran out, leaving the door open behind her. His blood boiled as he seethed over the visible abuse Susan had sustained. Infuriated with himself for turning her away, he charged across the room and slammed the door. He watched the vase of wildflowers crash to the floor and shatter just as their relationship and happiness had been destroyed by Sharon and Shane. Aster hung his head in shame; the disgrace weighed heavily upon his heart and mind. He knew if he was truthful with himself, the blame rested on his shoulders and his shoulders alone. She had just been within his grasp, but he allowed her to slip through his fingers like sand through a sieve. He could have confessed the truth while she stood next to him only moments before. He could have admitted to her he thought of her every day over the last five and a half years. He could have told her he loved her and always had. He could have said *yes* to her proposition, but he held his tongue and scolded her instead. *I should have run after her,* he fussed at himself.

Aster knew their love had never died. It had merely been postponed as a result of Sharon's deception and Shane's conniving. He also knew in his heart that Shane had been dishonest with Susan, and her naivety had kept her in the dark as to his lies, but Aster knew what Shane was capable of.

Aster stared at the broken vase scattered

across his office floor. A shaft of sunlight shined through the window Susan stared out of as she disclosed the events that kept her and Aster apart. It glistened on the shards of glass. Rays of colorful light sparkled across the room, creating multiple rainbows shimmering on three of the four walls in his office. Adrenaline rushed through his veins causing him to shake violently and flush red. He was acutely aware of the lust for blood Susan had left him with as she stormed out of his home. It was the same thirst for revenge he felt the night his little sister had awakened him, and it just so happened to be the blood of the same person he hungered for—Shane Garrish. *Not her,* he seethed. *Not my black-eyed Susan.* Aster's battle to repress the beast Susan tamed began. The monster inside him had been released. His heart told him to fight the fiend, but his mind assured him of the inevitableness of his own defeat.

Aster's junior year had just begun, and it wasn't going well. Frequent nightmares kept him awake at night, depriving him of sleep, and lack of sleep didn't help his attitude or his grades. Tired and frustrated, he stormed out of the school building, jumped on his motorcycle, and headed home to try and get a short nap before the first football game of the season.

The Bayville Bears were tied with the Biloxi Indians, so the game extended into overtime, causing Aster's night to linger. When he finally made it home, he felt as defeated as the Bears. He plopped in his bed and crashed.

*Tap...tap...tap...*Aster tossed in his bed and pulled the covers over his head, but the tapping continued. Kicking the covers off, he stumbled out of bed and flipped the light switch. Squinting, he scanned the room in search of the origin of the tapping. He rubbed his eyes and peered toward the source, his window. Eva stood on the other side of his bedroom window with a torn dress. Scurrying across the room, he raised the window. "Eva, what's wrong?"

Eva climbed through the window. "He hurt me, he hurt me," she stammered.

"What? Who?" he pressed.

"Shane...Shane Garrish...He...he asked me to sneak out...and meet him after the game." She trembled.

Aster placed his hands on his baby sister and persuaded her to sit on his bed. "Come on, sit down. You're shaking all over." He opened his closet door and grabbed the towel hanging on a nail being used as a hook. He wrapped it around her shoulders. "Here, this will warm you up some."

"He's so popular, Aster. All the girls feel privileged if he shows an interest, so..." her voice trailed off, "when he told me he liked me and asked me to sneak out and meet him...I thought...I was one of the lucky ones, you know."

"Tonight? You sneaked out tonight?" Aster struggled to figure out when Shane had done something to his sister.

"Yeah, tonight...I...I just ran away. I didn't know where else to go. I figured he wouldn't come here looking for me."

"Where is he and what did he do to you?"

"I left him on the pier. He asked me to meet him there, so I climbed out the window and walked to the bay."

"Did you tell Melody where you were going and who you were going to meet?"

"No...I didn't want her to snitch on me and cause me to get kicked out. At first he was being all nice. We walked on the beach for a while. He draped his arm over me, and then he started talking about us living dangerously. He wanted me to climb the gate with him to get on the pier. He said the city shouldn't be able to put a time limit on what his parents' tax dollars pay for, so I laughed about it and thought it would be fun. We climbed the gate. He even went first and helped me over."

Tears welled in her eyes as she continued, "We were sitting on the bench at the end. At first he was just kissing me, but then he started rubbing his hands all over me. I kept pushing his hands off me, but he just touched me harder. I told him to stop; he just laughed and said *no*, so I stood up to walk away." Eva's tears rushed over her cheeks. "He grabbed me and knocked me down. Then he...he...he forced himself on me." Eva broke and threw her arms around her brother and sobbed into his chest.

As Aster held his sister, murder grew in his heart. "I'm gonna kill him," he spit.

"No...no, Aster, please don't. You'll go to prison like dad. Please don't," she cried and begged.

Aster sat fuming in silence listening to his sister's sobs. Finally he could take no more of her worry, so he soothed her fears with his words, "Okay, okay, calm down. I won't kill him, but you need to go to the hospital and report it. You can press charges...send him to jail. That's where he belongs."

"No." She shook her head violently. "I can't...I'm...it's...it's so humiliating. I don't want anybody to know, Aster. Please, please don't tell anybody," she begged.

Comforting his sister, Aster held her in his arms while his mind concocted a plan. "Hey, Mom's passed out. Why don't you go take a nice, long shower and clean yourself up? You can't go back home like that. I'll throw your clothes in the wash while you're in, okay?"

Sniffling, Eva pulled away from her brother. "Okay."

Eva crept through the house to the bathroom and turned on the water. She undressed, wrapped a towel around herself, and opened the bathroom door. Aster stood right outside waiting to retrieve her clothing. He stepped outside to the small laundry room situated off the front porch and threw them in the washing machine and slipped out to the shed. He pushed his motorcycle down the road a short piece before cranking the engine. He didn't want Eva to realize he was gone.

He drove straight to the bay in search of Shane Garrish. He found him slouched under the pier leaning against a piling drinking a beer. Aster approached him from the side and knocked the beer from his hand.

Startled, Shane yelped, "What the hell?"

"You bastard, I'm gonna kill you for what you did to my sister," Aster growled as he punched him in the mouth.

As Shane's head bounced off the piling, Aster grabbed him around the neck and slung him to the ground. While having his face smashed into the sand, Shane writhed, attempting to break free. Aster pummeled Shane multiple times in the back and sides of his head as the vision of his sister being violated by him continually pounded his mind and blurred all sense of reason. Scuttling to his knees, Shane tucked his head into his arms to shield himself from Aster's fists.

While in a fetal position, Aster repeatedly kicked him in his ribs, knocking him onto his back. Aster grabbed Shane's hair, holding his head in place, and continued bashing him with his fists. As Shane's blood splattered, he remembered his sister's plea not to do anything; he released his grasp and left him unconscious in the blood-soaked sand.

Aster returned as Eva pulled her clothes from the dryer. Startled at the sight of the blood covering his clothes, she screeched, "Oh, my God, What happened?" Eyeing his bloody knuckles, she demanded, "What did you do, Aster?" Eva raced inside to get a damp cloth.

Following her, Aster barked, "Gave him what he deserved, that's what I did."

"You didn't kill him, did you?" she asked as she wiped the blood from his hands.

"No, he's still alive, but he probably wishes he were dead."

"Aster, Why did you do that?"

"Because you're my sister, and I wasn't going to let him get away with hurting you."

"He's gonna tell them who beat him up. You'll be arrested!" she screamed.

"It's okay. According to half of this town, I was gonna end up there anyway."

"Please, Aster, you promised you wouldn't tell anybody what he did to me. He's Melody's cousin. Her family will believe him, and I'll have to come back here, and you'll be in jail." She broke down.

Aster sighed, "I won't say anything, Eva. No one will ever know what he did to you. They won't know it even had anything to do with you, I promise. As far as anyone will know, I just don't like him. Okay?"

"Okay," she whimpered.

Eva returned to Melody's without getting caught. The following morning she awoke to Mr. Smith screaming and Mrs. Smith crying. Shane had been found and hospitalized.

Mr. Smith charged into Eva's room. "Shane was nearly killed last night, Eva, and he said your brother did it. He said you two had gone out a couple of times, and he broke up with you last night. Did you put your brother up to it?" he demanded an answer.

Eva's eyes bulged. "No, Sir, I swear. He did...he broke up with me, and I told Aster, but I didn't ask him to hurt Shane. I wouldn't do that. Is Shane going to be okay?"

"Doctors have him stable. Your brother worked him over pretty bad. I guess he's really got your father's blood. Cops have already arrested him, but he's not talking as to why he did it. Just said he didn't like him," he grumbled.

"I'm so sorry. I swear, if I would've thought he would respond that way, I wouldn't have told him," Eva cried.

"Well, you're definitely not responsible for your brother's actions, but if you expect to continue living in this house, you're going to have to cut off all communication with him," he commanded. Eva curled into a ball and nodded her head acknowledging Mr. Smith's demands.

Aster was held in the juvenile detention center until Shane recovered and eventually dropped all charges against him. Aster and Eva both kept secret what Shane had done that night. As Shane lay in the hospital bed recuperating, he feared Aster may snap and tell all; there was no way for him to know if there was any evidence of what he had done, so he told his parents Aster had already had such a hard life that he didn't want to be someone to make it more difficult for him to straighten up. His only request was for Aster to be sent to alternative school so he didn't have to face him at school every day. Although the beating did not take place on school property, the deal was shared with Aster, and he agreed to spend the remainder of his junior year in alternative school as opposed to being tried as an adult and being sent to the penitentiary to spend a few years with his father. The public defender assigned to Aster was unquestionably convincing when it came to that possibility, assuring him as a result of the horrific brutality he used, the judge had already consented to his being tried as an adult. Considering the fact Aster would never use what had happened to his sister as a defense, he conceded to the offer.

Sharon climbed back in the car after dropping off her granddaughter with Susan's friend Angie. When she slammed the door, Aster awoke from his memory of how the beast loosened his chains. He sat quietly in the passenger seat and twiddled his thumbs.

Sharon glanced at his obvious uneasiness as she pulled out of the drive. "You know, you don't have to be nervous around me anymore, Aster. I'm not going to bite."

"Ha," a chortle slipped through Aster's lips. "I'm not worried about you biting me, Sharon. Your former threat is irrelevant at this point in my life."

"Yeah, about that threat." She pulled up to a stop sign and turned right, heading to the police department. "I should apologize. I thought I knew what was best for my daughter, but I didn't, and despite the fact I don't believe there is a God out there like my daughter did, you turned out pretty good. You beat the genetic odds, you know?" She cut her eyes toward him and smirked.

"Yeah, I know, Sharon." Aster glanced out the passenger window watching the trees go by as they headed toward the police station. Trying to gain the courage to speak up and make his confession, he inhaled a deep breath. His eyes landed on a patch of daisies growing on the side of the road causing his mind to drift to the hospital where Susan's battered body lay dying.

Aster had been sitting and caressing Susan's hand while praying for God to spare her for thirty solid minutes, yet she did not open her eyes or respond. She had apparently slipped back into a deep sleep as a result of the medications being administered to keep her out of as much pain as possible. He listened to the constant dripping of the IV and the constant beating of her heart through the monitor. Life still coursed through her veins, and that gave him hope she would return to him.

Penny, the nurse, cracked open the door. "Her mother just called; she said she was leaving immediately. She will be here in four hours or so. Thank you for coming in and identifying her for us. I'm going to have to ask you to leave for a bit. I've got to tend to some of her needs. You can come back if you'd like to and check on her. It won't take me too long."

Aster placed Susan's hand back on her bed and stood. "Thank you. I'll be back at eleven then. I need to go take care of a few things. Please take care of her," he whispered before passing through the door.

Aster drove to a small diner and ate a miniscule breakfast before returning to the hospital at eleven-thirty a.m. carrying a vase full of daisies.

He hit the buzzer and was greeted by Penny. "Reverend, that's so sweet of you to bring her a bouquet of daisies. She'll be happy. She woke up once since you left and asked for some. She asked for you again too." The nurse smiled. "Her meds are about to wear off, so maybe she'll wake up for a little while before it's time to give her more."

With that hope Aster's eyes beamed. He entered the cubicle Susan lay in. As he walked through the door, Susan listlessly opened her eyes. Aster's mouth twitched and stretched into a weak smile. "You're awake."

Chapter 24

The Breaking

Sharon slammed on the brakes causing the tires of her car to squeal to a stop. "Damn it," she grumbled. "I know you had to have seen me, you stupid ass," she fussed at the car pulling out in front of her and speeding off. The stench of burning rubber and the annoyance in Sharon's tone jerked Aster back to reality.

Sharon was breaking apart. Aster knew he needed to help her to remain calm, so with a broken heart he craned his head to gaze upon the woman who had robbed him of happiness and love. "Young drivers just don't pay attention, do they?" he said, his voice smooth and relaxed.

Sharon sighed, "No, they don't, do they?"

"It was probably a reckless teenage boy trying to prove he's hot stuff to some pretty girl sittin' in the passenger's seat." He laughed. "We do crazy things as teenagers when we wanna impress someone we like."

"So, is that what you did to win my daughter's heart, spin out on your motorcycle or something?" She smiled.

"Yeah, something like that." Aster's smile faded. He stared at the lights on the console revealing the time of day. "Sharon, now that we're alone...There's something I need to confess. What happened to Susan—"

Sharon interjected, "Is not your fault, Aster."

Aster jerked his head and stared at Sharon's intent eyes gazing straight into his. "But it is...and I wanted you to know before we got to the police department. I wanted you to know everything that happened that day."

"Susan told me she went to your home. I already know, Aster. That's the reason I asked you along. I figured you would want to tell the police what you knew. They need all the evidence they can get against that bastard!" she raised her voice. "Sorry, I know you're a preacher and all, but I'm just so angry right now," she apologized.

"I know; so am I," he whispered.

"If it wasn't for my Mae Mae, I don't know what I might do when I got my hands a hold of Shane Garrish. I'd like to strangle the bastard. He better hope the police find him before I do."

"Don't even think like that, Sharon. Your granddaughter needs you. She may be all you have left, but you're all she has now too. It's not easy growing up with a father in prison. I should know..." his voice faded.

Silence filled the car for the remainder of their ride. When they arrived at the police department, Sharon marched straight to the front desk. "I'm here to see Lieutenant Watkins," she said, her voice stern.

"Sure thing." The young woman behind the

desk picked up her phone and dialed the extension. "Lieutenant Watkins, there's a couple here to see you." The woman covered the receiver. "What's your name, Ma'am?"

"Sharon Blackman. I'm here about the murder of my daughter, Susan Blackman Garrish."

Removing her hand, she informed the Lieutenant, "It's Mrs. Blackman here about the Susan Garrish case." After a moment the young woman hung up the phone. "If you go down that hallway." She pointed in the direction for them to go. "You will take a right through the first door. The Lieutenant is in the second office on the left."

"Thank you," Sharon uttered.

Sharon and Aster briskly strode through the hallway. The building was new. The smell of fresh paint wafted through the wide halls with multiple offices nestled on both sides. They made the appropriate turn and entered Lieutenant Watkins's office. As they passed through the door, the fair-skinned, blonde female approached them. She held out her thin hand and gave them both a firm handshake. "Mrs. Blackman...Mr.?"

"Reverend McGrath," Sharon corrected.

"Reverend," Lieutenant Watkins revised her welcome. "What can I do for you two?"

"We wanted to see where you were in finding my son-in-law, and I brought Aster down to tell you about the visit he received from my daughter the day she was beaten and left for dead by that monster. I know I've already talked to the detective briefly, but I need to make a formal statement. Detective Marshall seemed pretty pissed off when I refused to come down here until after the funeral, but I had too many things to take care of, and I was overwhelmed at the time."

"I do understand, Mrs. Blackman. You were

probably in shock, but Marshall knows the quicker we get things headed in the right direction, the faster everything goes. Have a seat." She pointed to the two chairs seated across from her side of the desk. "I want you to know we are doing everything we can to find him so we can question him. All the evidence we can gather showing he is responsible is needed to put him away. I would love nothing more than to personally watch him rot. I despise men who think women are beneath them. Working here, I've seen my share of battered wives." She sat in her seat.

As Aster went to sit down, he scanned the documents and pictures strewn across her desk. His eyes fell upon several pictures of Susan taken at the hospital. The most visible one showed her broken and bruised body when she first arrived at the hospital before the doctors had the opportunity to stitch her up. Lieutenant Watkins swiftly shoved the pictures back within the envelope lying next to them but not before Aster had ample opportunity to see the damage done by Shane.

As Susan awoke from her unconscious state, she eyed the bouquet of flowers in Aster's hands. "Daisies," she whispered.

"Yeah, the nurse said you were asking for them, so I wanted to bring you some," Aster proclaimed as he set the vase on the small table at the side of her bed.

"Oh, I don't remember. I've been so groggy."

He pulled the only chair in the room back closer to her side, sat down, and grabbed her hand. "Yeah, I imagine you have."

"Thank you," she whispered, her voice barely audible.

Aster gulped, "Susan...I'm so sorry. Please forgive me."

Susan pulled her hand free from his and reached for the side of his face. Aster leaned in. Tracing the line of his jaw with the tips of her fingers, she breathed, "There's nothing to forgive." A tear spilled from Aster's eye. "You didn't know...but...there's more I have to say."

Shaking his head, Aster insisted, "No, save your strength, my black-eyed Susan."

A smile flitted across her bruised and swollen face and quickly fell as the door creaked open. "Nurse, what in the hell is he doing here?" Sharon demanded.

Penny stuttered, "She...she asked for...for her preacher to come. He helped the police to identify her so they could contact you, Mrs. Blackman."

"Mother," Susan gurgled in pain. The numbers on the blood pressure monitor quickly shot through the roof and Susan's heart rate increased dramatically.

"Ma'am, I'm going to have to ask you to leave for a moment. I've got to get her stabilized again," the nurse insisted.

"She's my daughter," Sharon gasped.

"Yes, Ma'am, I know that, but she's obviously been upset, and her heart rate and her blood pressure are skyrocketing. In her condition that's not good. I just need a moment with her."

"Is someone going to tell me what's going on with her?" Sharon challenged.

"Yes, Ma'am, I will be right out and explain everything."

Susan grasped Aster's hand, unwilling to let go.

"You have to step out too, Reverend," Penny stipulated.

"Of course," Aster conceded. Studying the emotions exposed through Susan's eyes, he assured her, "I'll be right outside. I'll come back in as soon as she gets you settled down, okay?"

"Promise?"

"On my life," he pled with a kiss on her hand.

The nurse eyed the kiss and glared suspiciously at Aster. She shut the door behind him, leaving him standing in front of the nurses' station next to Sharon.

Sharon glared. "So, what happened to her? Was she hit by a car or something? She looks horrible. Tell me what you know."

"According to what I've been told, she was beaten. The nurse will have to divulge the details. I don't know them." Aster folded his arms across his chest.

"Beaten? By who? And why are you here?" she snarled.

"I'm sure they're investigating that, and Susan asked for me when she awoke. The police found my card in her pocket, so the detective investigating her case called me in thinking she was a member of my congregation. They were hoping I could identify her. She wasn't saying anything else," he explained.

"And you told them who to contact?" Sharon narrowed her eyes.

"Yes, Ma'am, I told them she was Dr. Blackman's daughter and that you lived in Prentiss, Alabama. They looked up your number. I didn't have it."

Sharon's callused countenance softened. "Well...thank you."

"You're welcome."

Sharon waited impatiently, constantly tapping her feet for fifteen minutes. The nurse opened the door and signaled for them both to return, but as soon as they crossed over the threshold, Susan mumbled, "Aster, if you don't mind, I need to speak to my mom alone."

Sharon gleamed. "You called me mom and not mother."

Susan held out her hand for her mom. Aster gave his head an indiscernible nod and backed out of the room. "I'll just wait out in the waiting room, Penny. If you would, just let me know when she's ready to see me."

With a gentle pat on Aster's shoulder, Penny assured him. "I will."

Aster sat waiting until two o'clock when Sharon staggered into the room, her face forged with shock and drained of life. "She's asking for you now," she uttered.

Knitting his brow, he asked, "Will they allow me in at this point?"

"They said they would. They aren't imposing visiting hours with her."

Briskly, Aster made his way to the hall and mashed the buzzer. Penny opened the door and let him in. "I know you're not her pastor." She eyed him.

Removing eye contact, Aster cut his eyes to the floor. "No, Ma'am, I'm not, but I am a pastor."

"You love her, don't you?" she pried.

"Yes, I do," he somberly declared.

Placing her hand on his back, she informed him, "You should know, her breathing is slowing, and her blood pressure has started dropping. She doesn't have much time left."

Penny closed the door allowing Aster and Susan privacy. Aster moved the chair closer to the bed; it screeched across the floor. Sitting, he grasped Susan's hand in his. "I shouldn't have sent you away yesterday morning, Susan. Why didn't you tell me Shane had been hurting you?"

Susan's breathing was shallow, but she managed to explain in broken sentences, "Because, Aster...I know...what you did to him...before...when he hurt your sister. I...I didn't want...you to lose your cool...and beat him to death."

"How long has he been abusing you?"

Gurgling, she answered, "Forms of abuse...started as soon as...the baby was born. He became extremely...jealous of her. Got mad...when I spent time...rocking her. He started..." She sucked in a deep breath. "Demanding I give him a son...almost right away. I...wanted to enjoy her a little, so...I refused, but he started...drinking heavily and coming home...from work plastered and forcing me to...have sex with him." Susan tightened her grip on Aster's hand and inhaled as deep a breath as she could. "When I resisted, he ordered me that...it was my wifely duty. He even went...so far as to tell me he'd...go find someone else if I didn't, so...I always gave in—even when I didn't want to. He shoved me into the wall a few times...and slapped me once or twice, but the...real abuse started when you returned."

"Why didn't you tell somebody?"

"I did," she gurgled.

"Who?"

"I went to our pastor. I told him...I was planning...to leave Shane."

Lowering his brow, he asked, "And you told him why?"

"Yes." She nodded her head slightly. "I told him Shane...was apparently jealous...of our little girl and the time...I spent with her. He said it...was natural for a man to be...a little jealous of my attention being elsewhere, so...I explained he was demanding...I give him a son and was using...the threat of sleeping with someone else...to get me to sleep with him. I told him...Shane had beaten me...several times as well. To that...he stated my husband...maybe needed some counseling."

Susan closed her eyes to rest for a moment. When she opened them again, she continued, "I tried explaining I didn't want Shane to know...I had come to him because...he might hurt me. He thought...I was being a little...ridiculous with that. He insisted...he had been Shane's pastor...for Shane's entire life, and he knew...him well. He told me while...he didn't know me that well, he thought I was...a nice young woman but...it sounded to him...like I was simply looking...to get out of a marriage I only entered...because of being pregnant."

"Susan, you do know not all ministers treat people that way, I hope," Aster assured her of the purity in the motives of most of the Church.

"I know. He was a family...friend, and he couldn't believe...that precious Shane would do such. I...went back to him after you...moved back and the real...beatings started. I explained to him...my first love...had moved back into town and...Shane had started making comments about me...sneaking out to see him. I...I didn't tell him your name, Aster. I didn't want him...to know that. I told him Shane started...calling me fifteen to twenty...times a day grilling me about where I was...and what I was doing, and then...he started telling me...I couldn't go places. He made me take our little girl...out of her K-four class...said she needed to be at home with her mom for a while..." Susan gasped for breath. "Chalked it up to finances too. Then he started degrading me...calling me a whore, and then when I tried...to stand up to him, he shoved me into the...shower door, busted my...head, and told me...the next time I mouthed off...to him, he'd make me pay. He held my head...under water one time. I thought...I was going to die," she sobbed.

"What did your pastor tell you to do?"

Tears rolled down Susan's blue and purple, swollen cheeks. "He told me it...was my Christian duty...to pray for him. He said I needed to go home...be a good wife...be sure to obey my husband...and not give him any reason...to question my loyalty. He was certain...Shane had to have reason...to think I would cheat. He assured me...God would not be pleased...with me if I left, that the Bible...instructs us we can only...be released from our vows if...the other person has committed adultery. He reminded me that my vow...said, 'for better or...for worse, in sickness and in health.' He advised me Shane's jealousy...and abuse, if there was...indeed any, was a sickness, and then...he told me I was...faced with a choice. He said...I could choose to be an...instrument of God's deliverance by sacrificing my own selfish...desires and staying, or I...could be a tool of the enemy...by stepping out of...the will of God and bring destruction...to both myself and Shane. Then he looked...me in the eyes and asked me if I...wanted to help my husband...with his issues or if I wanted to...hinder him. He didn't even really believe...Shane had issues."

Aster turned his head in shame at the way Susan's pastor had imprisoned her to a man with an unrepentant heart. "He should have been concerned about your safety...even if he didn't discern the scriptures to release you from your marriage. He should have never advised you to stay in abuse, Susan. Maybe I'm not...well, I know I'm not able to completely remove my emotions from this and speak on the scriptures without any predisposition concerning you and Shane, but he'd already broken his vow to you. He vowed to honor and love you. He didn't honor you in the beginning when he drugged you and raped you."

Susan broke. "But he didn't, Aster. He didn't rape me."

"Yes, he did." He caressed her face and dried her tears.

Susan's heart rate spiked, and she struggled to breath. "Please, no more. I'm dying, Aster...I don't want my last thoughts to be bad."

Aster winced. Tears rushed to his eyes. "Don't say that. You're gonna be fine." Aster leaned over and ran his hand through Susan's hair. "My black-eyed Susan," he breathed.

Susan smiled. "I love hearing you...call me that. We're just a couple of...wildflowers, huh?"

A broken smile inched across Aster's face. "Yeah, we are."

The two of them sat in silence for a while before Aster began to break. Gazing at her broken, beaten body, he fell apart. Crying, he whispered, "There's something I need to tell you...something I should've told you a long time ago."

Susan glanced into Aster's eyes. "What's that?"

"I love you, Susan. I was completely captivated by you the first time I laid eyes on you, but I didn't think someone like you would ever be interested in someone like me. I wanted to kiss you so many times before I actually did, but I was afraid of truly admitting what I felt. Before you came into my life, I had my share of girls, but I can say with all honesty there hasn't been another woman in my life since Mrs. Howard forced me to carry your books to the office. I think about you every day, Susan. I love you with every fiber of my being...I always have." He caressed her hand. "Now I want you to do something for me." Aster gazed intently into Susan's eyes.

Pools of tears filled her swollen eyes. "What?" She grinned despite the pain of moving her face.

"I want you to concentrate on getting better, and...I want you to marry me. Will you do that? Will you marry me? I know you have to take care of the other first, but when we get you out of here, we'll make sure your divorce goes through quickly. I promise. We'll run away, just like you wanted."

Susan grazed the side of Aster's face with her hand. "Okay," she cried.

Aster lightly pressed his lips against hers. "I love you so much, my black-eyed Susan."

"Aster?"

"Yes?" he sniffled.

"Will you hold me?"

Desperately trying not to cause her any physical pain, Aster crawled in the bed with Susan. He wrapped his arms around her and repeatedly kissed her forehead. Time seemed to stand still as Aster comforted her. He wasn't sure how much time had passed when he heard her whisper, "Aster?"

"Hmmm?" he mumbled.

"Will you...take care...of my daisy?"

"Of course," he promised, and then Susan's lungs heaved a long breath, expelling her spirit and soul from her body. Completely broken, he sobbed uncontrollably and tightly held her lifeless body close to his.

Chapter 25

The Daisy

Aster and Sharon sat in Lieutenant Watkins' office as he recounted his statement about the day Susan had been beaten to death by Shane. He painfully told the story of how she told him she was divorcing Shane and how it wasn't until she left his office and caught her sleeve on a hook that he became aware he had been responsible for sending her back to an abusive man. He admitted Susan hadn't confessed any abuse until they were in the hospital together, and then he explained what Susan said about how the abuse started and how long it had taken place.

Sharon sat quietly and listened to Aster regale his story while Lieutenant Watkins took notes. As soon as Aster finished, Sharon opened her mouth. "I need to make my statement as well, Lieutenant Watkins," Sharon insisted.

"All right, go ahe—" *Brrring brrring brrring...* The phone interrupted Lieutenant Watkins. "Hold that thought." She held her finger up signaling Sharon to give her a minute. "Lieutenant Watkins speaking...yes...yes...*really*? You don't say. Thanks, that's wonderful news." A bright smile beamed across her face as she glanced to Sharon and announced, "We've got him. They just picked him up in Florida. One of my men is heading over right now to get him."

"Ahhh...You got him? Oh my..." Sharon threw her arms around Aster and sobbed.

Lieutenant Watkins excused herself while Sharon reveled in the victory of Shane's being captured, "I'll give you two a minute, and then I'll be back to get that statement, Mrs. Blackman." Lieutenant Watkins shut the door behind her.

Aster pulled away from Sharon and questioned, "Can I ask you something?"

"What do you want to know?"

Aster sighed. "Why the change of heart? Did Susan say something to you at the hospital to change your mind about me?"

"Yes, she told me what I'm about to tell the Lieutenant. She insisted you were completely unaware of what she had been living in, and she assured me had you known, you would've done everything in your power to save her from that situation."

"But I didn't save her...I wish I had. I just keep racking my brain trying to figure out the last thing she said to me...Does she have a bed of daisies at her house?"

"Yes, she does as a matter of fact," Sharon uttered just as Lieutenant Watkins opened the door.

"Now, let's get that statement and get all the information we can to put Shane away," she prompted Sharon to give her statement.

"At the hospital Susan asked to speak to

me alone. She wanted me to know what had happened to her. She didn't want to tell Aster the details of it all. She feared he may go looking for Shane himself," Mrs. Blackman began her story. "Reverend McGrath and Susan have a history, you see. I didn't like it so much when they became friends. I was a little on the controlling side. I wanted my daughter to marry well..."

Aster and Sharon watched as Susan's nurse, Penny, injected a needle into the IV, pulled the chair next to her bedside, and sat. It appeared she was writing in her chart. They both wondered at the amount she wrote; it seemed to be a lengthy addition to her chart. As soon as Penny completed her writing, she bent over and slipped something into the nightstand next to Susan's bed. Penny opened the door and Aster and Sharon crossed into the unit housing Susan's battered and bruised body. Penny stood next to her, keeping a close eye on the monitors. Susan gasped, "Aster, if you don't mind, I need to speak to my mom alone."

Susan held her hand out for her mom. "You called me mom and not mother." Sharon gleamed.

Aster gave his head a slight nod and backed out of the room. The nurse followed close behind. She shut the door to give them the privacy they needed.

Sharon ambled her way to her daughter's side, grabbed her hand, and kissed it. "How are you, Sweet baby?"

"Not too good, mom," Susan wheezed.

"Who did this to you, Baby?"

"Shane...I left him, Mom. I wasn't honest with you...when I brought Mae to you. I left a note for him...telling him my intentions. I have...an appointment with a lawyer on Monday...What day is it, Mom?" Susan asked, confused.

Sharon rubbed her teary eyes. "It's Sunday, Sweetheart," she answered. "I don't understand. Why? Why would you want to tear your family apart? You've always had such conviction over the way you should live your life. I just don't understand why you would want to leave him? And why in the world would he do this to you?"

"He's been abusive our whole...marriage, mom. I just never...told you. You've always despised Aster and...clearly wanted me with Shane. I was...afraid you'd think it was just my way of trying to find Aster...and be with him," Susan explained. Her breathing was labored and her sentences were broken.

"So, you're telling me he's been abusing you the entire time you guys have been married?"

"No, he was nice at first. It was only...once the baby was born. He changed. It was like...he looked at her with hatred. I...thought he was just jealous...of how much time I was devoting...to her and not to him. I took the blame...on myself because I knew deep down inside...I wasn't being the wife I was supposed to be...because I never loved him. I only married him...because I was pregnant," Susan cried.

"Well, Susan, you already admitted that to me, but why did you sleep with him, if you didn't want to be with him?"

"Someone spiked the punch at the prom, and I ended up...waking up the next morning at Shane's...house. He told me we did, but...I didn't remember anything. I found out...after my graduation rehearsal that...I was pregnant. I'm so sorry I lied to you...and daddy about all of that. I know I told you...I slept with him...around graduation time, but...that was the day I found out...I was pregnant. I tried...to find Aster to...tell him. I knew he would marry me, but...I couldn't find him."

"So, you wanted to marry that thing out there?" Sharon snarled.

"Yes, I love him; I have...for a long time. He's such a...sweet, kind person, and he loves me. I know...he does. He broke up with me...once because of you, you know?" Susan gazed at her mother.

Sharon hung her head. "I've no idea what you're talking about, Susan."

"Yes, you do, Mom. You threatened...that you and Dad wouldn't pay for my college if we were together, so...he broke up with me, and then...when his mother died, I went to see him. It...all happened so fast. I felt so bad for him. He...was so sad, and my heart was breaking...for him. I kissed him, and the next thing...I knew, we were making love. It was the only time...I've ever been touched...and I actually wanted to be..."

"Are you telling me you and Aster..." Sharon choked.

"Yes, Momma, I am. We were...gonna get married. He moved off...to go to school to get a degree as a motorcycle," Susan stopped mid-sentence and took a deep breath, "mechanic so he could get a good job and maybe earn...your respect. He wrote me, and he called me, but you...already know about that, don't you?"

Sharon stuttered, "I was doing what I thought was best for you, Susan. He was no good for you."

Susan heaved and gasped for breath. "Yes, he was good for me. He was more than...good for me; he was perfect." Susan turned her head away from her mother and finished her story, "When I couldn't find Aster, I felt I...had no choice but...to marry Shane, so I did. The abuse was bearable...until Aster moved back into town. At that point he hit me...harder and accused me constantly of having an affair. I went to see Aster...this morning to tell him I was leaving Shane and to...get closure I guess. I wanted to know why he had not...written me. He showed me the letters, Mom. I read them...*all*. I know your handwriting...Mom. I know it was you who...scribbled return to sender."

"You read them?" Sharon looked away.

"Yes, but I forgive you. I know...you only wanted what was best for me, and I understand...you truly believed Shane was that."

Tears streamed down Sharon's face. "I'm sorry, Sweetheart. I really messed up, didn't I?"

"Yes, you did, but now...you have a chance to make it up to me."

"How?" Sharon raised her brow.

"I'm not going to make it, and I want Aster...to officiate my funeral. I know it will be a lot for me...to ask of him, but he knows me better than...anyone else on the face of this earth. And you are going to be...the one to ask him to do it."

"You're gonna be fine, honey."

"No, Mother, I'm not. Now promise me," Susan demanded, squeezing her mother's hand.

"Okay. I promise. Now you tell me how this happened."

Susan gathered her thoughts. "I guess it was around ten a.m. when I left Aster's place...yesterday morning. The last thing he said to me...was to go home to my husband, but he didn't know Shane had...been hurting me. I never told him. What he said hurt, but I knew...he didn't want me to regret a failed marriage. He didn't want me...to ever be accused of having left my husband for him. I drove down to the bay...to sit and think for a while. Shane must've seen me there...because he came up from behind me, put his...hands around my mouth, and...dragged me into the car. I bit him. He drove me to the east side...of town, climbed out of the car, yanked me...out by my hair, and told me he was going to leave me...for dead in the place I belonged—in the slums with the man...I had always whored around with. He started beating me so...hard I nearly lost consciousness. He was kicking me...in the ribs and gut. He slammed...my face into the concrete sidewalk...several times. He told me over and over again...he was going to beat me as ruthlessly...as Aster had beaten him when he...raped Aster's little sister," Susan broke into sobs.

Sharon gawked. "He raped Aster's little sister, and you never told us?"

"I didn't know. Aster never told me...what Shane had done to hurt Eva, only...that he had. He begged me to be careful...around Shane. He was constantly warning me...he was dangerous. I even promised him I would keep...an eagle-eye on him, but you were insistent about...the prom, and I feared you would figure out I was back...with Aster, so I went with Shane, and I...pretended to be happy."

Lieutenant Watkins scribbled away as Sharon recalled everything Susan had told her that day in the hospital. "The bite mark will be great evidence." She picked up the phone. "Let me call Florida right now and have them look for it." Sharon stood and walked to the window. She looked out over the parking lot and watched the cars drive by on the highway.

"Is that it?" Lieutenant Watkins asked.

"Not quite. I just need a moment."

"I understand."

"Lieutenant," Aster interjected.

"Yes, Reverend."

"The last thing Susan said to me has been bothering me. She asked me to take care of her daisy. Mrs. Blackman told me that she does have a bed of daisies at her house. Maybe she's hidden something there, something that will help to seal the deal in getting Shane."

Sharon jerked her head around and stared at Aster. "That's what she said to you?"

"Yes, Ma'am," Aster acknowledged.

Turning her gaze upon the Lieutenant, Sharon stated, "You won't find anything in her bed of daisies."

"And why is that, Mrs. Blackman?" Lieutenant Watkins pressed.

"Because that bed of daisies was planted for a reason. It was planted in honor of her daughter Daisy." Sharon marched to Aster's side, placed her hand on his shoulder, and looked him square in the eyes. "Susan was asking you to take care of her daughter."

Aster peered into Sharon's eyes. "You...you introduced me to your granddaughter as Mae," he stuttered.

Sharon stood tall and proud. "Yes, Aster. Her name is *Daisy* Mae. I call her my Mae Mae. She's my heart and all I have left of my daughter, but you see, that wasn't the end of my conversation with Susan. She had me get an envelope from her bedside table. She asked me to give this letter to you, but I...I just haven't been able to bring myself to do it until now." She pulled a folded envelope from her purse. "I'm sorry. Please forgive me for all the wrongs I've done against you, Aster." Sharon handed Aster the letter. "She said she had the nurse write it for her."

Hesitantly he opened it and read:

My Aster,

I'm writing this because I'm not sure if I will have the strength or guts, whatever you want to call it, to tell you in person. There was no way for me to know for certain if Shane was the father of my baby, just like I told you standing in your office. You and I had made love only a week before my nightmare began. I hoped beyond hope she was yours, but I was afraid to admit to Shane I was not a virgin the night we were together. I know it was wrong of me to deceive him in that way, but I was so frightened when I couldn't find you, and I didn't know what else to do. I pray that one day he'll forgive me for my deception.

I named her Daisy in the hope she was yours. Because of when she was born, my hope had dwindled to nearly non-existent, but I wanted to be able to say we were just a bunch of wildflowers. It wasn't until Shane was beating me earlier today that I learned he already knew about what happened between us.

Shane grabbed me by the hair on the back

of my head and made me look him in the eyes when he told me he had slipped something into my drink at the restaurant because he planned for us to sleep together, but when I had the two drinks at the prom that were spiked and got sick, I passed out in the car. He carried me into his home and undressed me anyway, but he said he lost interest because he wanted me to be conscious. He said he knew the minute I told him I was pregnant that the baby was yours. That's why he wanted me to have an abortion—to pay you back for what you did to him, but then when I wouldn't go through with it, he said he decided that marrying me would be enough punishment. He would always have what you wanted.

Aster, I know this is probably overwhelming for you right now, and I'm truly sorry about that, but I'm also happy. I have lived a lie for the past five and a half years, and I can die knowing that day when we made love, even though we both felt we had given in to our passion and sinned, well, God saw fit to bless us both with a little girl.

Do you remember when we were on the beach in Paradise Shore, and you asked me why there was bad in the world? I told you there is bad because there is evil, but God can take the bad and bring good out of it, and He did, Aster. It is only in my death and the evil in Shane that I was able to learn the truth, and that truth has made the last moments of my life truly happy. And for you, it is only in losing me that you will be able to gain your daughter. There was always a part of me, deep down in my being, that believed she was yours, but I was afraid to really believe it. She reminds me of you with the way she smiles. Now you will always have a part of me with you. When you look at her, I hope you see me in her eyes.

I want you to know how much I utterly love you. I never stopped. Kiss my Daisy for me and tell her I'll meet her in my field!

Your Black-eyed Susan

Schledia lives on the Gulf Coast. The mother of five is the author of YA companion novels Pretty Boy and Plain Jane and the NA romance novel Wildflowers. She dedicated eight years of her life to working with teenagers as a youth minister and has been invited to speak to high school students and women. Her goal as an author is to write stories that touch the hearts of readers and to tackle issues such as bullying, abuse, depression, domestic violence, and suicide. In addition to writing novels, she has taught creative writing at a small private school and has written skits and human videos for a drama team. She attended MGCCC. She was the Keynote Speaker for The Key Club International's Division 14's Divisional Rally. In her spare time, she enjoys reading, spending time with her family, and visiting over a cup of coffee.